The WATCHMAN'S WIDOW

Joanne Clague

First published in the United Kingdom in 2023 by

Canelo
Unit 9, 5th Floor
Cargo Works, 1–2 Hatfields
London SE1 9PG
United Kingdom

A CIP catalogue record for this book is available from the British Library.

Print ISBN 978 1 80032 952 2
Ebook ISBN 978 1 80032 951 5

This book is a work of fiction. Names, characters, businesses, organizations, places and events are either the product of the author's imagination or are used fictitiously. Any resemblance to actual persons, living or dead, events or locales is entirely coincidental.

Cover design by Diane Meacham

Cover images © Gordon Crabb, Shutterstock

Look for more great books at www.canelo.co

Printed and bound in Great Britain by Clays Ltd, Elcograf S.p.A.

The Watchman's Widow

Born and raised in Sheffield, Joanne Clague lives in the coastal village of Laxey in the Isle of Man with her husband, children, dogs and other assorted wildlife. She has worked in print, radio and broadcast journalism in the north west for the past three decades and is now a full-time writer of historical fiction set in nineteenth century Sheffield.

Also by Joanne Clague

The Sheffield Sagas

For Alan

Chapter 1

Rose Butterfield came to an abrupt halt on the edge of Paradise Square and wondered what had possessed her to think she could cross the cobbles on this day of all days. Perhaps the men who filled the space like sheep squashed in a pen would raise her up into the hazy air and pass her over their heads. The thought brought a wry smile to her face. She'd not felt a man's hand on her in more than half a dozen years.

The noise from the crowd had carried from streets away on the stifling heat of high summer – cloudbursts of applause that erupted suddenly then petered out to allow the orator to continue, the occasional solitary heckle or whoop piercing the air. Still, she hadn't been expecting to turn the corner to find thousands of men facing her, all focused on a speaker in full flow, pacing on the balcony of the Freemasons' Hall near the top of the side of the square Rose had emerged onto.

Standing at the foot of the steep gradient, Rose could see the spire of St Peter's rising from behind the chimney stacks in the diagonally opposite corner. The narrow alley that gave access to the church and the high street was just as packed with people.

She pursed her lips and swept her gaze over the crowd. In the brick, flat-fronted buildings that fringed three sides of the square, people braced their elbows on the ledges of second- and third-storey sash windows, while others were hanging like acrobats from the struts of the lamp post in the middle of the square.

Knowing it would be impossible to strike out across the square but keen to avoid having to retrace her steps, Rose fought her way along the pavement between the crowd and the buildings, earning irritated looks – and the occasional speculative glance – from the men who hemmed her in. She was now close enough to the speaker to see the sheen of sweat on his forehead and the silver threads in a fulsome beard that straggled across his upper chest like a hairy bib. He was elaborating on the virtues of his political party, which was all very well and good but there was a grocer's in that still-distant alley she needed to get to.

Rose used the corner of her thin headscarf to wipe perspiration from her upper lip. A smatter of applause rippled through the crowd. It sounded, deliciously, like rain. She longed for a proper downpour that would clear the filth from the streets and the grit from the air. Instead of embarking on this fool's errand, she ought to have taken her children for a walk to the high fields, away from the stench of the town. Across St Philips Road and up towards Crookes Moor, where she could breathe in lungfuls of fresh air. She and Jane could have lain in the cool green shade and made daisy chains while Bobby and Jack stalked the wild goats that balanced on the crags, straggly-haired creatures that fixed intruders with a slotted eye and always stayed just out of reach.

But here she was, melting in the heat. There was a flurry of cheers from the crowd, and polite applause from the town luminaries sharing the balcony. Rose reached a trio of top-hatted gentlemen who were working their heads up and down as vigorously as she worked the handle of the water pump at the end of her street. One of them caught her eye and smiled at her and she gave him a resigned smile in return.

'Who've we got pontificatin' today, then?'

'Why, it's our esteemed member of parliament, Mr A. J. Mundella. I wonder you don't recognise him?'

'I don't know why I would,' Rose said. 'I suppose there must be an election comin' up.'

'Indeed so. And the common man will get his vote, which gives the opposition long faces, I can tell you.' The man laughed. 'All that lot is good for is blundering into some little war or other. Our liberal member wants a vote for every man and every woman in the land. It'll be young ladies like you next, mark my words.'

Rose snorted. 'I've enough on me plate, thanks all t' same.'

She peered around him. The mass of bodies seemed as solid as a brick wall. Rose sighed, finally resigned to the prospect of retracing her steps, then her brow cleared. There might be a way, after all. A gang of men, seven or eight in number, emerged from the Q in the Corner – the tavern adjacent to the Freemasons' Hall – and began striding along the top of the square. Rose could take advantage of the clear wake they left as they pushed through the crowd. She kept on the heels of the man at the back of the pack, close enough to touch the metal buckle on the back of his waistcoat.

Following them was a mistake.

She realised too late why the men were moving so decisively, enough so that those in their path took one look and shifted quick-as-you-like to allow them through. They were almost upon the unsuspecting group of men who stood outside a beer-house, waving their tankards about like flags, splashing ale onto the pavement and each other. Rose glanced behind her but the crowd was a solid wall once more. The men outside the beer-house clocked the gang, and a shout, an indecipherable cry of alarm, rang out. Some lunged forward to meet their attackers. Others disappeared back inside, and the door was slammed shut.

Rose's stomach lurched. She had a ringside seat at a mass brawl, a planned attack carried out in plain sight while all eyes were focused on the rally. The police would come to break up the fight and she imagined herself trampled under the hooves of a horse, her skull stove in, and her children waiting at home in vain for her return. Her mind was racing as fast as her heart. She had to get away but there was nowhere to go. She cursed herself. She had lost focus for a moment, acted recklessly, and put her children in danger. When a bottle flew through the air towards her, she cried out, cowering behind a man's broad back. The bottle hit him square on the forehead and he lurched backwards. He was coming down on her like a falling tree, and she pushed at his back but she didn't have enough strength in her arms. He was falling, and she would be pinned under him. Then her arm was gripped and she was yanked sideways and pushed against a wall. The man who had saved her was cackling with laughter and she was sickened to see the black stubs of his teeth. A cut on his lip oozed blood and his breath stank of hops.

'Gi' us a kiss, love.'

Rose shook her arm free. 'Get off me or tha'll be sorry.'
The man reeled away, back into the fray, and she sagged
with relief. Shouts of warning signalled the arrival of the
police. She could see their blue tunics infiltrating the
crowd, which immediately began to melt away, leaving
Rose alone on the cobbles. She pressed her hand against
her forehead, which was damp with perspiration.

'Are you all right?'

An attractive woman with friendly eyes stood before
her, dressed stylishly for the weather in pale gingham and
a light summer bonnet. She looked to be in her early
thirties, so not much older than Rose, but had a confident
bearing that made Rose immediately feel like a small
child.

'Aye,' she said, brushing down her skirt, 'I am now.'

The woman gestured towards the alley Rose had been
trying to reach, which was now only a few feet away.
'I think that leads to the high street. Shall we make our
escape?' Her eyes sparkled. 'I wasn't expecting a political
rally to be this exciting.'

'That's one word for it, I s'pose,' said Rose. She picked
up the basket she had dropped, and checked to see if her
purse was still inside it. It was, to her astonishment. A
bead of sweat ran down her side, the tickle of it making
her shudder.

'I hope you're not too shaken,' said the woman. 'I saw
that ruffian grab hold of you.'

Rose put the back of her hand to one cheek then the
other in a fruitless attempt to cool them. 'It's hot enough
to boil frogs.'

'It is indeed.'

Rose kept up with the woman's brisk pace, following
her through the alley, throwing a glance at the grocer's

shop that had been her destination but obeying the urge to get as far away from the square as possible. They emerged onto the high street, which was thronged with men walking up from the square into town.

'I'm goin' over yonder,' said Rose, pointing across the road.

'I'll leave you, then, provided you are sure you don't require any assistance.'

'No harm done,' said Rose.

'Then take care.'

'Sithee. An' thanks for lookin' out for me.'

She watched the woman walk briskly away towards the lower end of the high street, then waited for a gap in the traffic and crossed over to the pork butcher's shop, reassuring herself she was clear of the melee and wouldn't have the bother of being detained as a witness by the police. It had been frightening but it was over. *You need to put it behind you.* How many times had she been advised to do just that, in the weeks and months after Archie died, when the police lost interest in the case and she was left to deal with the senselessness of it all.

Flies buzzed on the cured meat hanging beside the curtained entrance of the shop. Rose wrinkled her nose and ducked inside. The butcher stood behind his wooden block, wielding a cleaver over the carcass of a pig. The air was thick with the metallic tang of blood.

'Ey up, Rosie.' The man put down his cleaver and wiped his hands on his apron before clapping them together. 'What can I do for thee?'

'I'm after half a pound o' sausage-meat an' I'll take a couple o' them trotters, please, if they're not spoken for.'

'Reight enough.'

The room was illuminated in stripes from the sunlight filtering through the window, giving everything a curious underwater effect. The butcher busied himself chopping at the pig's feet. Rose's gut squirmed, but it had nothing to do with the blood, bone and sinew. She had not been able to meet Sid's eye since she had rejected his proposal a few months earlier, although he'd accepted the excuse she gave with equanimity, and seemed unbothered now. A butcher was a catch, she supposed. He'd soon find himself a wife.

She could shop elsewhere but she'd always come to Sid's for her meat and it would add insult to injury to start avoiding his premises.

'Catch owt o' the rally?' He ripped a length of brown paper from a roll and began packaging up her purchases.

'Could hardly avoid it.' She didn't want to tell him about the fight, didn't want to remind herself of the panic that had had her in its grip. 'Big crowd, an' all. I were tryin' to get to Hanbury's. You know, the new grocer's?' She was grateful to talk of inconsequential things. 'He's got a cart an' is doin' free deliveries. I'm wantin' to get on his list if I can.'

Sid straightened up and snorted with laughter. 'Free deliveries? Aye, free for now. That's to reel thee in.' He handed her the wrapped meat. 'Then it'll be a penny a time, then a shillin'. I'd take bets on it.'

Rose smiled. 'I don't like to gamble.'

He smiled back, one eyebrow raised. 'Aye, love, I know.'

—

It was as hot as a furnace but Rose stamped home in half the time she'd taken to walk into town. It had been sly of

Sid to make that remark. Perhaps he wasn't as untroubled by her decision as he appeared. And she had rejected him as gently as possible. She had told him she had invested all of her heart in Archie Butterfield, and look what had happened there. She had been left all alone. That was the simple truth of it. Well, she had picked herself up. She was making ends meet and was, at the age of thirty, a respectable widow woman. Her girl and the twins were thriving. Why risk all that by placing their fortunes into the hands of another man who might be there one minute, gone like a spent match the next?

Or had her mood, which was as black as the smoke that rose from the factories in the bowl of the town, more to do with the altercation in Paradise Square? She had taken a foolish risk, getting near a crowd that size, and her heart raced again to think about it. Had she always been this cautious, even before Archie died? Rose couldn't remember. All she knew was that she had never wanted so badly to close her own front door behind her.

The street she lived on was a short but vertiginous slope she remembered running down as a child, certain she would take off and fly like a bird at any moment, longing for it. She shivered. One slip, one stone to strike her temple, and her children might be orphaned in a moment. Or she'd break a leg or an ankle and be put out of work, and have to pay for a surgeon that wasn't a butcher, and it was no great leap from there to the workhouse. She no longer felt she was teetering on the cliff-edge of Archie's absence, waiting to fall, but there was no call to take unnecessary risks.

A headache started at the back of her eyes as she neared the small terraced cottage that she had shared with her husband and now lived in without him. There would be a storm tonight. That might even account for the dragging heaviness in her body. To cheer herself and comfort the children, they'd watch the storm from her bed, wrapped up in blankets, and count the number of seconds between the thunder and lightning, safe and warm against the commotion in the heavens – Archie liked to say it was the sound of the gods quarrelling – and the downpour that would follow.

But the first thing she'd do would be to put the kettle on. Her lips were as parched as the cracked dirt beneath her feet. Rose nodded to a passer-by but the woman was labouring uphill and did not lift her head in acknowledgement. All Rose could see of her was a rounded cheek and a tendril of blonde hair escaping her headscarf. She did not seem familiar and Rose wondered what her business might be. Considering its proximity to the town centre, this road was little-used. Most people took the slightly more circuitous route into town rather than tackle this short hill, which was a hazard in either direction for a loaded cart.

She pushed open her gate onto a patch of scrub enclosed by a low stone wall. Archie had promised to cultivate the ground, plant potatoes and carrots, but then complained it was too stony and had abandoned the scheme. The windows of the front room and bedroom above were open but there was no breeze to stir the nets. The front door stood slightly ajar and Rose hurried inside, the fearfulness that had settled in her heart six years earlier now blooming like blood on fabric.

Relief washed through her when she heard the scolding tone of her daughter's voice coming from the kitchen. Jane was using a rag to scrub at the blackened face of Bobby, who sat on the countertop next to the sink, his little hands clutching his bony bare knees, while his twin brother, Jack, looked on solemnly. There was an almost perfect black handprint on the wall next to the cellar head. Rose tutted and Jack turned his large brown eyes – Archie's eyes – on her. Bobby peered over his sister's shoulder. His eyes – also his father's – were reddened and his chest hitched with a fresh sob when he saw his mother.

Rose put the basket on the kitchen table and unwound her headscarf. 'Can't I leave you three alone for five minutes?'

'It's not my fault. This 'un got in the coal 'ole,' her daughter said.

'*I* never,' said Jack.

'Shurrup,' said Jane. 'Nob'dy mentioned thee.'

'You're supposed to keep an eye on 'em.' Rose held up her hand to fend off the objection she knew was coming. 'I'll deal wi' it. Peel some potatoes for us, an' let's get a stew started. I'm on a night shift at six an' I'll need a sleep first.'

'So I've got 'em still, an' all night again.' Jane pouted. 'An' I've got a load o' sewin' to do for Mrs Brady.'

Rose raised her hands in defeat. 'What else can I do?' She lifted Bobby from the counter and set him on his feet. 'I'll help thee wi' the sewin'.'

Bobby hopped from foot to foot. 'Ma, I could'a jumped that!'

'Big babby,' whispered Jack.

Rose sighed. 'Right, you pair, go an' fill that.' She pointed to the bucket that sat on the floor by the back door. 'An' no messin' about!' The street pump was only a short distance from the house and they could carry the bucket back between them. Rose fanned her face with the edge of her apron. 'Just be careful.'

She touched Jane's arm. Two months off her eleventh birthday, and the girl was already nearly as tall as her mother. Almost a woman. 'Sorry, love. I don't know what I'd do wi'out you.' She rubbed at the crease between her daughter's eyes. 'Allus frownin'. Gi' us a smile.' Jane obliged, albeit grudgingly. 'Get the dinner started, eh? I'll be down at teatime an' I'll have mine then. If I don't get some kip I'll be fit for nowt.'

At the foot of the stairs, her eye was caught by a rectangle of white, bright against the dark wood casing of the mantlepiece clock in the front room. The clock, a wedding gift from Archie's parents, ticked placidly on as she approached the fireplace. There were harsher noises from the kitchen – a pan banging onto the stove, followed by the sound of vegetables being diced on the chopping board. Jane was occupied, and right now that was a blessed relief.

Rose plucked the envelope from the mantlepiece as if she was extracting a delicate butterfly from a net, or – more likely – handling the poisonous mottled bell of a foxglove. There was danger here. Danger of an unspecified kind, or perhaps just the fear of the unknown. It didn't matter. Cold fingers played on the back of her neck. She held up the envelope to the light, the contents sliding into the corner. She didn't need to look at it to know her name was printed on it – *Rose Butterfield* – in neat black script. There would be no address, and no other markings. When she turned it over she would find no return address or sender name. There would be no stamp or postmark to identify where it had originated.

Who was doing this, and why?

'What's that?' Her daughter stood in the doorway.

Rose started, crumpling the envelope in her fist. 'Nowt.' She made a show of yawning. 'Don't know how I'll sleep in this heat. Watch them for me, love?'

'I will. It weren't my fault Bobby...'

'I know. I know it weren't. I am grateful to you. Am just tired.'

She hesitated on her way up the stairs. 'Jane?' Her daughter gazed up at her. 'Did anyone call by today, anyone at all? Did you... were you given owt, an' put it on the shelf, against the clock?'

'No. Like what?'

'Nowt. It's all right. I'll be down in a bit.'

Someone had been inside her house, had crept about, and silently departed. Whoever it was had left the front door standing open. Perhaps they'd been disturbed by the sound of the kids coming up from the cellar, and had scarpered, all while Rose walked home, unawares. She slipped into her bedroom, quietly closing the door behind her, and dropped to her knees at the foot of the bed she had shared with Archie. She paused for a moment, resting her cheek on the counterpane and breathing in deeply. Six years he'd been gone and she could swear she could still smell him in the sheets, no matter how many times they'd been through the maidening-tub.

She reached under the bed and pulled out a heavy wooden box. Folded inside it was Archie's black cape, the one he had been wearing the night he died. She had been given it, had scrubbed the blood away and stashed it under the bed, and was grateful to the police detective who had made the gesture, although he had done very little as far as she could tell to apprehend her husband's killer. The cloak was a comfort. She felt protected having it close by.

And now it concealed a secret cache. Rose uncurled her fist and smoothed out the envelope, shaking out the coins from within. She sat back on her heels, staring at them. Three half-sovereigns, this time. She closed her palm over them, then decanted them back into the envelope and laid it in the bottom of the box, to join all the others scattered there.

She folded the cape back on top of the pile, replaced the lid on the box and shoved it back under the bed as far as she could reach. There were now twenty-four envelopes under her bed, each containing two or three or four coins. She could not spend them, however tempted she might be. What if they were hers for safekeeping only, and the owner would return and demand his money? She would not spend them. Perhaps, one day, she might use them to help the children get a foothold in life, a better start than she had had. But her mind shied away from this idea. The riches she was concealing felt like more of a threat than good fortune.

Rose sat back on her heels and rubbed at her temples.

Archie's cloak lay folded on top of a treasury of coins amounting to more than sixty pounds. A small fortune.

Chapter 2

When the member of parliament had concluded his speech, to cheers from most and catcalls from only a very few, Annie Whittaker moved away from the entrance she'd been standing in, keeping close to the walls of the buildings that fringed the square. Although it had thrilled her to see so many thousands cramming the square, she did not want to get caught up in the crowd, where fist-icuffs had broken out. She should not be here at all, unaccompanied as she was, but had wanted to listen to what the liberal politician had to say — to satisfy herself that the man, considered still by many to be of foreign stock and therefore suspicious, would once again win the townsmen's vote. Her husband had been so caught up in his new venture he had merely offered a distracted nod when she said she was venturing out for a moment.

Rob would probably assume she had walked up the high street to Cole Brothers to look at hats or curtain fabric or something suitably frivolous. Instead, she had hurried past the silk mercer's and general draper's store that dominated the bustling junction where Fargate met Church Street, and made her way to Paradise Square.

It was thrilling to be one among thousands, surging and shoving, and also a relief to see the police arrive to put a stop to the fighting that had broken out. Annie imagined writing something about it — she would start with the vast number of people come to listen to A. J. Mundella speak, and her exhilaration at being among the crowd. A commentary from the female perspective. She reached an alley she hoped was not a dead end and was about to hurry down it when she saw a woman – the first she had seen in the square – pinned against a wall not six feet away by a man wearing baggy trousers and a filthy coat. He looked like a beggar. The woman was a little thing, dark-haired and fragile-looking, but had managed to see him off before Annie got to her.

'Are you all right?'

The woman answered gruffly, a frown furrowing her brow, and Annie became uncertain. Was she about to become the victim of pickpockets? Had what she had seen been staged for the purpose of drawing her in? But the woman bent to pick up a basket and there was relief on her face when she looked up at Annie. She muttered something about frogs and the heat and took Annie up on her suggestion to escape down the narrow space between two buildings. The woman thanked her when they reached the high street and they parted ways.

Annie walked down the road along the bottom of Fargate, turning aside to avoid the cloud of dust stirred up by a passing wagon. She was becoming accustomed to the ripe aroma of the town, the smell of smoke and sulphur and animal waste, but didn't want to return to the shop plastered in dirt like a savage.

Rob had rented the ground floor of a building in Change Alley. The landlord's agent had wished them better luck than the previous incumbent when he handed over the keys. He'd tapped the side of his nose knowingly, succeeding in infuriating Annie and making her all the more determined to *not* enquire further of this man.

At the same time, she decided she would discover what had happened, without the agent's assistance. 'Whatever happened,' said Rob later, 'it sadly hasn't had any bearing on the astronomical rent I'm being charged.'

Annie entered the building through a side door that gave onto a narrow hallway, shabbily papered, with an uncarpeted staircase at the end, the wooden treads worn and dusty. Rob had told her there was a money lender on the floor above, and a jewellery maker on the top floor, so there would be plenty of passing traffic that was bound to be good for business. Annie unfastened her bonnet and brushed back the curls that had been plastered uncomfortably to her forehead and neck. She opened and closed behind her the only door in the hallway, entering the shop behind the counter that divided the room in two.

A cash register stood on the end of the countertop, partially obscuring a large board showcasing various fonts in the form of mottos or advertisements Rob had had mocked up. This board would be mounted on the wall by the end of the day. The opposite wall on the customer side of the shop was made up of floor-to-ceiling wooden shelving and cubby-holes, painted forest green and displaying packets of writing paper and envelopes, illustrated postcards, greeting cards, examples of monogrammed notepaper, brass letter holders, blotters and stamp boxes, and a large silver paperclip in the shape, delightfully, of a pineapple.

The shop door facing onto the street was flanked by two large plate-glass windows on which were etched advertisements for the services soon to be offered inside. Annie sat in one of the three leather-upholstered swivel chairs in the office behind the counter, rolling it slightly on its casters. She had picked out the furnishings, including the two large walnut desks, each sporting an elegant gas lamp, and the brightly coloured woven rug on the floor. She had decorated the small fireplace with knick-knacks and had hung a tapestry of a hunting scene above the narrow mantlepiece. All expensive items, especially the chairs, but purchased cheaply from a house clearance.

Behind the office was the case room, not much bigger than the table at its centre that held the letter frame. And beyond that, the machine room that led onto the back alley.

'Annie? Is that you?' The voice came from the machine room.

'Yes, Rob.'

She found him where she'd left him, leaning over a contraption that looked to her like some ancient instrument of torture, or a mechanical spider, with wheels and pulleys instead of legs reaching down from the ceiling. Perhaps when she saw it in motion she might feel differently. Her husband straightened and smiled at her, patting the machine's polished flank.

'If the steel factories are the guts of the town,' Rob said, 'then this is its beating heart.'

Annie smiled and tilted her head. 'I wonder where, then, the brain may be located?'

'Oh, I don't know. Probably there isn't one.' He laughed, a little wildly. He had seemed giddy from the moment he helped Annie down from the omnibus that had carried them two miles into town from their home in the leafy suburb of Walkley.

She wrapped her hand around one of the two handles protruding from the side of the printing machine. The dark wood was smooth and dry, reassuringly solid. She released the handle and surveyed the room – the fat rolls of white paper stacked against the wall, a guillotine knife, vats of black ink.

'Are we all set?' she said.

'We are.'

Annie wandered back into the other room to investigate the contents of a large oak case that sat on top of a waist-high bureau. This case was hinged open, revealing tiny built-in boxes in both the upper and lower compartments. Annie plucked a small piece of metal from one of them and examined it closely.

Rob smiled indulgently. 'What do you have?'

'A T,' she said.

'Capital. That's the type tray. All the capital letters are in the upper part, and do you see how much bigger the compartments are in the lower part for the most commonly used letters?'

'The power of the printed word.' Annie smiled back at him. 'There must have been ten thousand people at this morning's rally. There was a fight too' – she paused – 'or so I heard it said. What will you do, on Mundella? I was inspired to write a few words.'

'The rally? Oh, I sent your cousin to take a look at it.'

'Well, then, I wonder what our hungry young journalist will conjure up.' Annie scooped up a handful of the metal bits and sifted them through her fingers. 'Thank you for giving Jem employment. I think it will do him good.'

'How could I refuse a request from my beautiful wife?' He came up behind her and rested his chin on her shoulder, his whiskers tickling her cheek.

Annie tensed. 'Robert, I have an idea for an article.'

'Do you? You went there, didn't you, to the rally?' His tone was amused and when he wrapped his arms around her waist, she allowed herself to sink against his chest.

'No, no. Well, yes, but only for a brief look. I like Mundella. He's progressive. Listen, Rob, this idea I have…'

'Mundella has my vote, if that's what is worrying you.'

'I know that.' She took a breath. 'That's not what I want to talk about.'

'Wait.' He held out his hand and Annie dropped the tiny letters into his palm. She watched him replace them in their allocated box. 'The typesetter, and the compositor, will have my guts for garters if these get mixed up.'

'How long it must take to create even one sentence.'

'Not long at all! A skilled man can make up a page in no time.' He kissed her on the cheek. 'Will you miss me on Friday? We'll be here all night and our first edition will be flying through there' − he gestured to the back of the shop − 'at the break of dawn on Saturday, collected by handcart and delivered to libraries, public house news rooms, gentlemen's clubs.' He released her, only to take her hand and pull her into the front of the shop. 'And sold here.' He banged on the counter. 'And hawked out there for a penny a throw.' He stepped back and spread his hands. 'Tell me, Mrs Whittaker, what do you think?'

She knew there was a serious intent behind his question. It was Annie's dowry that had enabled Robert Whittaker to rent and furnish the property and it was Annie's dowry that would ensure the running costs and the wages of his employees were paid until the money began, as Rob would have it, *rolling in* from a tide of advertisers and subscribers. The romantic business of reporting the news of the day would be subsidised by a stationery and print shop producing pamphlets, posters and the like.

'Truly, I think it's marvellous,' she said.

'We shall make the investment back tenfold, a hundredfold. You'll see.' He patted his belly. 'I'm hungry. Shall I lock up? We could dine at the King's Head before we leave the town. I'm in the mood to celebrate.' He gestured out of the window, at the traffic passing on foot and in gigs and carts. 'See how busy the street is? How the town thrives, and us with it?'

He took her hands in his. 'Annie, do you see how we are at the very centre of things? We could not have hoped for a better location! See?' He released her to wave to a gentleman who had stopped to peer into the window. 'Interest already.'

The man smiled an acknowledgement and raised his eyes to the lintel above the door.

'He's reading the sign,' said Rob.

Annie smiled. She had stood on the pavement opposite the premises the day before and watched the painter on his ladder, rendering into reality their dream.

> Whittaker & Co. Print shop & publisher of
> The Weekly Tribune. Est. 1873

–

Jem Martin leaned over the detritus on the dining table to top up Rob's wine glass. Annie demurred.

'So, the stench from the ash pits, when they were at last scavenged, overwhelmed the entire neighbourhood around Broom Hall,' he said. 'Can you imagine, in this stultifying heat? Rich and poor alike staggering about the streets, pinching their nostrils.'

Rob laughed. 'That will give us a fine paragraph.'

They all flinched when a crack of thunder sounded from directly overhead.

'Then we ought to be especially glad of the change in the weather,' said Annie, 'and thank you, Jem, for waiting until we had finished supper to enlighten us on the town's overflowing middens, but might we change the subject?'

Rob laid his hand over hers. 'My dear, we can discuss any topic you like.'

A sound like the distant clatter of hooves grew quickly into the urgent drumbeat of rain against the windowpane.

'At last,' said Jem. 'I feel I've been waiting forever for that sweet sound. I think summer is bidding us farewell.'

'I'd hoped for spicier conversation to hold our Annie's interest.' Rob took a gulp of wine and wiped his beard. 'Is a weather report the best you can do?'

Annie leaned forward, pushing away her plate. She had prepared a supper of cold cuts, with radishes, lettuce and cucumber from the garden, thinly sliced and soaked in vinegar, with custard puddings to finish, and she would be clearing it all away once Jem, who had turned up with two bottles of hock, had left to return to his lodgings in the town. The household budget would stretch to a maid-of-all-work, and possibly even a cook, but Annie was reluctant to employ servants until the new business had begun to turn a profit. She could manage the modest villa they had bought in the outer-lying district of Walkley and Rob was enamoured of the deep well the builder had sunk near the scullery, and therefore not yet bored of operating the new pump himself.

'I have something that will interest you,' said Annie. 'My group…'

Rob moaned theatrically. 'Oh no, not this!'

Jem raised an enquiring eyebrow.

Annie smiled. 'Be quiet, Rob, or I shall take what's left of your wine away.' She turned to Jem. 'We're trying…'

'Who is?' said Jem.

'The ladies who like to agitate,' said Rob, earning a kick under the table. 'I think you'll find that was my leg, my dear.'

'Why, it felt as wooden as your head.'

She waited for the men's laughter to subside.

'I think – that is, my political association has resolved – that the woman in the factory deserves to have her voice heard. The men have it all, they can strike, they negotiate wages appropriate to their skill, while the woman must trail behind, even though she works much harder than her man, and for a lot less pay.'

'How do you work that out?' said Jem.

'How do I work it out?' Annie shook her head impatiently. 'A ten-hour shift with up to an hour's walk each way, then all the household duties she must perform, buying food, cooking that food, mending clothes. And if she is a married woman, looking after a brood of children too.'

She took a breath and glanced at Rob. Her tongue had run away with her and now her half-drunk husband would complain about their not having yet begun a family, in front of their company.

To her relief, Jem didn't give him the opportunity. 'But she's not doing men's work, is she? She's not ladling molten iron or leaning over a grinder's wheel.'

'Jem, some of these women – and girls, young girls too – are doing the same work as the men for half the pay. Have you seen the conditions they work under in some of these places?'

'Have you?' Jem fired back.

She hesitated. 'No, but I have heard about them, from the girls who come to the soup kitchen.'

'And shouldn't a woman who has, as you say, a *large brood* be devoting herself to her motherly duties and not going out to work at all? Isn't it the man's job to provide?'

'Jem, you're being disingenuous now.'

He laughed. 'I know. I enjoy arguing with you, my lovely cousin. I always have.'

'Are there any more custards?' said Rob.

Annie reached out and tapped his hand. 'I wish you would listen to me.'

Rob pouted in mock-sorrow. 'Ow.'

'It's better than a kick,' said Jem.

'All right, then. Tell us what you wish to achieve, Annie, instead of abusing me so.'

'I shall. I wish to bring these inequalities and injustices to public attention and have our political representatives act on them. If only,' she sighed, 'there was a soon-to-be illustrious organ willing to devote some space to…'

'O ho!' said Rob.

Jem nodded. 'Well played, cousin.'

'I can certainly fill a column or more,' said Annie. 'You'll still have plenty of room for salacious court reports and advertisements for twilled silk umbrellas and the rum and spiced porter at the Clarence spirit vaults.'

'Sounds delicious,' said Jem.

Rob gave her an affronted look. 'I beg your pardon! Those advertisements pay the wages. And Jem has much of importance to write about. The weather, for example, and the stinking privies, and the inadequacy of street lighting. This is what our readers want.'

'Bringing the townspeople the news, and all for less than the price of a cup of coffee or a half pint of porter,' said Jem. 'I'll tell you something, Rob. Get into the Q in Paradise Square. The landlord there reads the papers out on Sunday night. I hear it's quite the performance.'

'Are you changing the subject?' said Annie.

'I wouldn't dare.'

Rob reached for her hand. 'I will consider it.' He turned to Jem. 'What will you say about Mundella?'

Jem shrugged. 'He's boasting of reduced taxes, paying twenty-five million of the national debt off, bringing two hundred thousand children into school…'

'Lots of numbers,' murmured Annie.

'Free schooling is a way off yet.' Rob drummed his fingers on the table, an accompaniment to the rain outside. It made Annie drowsy. She concealed a yawn behind her hand.

Rob tipped the last dregs of the wine into his glass. 'It's all very good, but Annie's right, it is somewhat dull. Do you have anything else?'

She laughed, despite herself. 'You know that *I* have. Now I know you are trying to rile me.'

Jem struck his chest. 'Annie, I promise you that I will write a stirring editorial.'

'Why, I'm glad to hear it. You must interview the chair of our association, and talk to some of the workers at the factory gate. Or accompany me to the soup kitchen one afternoon.' She caught her husband's eye. 'You should both come. See for yourselves the parlous state in which some of the townspeople find themselves.'

Rob downed his wine. 'Ladies have more time and inclination for charitable work. Jem hasn't said what the subject of his editorial will be. I think I can guess at it.'

Jem rose to his feet and, clearing his throat, unrolled an imaginary scroll. Annie guessed he meant to tease her and was already shaking her head, a resigned smile on her face, when he made his pronouncement.

'The farmers always paid handsomely to empty the contents of our middens. With the ash pits overflowing, have the tables turned?' He flashed her a brilliant smile. 'Are we now expected to pay *them* to carry our – excuse me, madam – shit away?'

Chapter 3

It was reckoned that the tallest man could stand upright in the plush interior of the new buses that would soon be running on tracks along the main thoroughfares. Yet here Daniel Housley was, neck bent to an uncomfortable degree and no seats to spare. He backed out of the carriage and climbed up the curved set of steps that led to the exposed top deck. There was nowhere to sit here either, and the aisle was full of chattering men.

When the tram lurched forward, he almost lost his balance and let out an involuntary yelp. He tightened his grip on the cold metal rail, praying nobody had witnessed his stumble. All right, then, he'd remain where he stood, feet overhanging the top step, as if he had deliberately chosen this spot to enjoy the inaugural ride to test the track, ahead of the launch of the town's first tramline. He heard his name bellowed – '*Housley! Hey boy!*' It was Leonard Armitage, the landlord of the Golden Ball, from whom Daniel rented a room while he looked for more permanent accommodation. Leonard was leaning out from the seat he'd secured at the front of the bus and giving Daniel a cheery wave. Daniel waved back and settled his hat more firmly on his head. The gentle drizzle that had been falling since last night's storm rendered the step he stood on, and the rail he clutched, alarmingly slick.

The landlord of the Golden Ball had been quick off the mark when the horses were put in harness outside his Attercliffe alehouse, gulping the remains of his breakfast beer and scuttling off to find a seat on the top deck amongst the aldermen and engineers, as well as the highways inspector, who had travelled up from London. This inspector was the man who would, it was hoped, issue the relevant safety certificate and get the show on the road. The trams would catch the eye of everyone they passed and this one was suitably plastered with colourful advertisements for Zebra grate polish, Sunlight soap and Castle's milk. Daniel had been invited along by his boss, Edgar Bright, the owner of Bright & Sons wire mills, and one of the bigwigs who wanted to be seen on this journey through the town. Daniel had six months earlier taken the job of company secretary at Bright's and, although he hadn't really the time to spare for such a jaunt, was still keen to make a good impression with his new employer. He consoled himself with the fact he'd be away from his desk for no more than a couple of hours. He'd disembark back at the Golden Ball, near Bright's factory gates, and get straight back to work.

He'd established that the route would take them down to the Elephant & Castle tea dealers on Lady's Bridge and circle back again on a different track. The idea was that the horses, unused to the work, should not be unhitched on a busy street where crowds might gather to view the spectacle.

The landlord of the Golden Ball was calling to him again, eliciting laughter from his fellow passengers.

Daniel shouted back. 'I can't hear you, Leonard!'

The inspector, sitting behind Leonard, flinched away from the man's redoubled efforts to reach Daniel's ear.

'LET'S 'OPE SHE'S NOT A RUNAWAY CART, HEY?
HANG ON TO THEE 'AT.'

Daniel grinned and tapped the brim of his hat before
turning back to face the road behind him. The metal rails
were laid on cast-iron supports embedded in concrete, for
no wood had been used in the construction of this modern
track. These rails were presently obscured from view by
pedestrians, buggies and handcarts. He calculated at the
speed they were travelling it would take an hour and a
half to complete a return journey of some four miles. He
was in no danger of losing his hat. Only slugs and snails
would be getting a run for their money from this vehicle.
Daniel watched as a man drove his horse and cart through
the gap between pavement and tram with only inches to
spare. The old fellow was working his jaw on the stem of
a pipe and threw a contemptuous glance at the new mode
of transport as he overtook it on the slight incline.

So it was from this elevated position – balancing on the
top step of the horse tram, starting to admit to himself that
he was enjoying the ride – that Daniel looked down and
saw her.

His heart dropped like a stone into his gut and he
coughed out a harsh breath. He had composed a self-
conscious half-smile for those that had stopped in their
daily business to gawp at the new tram and the gentlemen
swaying on top of it like saplings in a copse. This now froze
on his face, a horrible caricature of a smile. She was only
yards away, crossing the street behind the tram, holding
on to the hand of a child, a smaller version of herself with
the same blonde curls and pink cheeks. The child stopped
to stare at the tram and Daniel held his breath but the
woman, dressed in the pale blue that had always suited
her so, her waist cinched by a lemon–coloured silk band

that matched the ribbon on her bonnet, didn't so much as glance his way. Instead, she leaned down to speak to the girl, taking her hand.

What was she saying? *Come on, love, quick march, else we'll be drowned rats.* Something along those lines, in a voice tinged with affectionate humour. She'd spoken to him in a similar tone, once upon a time, before she had seen through him with her sharp blue eyes.

If he had found a seat inside the tram, he would not have glimpsed her. He could not decide whether that might have been better. Ignorance was bliss, his mother frequently intoned. But he had seen her, was looking at her now, his eyes smarting. He quickly descended the steps, pulled towards her like the tide to the moon. The tram was moving so slowly he could easily jump off. He didn't care if he stumbled, or even fell on the rails, nor whether anyone would bear witness to his inevitable clumsiness. It was imperative he reach her, although he had no idea what he would say to her after all this time. And he was fearful of what she might say to him, even more fearful that she might refuse to acknowledge him at all.

Daniel swayed on the edge of the platform.

The woman and the girl were across the road now, and turning in the opposite direction. He watched her walk away. In a moment, the tram would round a bend and he would lose her. If he didn't leap off now, he knew that tonight he would lie on top of his lumpy mattress in the Golden Ball and curse himself for his cowardice. He gulped.

'Louisa.'

The word spoken too quietly for anyone other than himself to hear.

Daniel disembarked from the tram, thanked the driver, and set off on the dusty pavement that ran alongside the factory wall. He paused at the entrance to allow a wagon to pass into the yard. It was laden with blocks of iron and pulled by two bay-coloured shire horses, their muscular flanks gleaming. He followed in its wake, intending to climb the narrow staircase to his office and shut himself inside, where he would lay his head in his hands and daydream about the better outcome he was busy inventing, one where he had jumped down from the tram – gracefully, no stumbling – and crossed the road to ask Louisa's permission to accompany her to her destination. Perhaps they would pause to sit on a bench and watch her daughter chase the pigeons about, and he would take her hand in his, and apologise for abandoning her and blame his immaturity, or the shock of it. No, no, that might be too intense and frighten her into getting up and leaving.

Instead, he would ask her about Alice, tell her how much the little girl resembled her mother. They might talk about their mutual friends, Silas and Harriet Hinchcliffe, and he would wonder aloud how ridiculous it was that their orbits had never crossed, although he knew that had been deliberate on Harriet's part, that she had handled the situation delicately, whereas Silas might have blundered in and unintentionally made things worse. He would— Daniel cocked his head. Above the usual factory chug and whine he could hear a commotion, the swooping sounds of voices raised in anger. *What now?* he wondered wearily. In his six months at Bright's, he had dealt with two walk-outs over pay and given evidence at the inquest of a worker who had almost had his arm severed by a sheet of hot steel. The unfortunate man had subsequently died of lock-jaw. Edgar Bright had been reluctant to pay compensation, which had alerted Daniel to the parlous state of the company's insurance policy.

Daniel entered the yard to see a woman he didn't recognise standing near the tall cylinder of the brick boiler-house. She was remonstrating with a man twice her size who was wearing a thick leather apron. Daniel recognised him as one of the rollers, whose job it was to handle superheated metal, thinning it into wire to supply factories making crinolines and furniture springs. Arms folded, he was shaking his head slowly from side to side. The woman was pointing her finger accusingly at the man with one hand while her other hand was locked around the wrist of the man's apprentice, a boy of fifteen, who threw Daniel a mortified look as he approached the group. A handful of workers, including some boiler-house men and a few of the warehouse women, were either jeering at the woman or cheering her on. It was hard to tell.

The woman was shouting at the top of her lungs. 'An' like I keep sayin', he's apprenticed to thee! Tha should be makin' sure he's fit to work!'

'Tek it up wi' Bright,' the man said, more calmly. 'I can't help thee.'

'What's going on here?' said Daniel.

The woman turned on him, swinging the boy into his path. ''Ere he is at last!'

'That's not the boss,' one of the workers shouted, 'it's the company secretary.'

Another called out, 'Bright's right-hand man!'

A dubious accolade. Daniel nodded reluctantly. 'I'm Daniel Housley. What seems to be—'

'I'll tell thee!' The woman prodded his chest but then seemed lost for words. Daniel took a step back and looked over her head at the roller, who shook his head.

'No apron,' the man said. 'Even some o' the rollers don't have one, let alone the apprentices.'

''E's not workin' 'ere a day longer 'til he gets kitted out proper!' Now the woman – evidently, the boy's mother – bent to pluck at the thin material, almost worn through in places, covering the boy's thighs. He batted her away. 'Gerroff me!' She glared at Daniel through the tears in her eyes. 'This is the lad's last pair o' trews. He's come 'ome like this for 'is dinner. Will tha buy him some more because I can't afford it?'

'Gi' it a rest,' the roller said.

'Easy for thee to say! Should 'e gad about as nature intended?'

There were catcalls and whistles from the workers that had gathered, and some sympathetic clucks. Daniel hadn't thought the apprentice's face could get any redder, but it did.

'I will do my best to help you,' said Daniel. All he could think, for the moment, was that it was a blessing Edgar Bright had taken himself off to his club after the jaunt on the tram. If he had returned with Daniel, this crowd wouldn't be getting sent back to work, they'd all be fired on the spot. He caught the eye of a female employee standing slightly apart from the rest of them, observing the scene, a dark-haired woman with a solemn set to her mouth. She was the young widow who worked as a packer, who had managed to remain in Bright's employ for the past five years and, he knew from the warehouse manager, was well respected by the others.

'Mrs Butterfield?'

'Aye.' She eyed him reluctantly.

'Perhaps you could encourage your colleagues to return to their posts while I speak with the boy's mother. I don't think this audience is helping anybody.'

She frowned and he thought she was going to ignore the appeal in his eyes, but then she gestured to the others. 'Mr Housley's right. Come on. What will Bright say when he gets back an' sees nowt gettin' done?'

Several women and the boiler-house men turned to leave, mumbling about accidents waiting to happen and no good coming of corners being cut. They were correct, of course. Daniel removed his hat and scratched his head. There'd been talk of strike action after the last accident and those who had raised their voices in complaint quickly found themselves out of a job. It was laying-off season too, and Mr Bright had only this morning complained about the strain on the company bank balance of repairing the steam engine.

When the yard had emptied of all but the roller, his apprentice and the apprentice's mother, Daniel turned to her. 'Will you allow your son to return to work, and I shall raise your concern with Mr Bright and we will try to rectify the situation?'

She shook her head, in disgust and frustration. 'I'm tellin' thee now, nowt'll get done.'

The roller raised his hands in frustration. 'Am on piece work,' he said. 'This is costin' me.'

'All right.' She relinquished her grip on the boy's wrist. 'Get theesen back in.'

The boy followed his master into the factory, slump-shouldered. He didn't look back.

'Please come with me,' Daniel said to his mother.

In the privacy of his office, he took out his wallet and shook coins into the palm of his hand, sorting out four shillings and offering them to her.

'I don't want charity,' she said, taking the money from him, 'I want summat done. That's my lad workin' his guts out for people that don't gi' a fig for him, or any o' 'em. Just so long as a profit's made, eh?'

'You're a good mother, to stick up for her son.'

'And don't thee patronise me neither.'

After she had gone, Daniel sat behind his desk and made a note of the encounter. She was right. Something would have to be done. The factory was due to be inspected in two weeks' time and a lack of the correct equipment might result in a temporary halt in production. Bright wasn't concerned about the safety of his workplace but he did care about keeping the factory fully operational, so there was Daniel's argument. He sealed the note, walked into Bright's office to drop it on his desk, and then decided he would visit the warehouse to thank Mrs Butterfield for her help.

He asked the warehouse manager's permission to take up a few seconds of her time, knowing the man would not deny the company secretary.

'But there's no need,' Mrs Butterfield said. 'Main thing was that the boss din't witness it.'

He hadn't intended to, but Daniel ended up telling her about the parting shot fired at him by the apprentice's mother. He was gratified to see her lips twitch.

'What 'ave you done about it, apart from payin' for new trews?' she said.

'I've reminded Mr Bright of the inspection that's coming up.'

The woman standing next to Mrs Butterfield leaned forward. 'That's all very well, Mr Housley, but what if work's halted again, or there's another walk-out?'

Now the line was buzzing with chatter.

'There'll be a strike, I'm tellin' thee.'

'Well, I've got three from our house workin' 'ere, includin' the lodger. So, what'll happen when I've no wages an' no rent comin' in?'

'It'll take a death afore Bright sorts this place out.'

'It's not just this place, love. Factory work's dangerous, no two ways about it.'

'It pays the rent, though.'

'My brother-in-law were killed when 'is grindin' stone exploded. There were bits o' him stuck in the roof.'

'Ethel!'

Daniel grimaced at Mrs Butterfield. 'I'll leave you ladies to it,' he said.

She nodded. 'You can understand we want the factory run reight. I've got mouths to feed, we all 'ave.'

'I do understand.'

Outside, he loosened the collar of his shirt and gazed up at the hazy sky, and then walked heavily back up the stairs to his office. Rose Butterfield had mouths to feed. He wondered how many dependants she had, who was waiting at home to greet her on her return.

How lucky she was.

Chapter 4

A fortnight after the altercation in the yard, Rose was taken off the packing bench along with three other women and told to report to the company secretary. She guessed what was coming – all four of them did, and they walked across the yard in silence, each lost in their own thoughts.

Daniel Housley rose from his desk when they entered, his cheeks flushed, and stammered out a welcome.

'I'm sorry I can't offer you a seat,' he said, 'as you can see, I don't have much room in here.'

One of the women laughed. 'I'd be 'appy to take leave of thee so as to make more space.'

'No, no.' He wrung his hands. 'I am sorry. I wanted to give you this news rather than assign the warehouse manager to the... um... task, particularly as I'm aware some of you' – he looked at Rose – 'are employees of long standing. Additionally, I am sorry Mr Bright cannot be here in person but he wishes you to understand how deeply sorry he is.'

They all waited. The company secretary seemed to wither under their gaze. He took off his spectacles and laid them on his desk, then seemed to think better of it and hooked them back over his ears.

The same woman spoke again. 'Are we bein' laid off, or what?'

His brisk nod snapped the last thin fibre of hope Rose had been clinging on to. 'I'm afraid a large order has been cancelled,' he said, adding hastily, 'through no fault of our own, I assure you of that. And we are working very hard indeed to garner new business.'

Another woman, standing beside Rose, sneered at him. 'Ah well, that's a relief, then. That'll make tellin' me mister I've got the sack a much easier job, won't it?'

Rose put her hand on the woman's arm. 'Let's hear him out, love.'

Daniel Housley gave her a grateful look. 'There are others being laid off and I hope it will be a temporary situation but understandably you might want to find alternative employment.' He was falling over his words in his haste to expel them. 'You can collect what's owed you from Mr Schofield.'

Harry Schofield was the wages clerk. Rose frowned. 'Are we not workin' out the week?' she said.

This time, it was a shake of his head that confirmed her fear. 'No, I'm afraid not. Mr Bright, that is, we are... letting you go today. With immediate effect.' He cast his eyes down, then looked up at Rose. 'I'm very sorry, Mrs Butterfield.'

'Aye, me an' all.' She wondered whether the summary dismissal had anything to do with the fact that all the women crammed into this poky office had left their posts to watch the commotion in the yard over a leather apron. Mr Bright had not been present for that altercation but he might have persuaded the warehouse boss to part with a list of names.

'I promise each of you will be given a favourable reference.'

'So that's that?'

Rose glanced at the woman who had spoken, whose lips were folded tight against the tears she would not shed in front of this man. She had her pride. They all did.

Rose was the last to leave, and made as if to follow the others down the stairs before turning back. 'Can I 'ave a word?'

Daniel Housley was in the act of sitting down and sprang back to his feet.

'I'd like to speak to Mr Bright direct.'

He looked uncertain. 'I'm sorry. He isn't here. He's taken ill, I'm afraid.'

'Or can't face us lot, more like.'

Mr Housley's shoulders sagged. 'Or that, yes. His son is in America, drumming up new business, and I know you're a valued worker, Mrs Butterfield. Hopefully Bright's will be in a position to re-employ you very soon. I don't know if I can say that about everyone.'

'Well, I'm 'ere on my own behalf, not theirs.' Rose lifted her chin. 'I'm responsible for my family. I 'ave no husband to support me or my children.'

'I am sorry.'

'Don't you think I deserve better than waitin' around for that useless dollop to do his job?'

'I do.'

Rose nodded. 'Aye, I do, an' all. So gi' me Edgar Bright's address. I sharn't tell him where I got it.' She could see he was wavering, and pushed the point. 'I shall go an' see how he is, the poor soul, and appeal to his kind nature. You'd be helpin' me and nobody'd be any the wiser.'

A few minutes later, leaving the yard, she saw a group of women standing on the street on the other side of the road, including the three she'd been called to the office with. Rose lifted her scarf to cover her head, glad of the light rain that dampened the dust and dirt. She looked back at the factory gates. It was just a job. It paid the rent. But she'd spent most of her waking life at Bright's over the past five years and the idea she would not be returning was frightening. Grease and smoke clogged the hot and airless factory floor of the wire works and it was no better inside the warehouse, a draughty, mucky space where the finished product was cleaned and packed, ready to load onto wagons and travel far and wide. She would never travel as far as the springs she'd polished this morning. Although she'd gone a bit further today than she was expecting, finding herself turfed out on the street by dinnertime. Still, the place was as familiar as her own face, the wages weren't bad, and she would not be thrown out without so much as a by your leave.

She walked over to the women. 'Ey up, Ethel.'

Ethel cracked her swollen knuckles, making Rose wince. The older woman frequently complained her back was as stiff as a bar of steel from bending over the table, packing up boxes. If Rose were to complain, it would be about the taste of metal on her tongue and the smell of smoke always in her clothes. She looked across at the name above the main entrance. *Bright & Sons Wire Mills.* They now had a lot more to worry about than bad backs or stinking clothes, she and Ethel both.

She curled her fist more tightly around the scrap of paper the kindly company secretary had given her, which had the boss's address written on it.

One of the other women joined her in gazing up at the sign above the entrance. 'We're well rid o' this filthy place,' she said. 'Not safe to work in. What about that roller dyin' after that sheet o' steel whipped out o' the machine? Nob'dy got called to account for that, did they?'

'We can't do nowt about it,' said Ethel.

The woman curled her lip. 'We can march! Get a protest goin'. Strike like the men do. Women are allus the first to get laid off. I saw Eben wasn't pulled off the line, did tha see 'im smirkin'?' Rose wondered fleetingly if it had been Eben who had given her name to Mr Bright, if he was the reason she stood here. 'I tell thee what, I'd like to be earnin' what 'e is.'

'I know a plater's assistant, a woman, an' she's gettin' a pound a week,' said Ethel.

'An' I know a rubber on less than three shillin',' the woman retorted, 'where a man doin' the same job is gettin' two crown.'

Rose shook her head. 'Where do protests get you? I need work. I need to support me kids.' She was suddenly close to tears and clenched her fists. 'I've got nothin' to fall back on, nothin' except the workhouse.'

And a box full of sovereigns under her bed. But how far would they go? Each donation might be the last. And that money wasn't hers to spend until she knew where it was coming from.

'Aye,' said Ethel. 'Rose is talkin' sense.' She turned to walk away. 'No point standin' 'ere chewin' the fat. It'll all sort itself, just wait an' see what fate brings.'

Allowing fate to take its course was a luxury Rose couldn't afford.

She said her farewells and set off at a good pace, north towards Newhall Road, which spanned the fast-flowing waters of the Don, linking Attercliffe to Brightside village. Ahead, a towering expanse of red bricks that were not yet soot-blackened sprouted from the river bank. Another new factory. A pretty sight for sore eyes. There were always jobs to be had, in this town. Was she on a fool's errand? Rose slowed her pace over the bridge and stopped when she reached the other side. Her eyes followed a wagon as it clattered past, towards the town.

'Tha looks lost, love.'

A man was blocking the path in front of her. He was bare-headed, a short, burly figure in a dirty collarless shirt, blue britches and sturdy boots, one of the navvies that were shipped in for construction projects. He could be working behind that high brick wall, and would know what kind of manufactory was being created. No. She would continue on, have it out with Mr Edgar Bright. She shook her head and pushed past the man.

'Jus' tryin' to help,' he called after her.

Rose rounded a corner and stopped to examine the piece of paper in her hand. The address given was a residence near the church of St Thomas, which sat on the crest of a hill and should therefore be easy to find. It would be a long walk home through town but Rose reckoned she could manage it in an afternoon and be back when the children expected her, in time for tea. If not, Jane would feed the little ones. They could eat the crumpets and the rest of the strawberries and blackberries they'd picked last Sunday.

She spent the rest of the walk planning her approach. It was important to present a confident front, to remind Mr Bright that she had been an exemplary employee for several years, with never a day off sick nor slacking. She was a hard worker, as good as the men. She oughtn't to say she was better than them, though she was. She was young and strong. She would remind him she was a widow, but she would not beg; she had survived thus far without handouts. This reminded Rose again of the money she was concealing under her bed – the mystery of it nagged her constantly, like an itch just out of reach. Her benefactor might even now be counting out his coin, or waiting for an opportunity to place an envelope, slipping into her house as silently as a fox. She shuddered at the thought. But what could she do? She could imagine how the conversation would go if she reported it to the police.

There's somebody gettin' into the house, over and over.

And what have they taken?

Nowt.

So, they're not stealing from you?

No.

What are they doing?

Leaving envelopes of money.

Now, there's a problem I'd like to have!

Rose slowed her pace as she passed a chandlery at the foot of Holywell Road, a corner of her mind making a mental note to purchase candles and soap on the way back.

Perhaps the donations came from the family saved by Archie from the Dale Dyke flood almost a decade earlier, a way of offering financial support she would be too proud to accept directly. The man of the house had wept copious tears at Archie's funeral and had clutched her hand at the wake, telling her the tale she'd heard oftentimes from Archie's own lips. Rose smiled gently to herself. She would give anything to hear her husband tell that tale again, how he'd come home after work, gulped down his tea, rocked Jane to sleep and gone straight back out to do a seven o'clock to midnight watchman's shift. He had been in Neepsend when the monstrous wave poured into town in the dead of night, released by a shattered dam in the Loxley Valley. It had destroyed in a matter of minutes everything that lay in its path for more than eight miles, wiping out fifteen bridges and countless lives.

Archie told Rose he had heard the thunderous cascade before he saw the black curtain begin to rise up the street, a monstrous sight that had rendered him immobile. Then he had sprung into action, knocking up a neighbour to lay a ladder between the hill behind and the bedroom window of a house already halfway to being engulfed, no thought to his own safety.

He'd got them all out – mother, father, all six children including a babe in arms – before the cottage collapsed and joined the churning debris. Archie had worked on, soaked through, and returned home at dawn in a state of exhaustion. By the time he woke halfway through the morning of the following day, Rose had already learned about the flood, and his heroism, from the neighbours. She recalled, grimly, that she had been aghast at the thought that she might have lost him. He had gone and left her anyway.

Perhaps the money came from a kind-hearted neighbour? No. She would have seen some giveaway sign, a look or a weighted word spoken.

She passed a row of cottage workshops and a public inn; beyond that, a field of gently swaying crops that looked ready for harvesting; and finally, near the church at the top of the hill, a handsome redbrick house sitting in the shade of oak and sycamore trees. Two horses hitched to a curricle were tied up nearby. She had not counted on Mr Bright having visitors. Or had the doctor come to call? She did not believe his tale of ill-health, so perhaps he did have guests after all. Or it was his own gig and the stable boy had got it ready for a jaunt. It didn't matter. She was here now. She had to try.

The gravel path between the flower beds in the front garden crunched noisily under her boots as she approached the front door, the sound adding to the ridiculous feeling that she was trespassing, about to commit some crime, or overstepping the mark at the very least. She was foolish and should not have come. Nevertheless, she reached for the knocker. Before Rose could lift it, the door opened and she was staring into the wide-eyed face of a balding, middle-aged man in the act of putting on his hat. She was certain the same gormless look of surprise sat on her own face, and replaced it with a thunderous frown.

'My!' The gentleman lowered his arm, tapping his hat against his leg. 'What a furious expression. I merely opened the door.'

'Well, you startled me.' Rose attempted a smile. 'I've come to call on Mr Bright.'

'Why, my dear, let me show you in.' He stood back and bowed, with a mocking grin that set her teeth on edge. His manner seemed odd for a servant but Rose's experience of household staff was limited. Perhaps they were all this arrogant.

She hesitated, unwilling to leave the safety of the sunlit doorstep for the gloom of the interior of the house. 'Is Mrs Bright here?'

'She has gone into town, I believe. But you said you wished to see the man of the house?'

'I were told he's poorly. Least, he weren't at work today.'

'Why, he's fit as the proverbial!' Realisation dawned on the man's face. He looked her up and down. 'You're one of his women, from the factory, aren't you?'

'I...' She lifted her chin and met his curious gaze. 'Yes, I'm Rose Butterfield.'

'Well, this should be fun. Come in, come in.' He marched away and Rose took a deep breath and followed in his wake. 'Edgar! A lovely young lady has come to call on you, concerned for your health.'

She followed him into an orangery filled with exotic-looking ferns. Through the gaps between the glossy leaves of the lush plants and the glass walls that contained them, she glimpsed an immaculately kept lawn and ornamental fountain. A table in the middle of the room held the remains of a meal and a half-empty decanter of pale gold liquid. Edgar Bright was sitting nearby, half-swallowed by the cushions of a large wicker chair. His eyes were half-closed but he managed to hoist an eyebrow. 'Back so soon, Albert? Who's this...?'

'We breakfasted well this morning,' said the other man, with a wink. 'It bled into lunch, didn't it, Edgar?' He steered Rose to a seat at the table. 'I apologise for the debris. I believe Mrs Bright could use a better maid; what do you think? Accommodation is provided. The attic is quite roomy. I can vouch for that.'

'I already 'ave a house to look after,' said Rose, 'and children.'

She caught the glance he directed at the wedding band on her finger. 'And a hard-working and handsome husband, no doubt?'

'I'm widowed.'

'Young, to be alone in the world, if I may say. But very easy on the eye.' He laughed. 'There's that frown again, ruining your pretty face. You should learn to take a compliment. Shall I introduce myself, as Edgar here seems incapable?'

'No. I mean... I came here to...' Rose pursed her lips. 'I'm sorry, but I need to speak to Mr Bright.' She glared at the factory owner, who had remained seated. He shook his head as though to clear it.

45

'Oh, I know you. You're Mrs Butterfield,' he said, slurring her name. 'Are you one of them I've laid off? Why do you think I was absent today? I'm distraught.'

'Sorrows to drown,' said the other man. 'But you'll bounce back, Edgar, you always do.'

Rose opened her mouth to speak but Edgar Bright got there first. 'This is Mr Albert Boothby. He built this house, you know. Isn't it magnificent?'

Albert Boothby dropped into a chair, flapping one hand. 'You paid enough for it.' He gave Rose a lascivious look. 'And I *had* it built by a bunch of navvies. I don't get my hands dirty, my dear.'

She felt heat fill her chest and rise to colour her cheeks, and clasped her hands in an attempt to retain her temper. 'I'm sure it's a lovely house, er...' She had forgotten his name. 'Mr Bright, I've come 'ere—'

He interrupted her. 'Were you sent? You were sent, weren't you? It won't do you lot any good causing trouble for me. It's not my doing, it's simply the' – he burped – 'pardon me, the circumstances we find ourselves in. Temporary circumstances.' He sat up straighter, as if something had just occurred to him. 'Don't go telling people that Bright's is in trouble.'

'Why would I? An' I weren't sent. I'm here under my own steam to speak for mesen and nobody else.'

'You see,' the other man said. 'Such outspokenness is what comes of allowing these girls to work in factories. They become coarse. And they're taking jobs that rightfully belong to men, too. The domestic sphere is where you belong, my dear. Where all women belong.'

'And who feeds my family and keeps the roof over our heads then?' Rose cursed herself for rising to the bait. She had a purpose, and shouldn't allow this irritating creature to derail her.

'Find another husband. You've a fair face.' He smirked. 'There are other opportunities for good-looking lasses.'

Edgar Bright frowned blearily. 'Girls're cheaper to employ, y'know, Boothby. And I've not sacked 'em all, only a few packers, while we're quiet.'

'Ten, at least,' said Rose. 'You laid off a good few today with no notice.' She took a deep breath. 'I've been at your place for the past five years, since my lads were babes in arms. I'm willin' to take on other roles…'

He held up his hand. 'I've enough nagging from the masters wanting to bring more apprentices in.' He sighed. 'I suppose I can get you some nail-making work. I know a man who could use an extra pair of hands.'

She was expected to be grateful. 'Thank you, but that won't even pay the—'

'And I'm told you're a quick worker when it comes to wrapping and casing up, so I can place you top of the list when I'm ready to rehire. Will that satisfy?'

Rose pursed her lips.

Albert Boothby chuckled. 'Clearly not. I'm inclined to help the young lady.' He found a space on the ironwork of the tabletop that was not cluttered with crockery and drummed his fingers on it. 'Edgar. Your acquaintance who has the match factory at York. Do you remember telling me about the problem he has, with a certain employee? A most difficult dilemma.'

'I'd hoped you might take that unfortunate girl as a scullery maid, Albert,' said Mr Bright morosely. 'That was my reason for telling you the tale.'

'Would she be able to work, in her state? And do we want visitors catching a glimpse of her? That's why she's being spirited away, after all.'

'I'd rather you didn't use terms that imply she's being removed against her will,' Edgar Bright said faintly. 'I should never have confided in you. I thought you'd have her at your—'

The other man talked over him. 'You're repeating yourself. No, I have a much better idea.'

Had they forgotten she was there? Rose got up and turned towards the door. She should not have come. But Mr Bright's friend leaped to his feet and put his hand on her arm. He seemed unperturbed when she shook him off.

'Young lady, do you have space for a lodger, for a girl who needs to convalesce, with as little interaction with others as possible?'

She saw light dawn on Mr Bright's face. 'Oh, I see. Yes, but who would pay?'

'I will.' Albert Boothby puffed out his chest. 'Send some prospective house purchasers my way, Edgar, and we'll call it a favour returned. Well?'

He was directing the question at Rose. 'I've a large cellar space, next to the coal 'ole,' she said, 'but now the weather is turning, I don't know...'

'It sounds perfect! It's for a working woman, like yourself. Doesn't need to be fancy.'

Mr Bright added: 'It's not permanent, just until she recovers or...'

'Recovers, yes,' said the other man. 'An income for you, until Mr Bright re-employs you, as I'm sure he will, of five shillings a week out of my own pocket. That more than covers food and board.' He smiled, a grotesque attempt at modesty. 'It's the Christian thing to do.'

'I won't have the time to nurse her,' said Rose. 'What's wrong with her?'

'Well.' Edgar Bright tapped his mouth with a fingertip. 'She has developed a condition that requires rest. She needs to be away from any undue influences. She wouldn't be any trouble to you.' He made an impatient sound. 'Mr Boothby is making an offer. Do you accept?'

'All right,' said Rose. 'Six shillings would be acceptable.'

'Five shillings and sixpence,' said Mr Boothby.

Rose nodded slowly and shook his hand when he held it out. He squeezed her fingers – 'I would have paid six, my dear, if you had pressed it' – and turned her hand over to kiss the back of it. Rose recoiled, snatching her hand away. Both men laughed heartily.

'It might come to naught,' said Mr Boothby. 'But I should hurry home and make up a bed for your new lodger.'

—

Rattled by the encounter, Rose was seized by the need to unburden herself, to whisper her concerns to the only person she could trust. But the cemetery where Archie lay, where she sometimes sat on the grass beside his grave and told him how tall and strong his children were growing, was on the other side of town and she was footsore enough. There was another spot, closer to hand, that she visited when she felt strong enough. It was the location in the middle of the town where her husband spent his last, lonely moments. It had been a long time since she had laid flowers there.

Rose struggled through the undergrowth near the riverbank, her skirt catching on nettles and thistles, to reach a patch where wildflowers were growing in abundance. She picked yellow iris and meadowsweet, breathing in their heady scent, and walked further west before crossing another bridge, a rickety wooden footbridge that would take her back towards the town, to Change Alley, where her husband had met his end.

Chapter 5

Perched on the edge of a chair in the corner of the machine room, Annie leafed through the *Tribune*, a flutter of excitement stirring in her belly every time she turned a page. She could hear Rob conversing with a customer in the front of the shop, noting down the details of an advertisement for a new shoeing forge in Sycamore Street. Both the salesman and distributor were out drumming up business. Jem had sorted through the international and national news that came on the wire, made a list for Rob to approve, and had left to cover an inquest into a case of arsenic poisoning. He was due back any moment for the Monday afternoon editorial meeting.

She was happy for her cousin, she was. He had found his place, it seemed, but it was a niche Annie felt she could have slipped into quite happily, although as Rob pointed out, a woman would not be granted the same access necessary for news-gathering as a man. She had been forced to agree, annoyingly.

Impatience was gaining the advantage over anticipation as she scoured pages four and five. An advertisement caught her eye. J. Meekes was holding a clearance sale of summer stock – plain and fancy dresses, cloth and silk jackets, and the like. She would pay a visit. Annie was proud of a thriftiness that extended to buying fabric cut to size to sew into garments herself, but there were occasions that demanded fancier garb than anything she could run up on the sewing machine. On pages six and seven there were adverts extolling the virtues of new-fangled cooking ranges, Venetian blinds, spirits and spectacles. Rob was, as he had promised, reeling them in. A surgeon-dentist touted for business in text contained within a border in the shape of a molar tooth, and all manner of wonders were promised in a column devoted to tours of foreign lands.

It was with a bitter disappointment already brewing that she turned to the back page. Court cases, church meetings, concerts. Jem had written a paragraph about the progress being made on the creation of a new music hall in Barker Pool. This was due to open in late autumn with the capacity to seat over two thousand people. Courtesy of his job, Jem was now a source of free tickets to theatrical productions, concerts and plays all over town, in return for a review in the pages of the *Tribune*, and took Annie along when he couldn't find a pretty young woman to accompany him. She folded the newspaper and shook her head in exasperation. Six times the weekly *Tribune* had been published and distributed throughout the town – and still no promised column. She got up and stalked through the case room to the office, where she riffled through papers on the cluttered desks, then checked the contents of the drawers and examined the untidy bookcase. There was no sign of the layout book for the following week's publication.

At the shop counter, Rob was bidding farewell to the blacksmith. He turned to watch her.

'What are you looking for, my love?'

'You know very well.'

When he laughed, she shook her fist. 'You infuriate me.'

'Not very ladylike,' Rob said. 'I will try to find space in the next issue.'

'I've heard that before.'

He leaned back against the counter, grinning. 'You can't find the pages because I haven't started them yet. My darling, I'm not concealing them from you.'

Before she could respond, the bell above the shop door tinkled and Jem rushed through like a whirlwind, vaulted the counter and crouched beneath it. He peered up at Annie and Rob, merriness in his eyes. He put one finger to his lips and at that moment a portly man ran through the door Jem had left open, coat tails flapping, and came to an abrupt halt, breathing heavily.

'Alderman Prestwick,' said Rob smoothly, 'what can we do for you?'

The man's colour, in Annie's opinion, was dangerously hectic.

'Mr Whittaker. Madam. I was trying to attract the attention of your reporter. I saw him enter, only a moment ago.'

'Ah yes,' said Rob. 'He had urgent business to attend to – in Fargate – and took the shortcut through the back. Always on the go, that young man. Perhaps I can help?'

Alderman Prestwick took out a handkerchief and pressed it against his temple. 'I wish to make a complaint about your report of the council meeting, that I have to say I have had shown to me, as the *Tribune* is not one of the newspapers I take.' He took a breath. 'A personal slur was made against my person by that reporter of yours. Damn the man.'

'I see.' Rob lifted the hatch and for a moment Annie thought he was going to invite the alderman into the office, and darted a glance at Jem, but Rob walked through to the other side, closed the hatch behind him, and laid a consoling hand on the man's arm. 'There is a new coffee house across the way. Let us go and sit and resolve your issue in a calm and gentlemanly manner.' He made a point of looking at Annie, who smiled demurely.

'Of course, of course. I apologise, madam.'

Now sitting cross-legged under the counter, Jem reached out and pulled the hem of Annie's skirt. She coughed to cover a squeal of surprise and kicked him in the shin.

'Not at all,' she said. 'Goodness knows, Jem can be exasperating.'

'Perhaps he sometimes fails to consider the sensitivities of others,' said Rob. 'I think I can guess the matter to which this pertains. Come.' He stood back to allow the alderman out and followed him, grimacing over his shoulder at Annie as they left.

She watched them cross the street and tapped the counter. 'You can come out now, you rascal.'

Jem stood up, and brushed down his trousers. 'Dusty under there,' he muttered.

'Well? What was all that about?'

'Well, Annie, I can tell you there was nothing wrong with the report of the council meeting.' He couldn't keep the smile off his face.

'You're very pleased with yourself, considering you were hiding from the gentleman a moment ago.'

'Oh.' He waved a hand. 'I can't be bothered with his bluster and nonsense. I wrote a paragraph about him and he's taken offence. You know, he almost went under the wheels of a cart when he spotted me and gave chase.'

'I'm surprised Rob agreed to print a criticism of one of the town worthies.'

'It was a paragraph, an editorial comment, containing a harmless quip.'

'Even so. I'm trying to persuade my husband to publish an editorial on behalf of my sisters in the political association and he is curiously resistant.' She tapped her fingers on the counter. 'No matter. So, Alderman Prestwick has not appreciated your witticism. What did you say to offend him?'

'Nothing that hadn't a kernel of truth at the heart.'

'What was it?'

'Only that he seemed a slate short of a full roof.'

He followed her gaze to the ceiling. 'Have you lost something, Annie?'

'Only my patience, cousin.'

'We had better find it before your husband returns. I remember bearing the brunt of your bad temper when we were children.'

'Your punishments were always well-deserved.'

Jem pulled a mock-sorrowful face. 'Being shut in the wardrobe has made me forever afraid of the dark.'

'It's Rob I'm cross with.' Annie gazed out of the window, where a woman carrying an armful of wild-flowers stood on the pavement. She looked familiar but Annie couldn't place her. 'He will print your infantile comment but won't allow me to write a column about the injustices being faced by the working woman.'

'Because nobody would read it,' said Jem. He kissed Annie's cheek, then followed her gaze. 'Is she coming in, d'you think?'

To Annie's surprise, the woman crouched below the low frontage wall and was lost to view.

'Someone else you've upset, Jem?'

'I hope not; she's rather comely. And she's brought flowers, which is an odd weapon of choice.'

'Stay here. Try to refrain from getting into any fresh mischief.'

Annie didn't wait for his reply. She could see the top of the scarf that covered the woman's head from the window, and stepped onto the pavement to find her engrossed in the task of arranging the flowers against the wall. Her face, when she tipped it up to look at Annie, was streaked with tears. Annie recognised her immediately. It was the woman from Paradise Square, who had followed Annie down the alley to get away from the crowd.

'Oh dear.' Annie held out her hand and after a moment of hesitation the woman took it and rose to her feet. 'I don't have a handkerchief.'

'I don't need one.' She swiped her cheeks with the back of her hand, a gesture that a child would make. 'You must think I'm addled.'

'No.' Annie spoke slowly. 'I'm wondering what has happened to upset you so. Will you come inside? Or is it our publication that's brought you to tears? I do hope not.'

To her relief, the woman smiled and her solemn eyes sparkled for a moment. 'Don't worry, what's upset me 'appened long before your time.'

Annie stuck out her hand again. 'I'm Annie Whittaker, the proprietor's wife. We've met before.'

'Aye. I remember. You came to my rescue. I'm Rose Butterfield.' She laughed self-consciously when she shook Annie's hand. Her grip was firm and strong.

'I rather think you rescued yourself. Are you thirsty? Come inside, and tell me what you think of my elderflower lemonade.'

—

'They arrested the driver *and* the stoker.'

Jem was gossiping about the fish train that had departed Doncaster early that morning. Somewhere along the line it had ploughed through a signal house, leaving it as flat as a scattered pack of cards. It had then dashed into an excursion train taking holidaymakers from Sheffield to Cleethorpes, shearing it in half.

'What a terrible tragedy,' said Rose.

'I wonder how it got out of control?' said Annie.

'Four dead, unfortunately.' Jem paused when the office door opened. Rob entered, alone, and closed the door behind him. 'Scores injured.'

Annie introduced Rose to her husband. 'I've discovered something about the history of this place,' she said, reaching out to take Rose's hand. 'This poor lady's husband passed away outside our premises, Robert. I knew that realtor was getting at something but I wasn't expecting it to be so tragic as this.'

'It was six years ago,' said Rose. 'There's no reason you'd know of it.' She turned to Rob. 'My Archie – he was a night watchman – he was just in the wrong place at the wrong time. He was passing by when a bomb went off.'

'Oh, my goodness,' said Rob. 'I'm terribly sorry.'

'It was the tenant before us,' said Annie. 'Rose says the place has been empty since. They were publishing pamphlets that criticised the unions and one of the union bosses was ordering shootings, bombings, stealing tools—'

'Oh!' Rob interrupted. 'I know of this, of course. It's been going on for decades.'

'It's settled down a lot,' said Jem, 'now that these unions are recognised in law.'

'Too late for my husband.' She smiled but Annie saw the anguish in her eyes. 'But as I say, it were a long while back.'

Jem was seated next to Rose. He leaned towards her so their shoulders were almost touching. Annie saw her stiffen but Jem seemed oblivious. 'So, Rob,' he said, 'what of our esteemed Alderman Prestwick? Did you manage to placate him?' He lowered his voice so that Rose was forced to incline her head towards him. 'I may have hinted that the man was a shilling short of a crown.'

She laughed and Jem moved away, a satisfied smile on his face.

'That wasn't quite the expression,' said Rob. 'Perhaps you will learn to be a little more circumspect in your views.'

'It does no harm,' said Annie, 'for the proprietor of a new publication to be witnessed drinking coffee with one of the town's leaders.'

'I count myself lucky Alderman Prestwick did not pour his cup over my head!'

'As Annie rightly points out, a little notoriety doesn't hurt,' said Jem. 'We're adding spice to reading rooms and parlours all over Sheffield. I called into the King's Head Hotel earlier, in pursuit of a story, and we're sitting on the counter of that fine establishment too.'

'In pursuit of a story,' said Rose contemplatively, and they all turned to look at her. 'Sorry. It sounds excitin', your job.'

Jem smiled broadly at Rose. 'I've had a few jobs. Clerking was the most boring. But I think I've found my metier at last.' He turned to Rob. 'I have a snippet from the town hall that will mollify the alderman. Work is starting in the grounds of Weston Hall to create a park for the people of the town, thanks to the munificence of our leaders. I'll take you there, Rose, for the grand official opening. What d'you think?'

'I think you're a bit full o' yourself.'

Jem burst out laughing. 'Ah, but is that a yes?'

Rose joined in the laughter, a little nervously in Annie's opinion. She was twisting her wedding band around and around.

'I apologise for my cousin,' said Annie. 'Husband!'

'What?' said Rob, startled.

'How is it that you can't find space for a report from my political association, whereas Jem's puerile insults' – she raised her voice to cover Jem's protests – 'get the column inches.'

Rob hopped off the desk. 'Not now, my love.'

'Not now?'

Rose cleared her throat. 'Your association sounds interesting, Annie.'

She leaped on this. 'Yes! It's a women's group. We meet at the temperance hotel in Queen Street.'

'To sit with their embroidery and talk about recipes and the like,' said Rob.

Annie threw him a furious glance. 'Really, you are becoming tiresome now. We have just written to Mundella to complain about conditions for factory workers, especially the women. You could join us, Rose. We're always looking for new members.'

'I work in a factory. A wire mills in Attercliffe. Well, I did.' She shrugged. 'I've just this morning been laid off.'

'I'm sorry to hear that,' said Jem.

Rose acknowledged his comment with a wan smile. 'It's not the end o' the world. The women I worked wi' were all right but the place weren't up to much.'

'How so?' Jem glanced at Annie. 'If you don't mind my asking.'

'I don't mind.' Rose sighed. 'We've 'ad a few accidents, and a bit o' trouble over defective machinery. One lad's mother turned up in a rage because he din't have a leather apron and his trousers burned through.'

Annie threw up her hands. 'You see?'

'What will you do now,' asked Jem, 'if that's not too personal a question?'

'Find another. Or wait for things to pick up at Bright's. I've been there five years.'

'What's it like?' Annie leaned forward. 'On the factory floor?'

'Hot, noisy, dirty. But I was in the warehouse, packin'. I did a bit of finishing, an' all, but that's mucky work. You scrub an' scrub but your hands won't come clean.'

Rob clapped his hands. 'A little like us with our ink-stained fingers. We need to have our meeting, Jem.'

'I'll be off, then,' said Rose.

Annie was mortified. 'I do apologise, we're not chasing you away, Rose. In fact, I'd love to stroll a little way with you, and chat more?'

'She'll have her claws in you, for her group,' said Rob.

'Why not?' said Annie. 'It was started by working-class women, like Rose here.'

'Oh, I don't have time for that sort o' thing.' Rose smiled at Annie. 'Or to stroll about, neither. I've outstayed my welcome an' need to get home to the children.'

On the pavement outside, the flowers wilted against the wall, already losing their lustre. Annie bent to scoop them up.

'Shall I take them inside? I can put them in a vase.'

Rose raised her gaze from the pavement, her eyes distant. 'You don't need to. I don't want to put you out.'

'Oh, you're not!' Annie shook the flowers, intending to remove the street dust. Petals and leaves fell to the ground. 'Oh dear. Well. I shall hope to see you again soon, Rose. It's lovely to meet you, properly I mean, and despite the circumstances.'

'And you, an' all.'

Annie watched Rose walk quickly to the end of Change Alley and turn the corner. She looked down at the pavement, trying to imagine a man taking his last breaths here. Rose had told her the culprits were never brought to justice. They could be walking around the town now. Rose might see them every day, and not know.

How terrible that must be.

Jem appeared. 'She's a pleasant girl.'

'I could tell you had noticed.'

He nudged her elbow. 'Don't tease me, our Annie. Are you going to keep in touch?'

'Yes,' said Annie. 'She gave me her address and I've arranged to call on her. I'd like to find out more about her.'

'So she can help you with your cause?'

Annie hesitated. 'Yes, but not only that. I like her.'

'So do I.'

'She seems impervious to your charms.'

'You think so? I might come along with you, when you visit her.'

'To keep me company?'

'Yes.' He turned innocent eyes on her. 'What other reason could there be?'

Chapter 6

Daniel would have preferred to return to the Golden Ball after work and sup an ale or two in genial company, but he had promised to call on his mother today. She lived on Fitzwilliam Street, and a five-and-twenty-minute stroll in the smoky autumnal evening appealed to his senses even if the destination did not. Drifts of fallen leaves lay on pavements that had been decorated by cherry blossom only a matter of months ago, and the pearly light of early evening clarified the mustard-yellow leaves and the rust-coloured ferns that poked from dark hedges. It would soon be winter, and another year gone by without making amends.

He found his mother in her front parlour, hunched in one of the plush velvet armchairs that had replaced the dining furniture. *What use have I for table and chairs*, she had said, *when the days of entertaining company are long gone?* The grate was empty; his mother would not light a fire in the parlour until the first day of November, whatever the weather. He could appreciate why Mabel was lingering in the kitchen, where the temperature was several degrees warmer. A pianoforte that was never played stood against the flock wallpaper, a velvet-coloured stool tucked between its feet. His mother frequently lamented the lack of a daughter-in-law who would fill the house with music, a complaint Daniel never rose to, although he silently seethed.

She was pretending that she hadn't noticed him enter. She held a folded newspaper in one hand and magnifying glass in the other, her head bent close to the page she was reading so that only the top of her black lace cap and a few tendrils of white hair were visible. It had been four years since his father's death but his mother had chosen to adopt the trend for long-term mourning clothes, as favoured by the Queen, and seemed determined to remain in her black crepe.

'Good evening, Mother.'

'Oh!' She straightened, her hand going to her heart. 'You startled me. I must have lost track of the time. Where's Mabel? Mabel! Where are you?'

'Don't fret so, Mother. Everything is in hand. Mabel's in the kitchen, preparing a pot of tea and sandwiches.' He had only been in her presence for a few moments and was already exhausted. 'I came in the back as I discovered the front door was bolted against me.'

She gave him a scornful look, wrinkling her nose. 'Well, of course the front door is locked. Can't have people wandering in off the street.'

'When has anyone ever wandered in off the street?'

'There's a first time for everything.' She put her hand to the silver and onyx brooch at her throat. 'And a last. An elderly gentleman who lives only a few streets away was robbed and left for dead. He expired a few days later, from the shock of it. I don't know what the world is coming to.'

Daniel gestured at her lap. 'Is that what you've been reading about?'

'Hmm?' She stared at the newspaper as if it had jumped into her hand of its own volition. Then, for a second, he could have sworn a shifty look crossed her face. 'Oh, this. No, my neighbour told me about the robbery. She was kind enough to pay me a visit to ensure I wasn't too badly shaken. No, this is the new weekly, the *Tribune*. I thought I would try it and asked Mabel to bring me a copy. If I'd asked you, I'd never have got one, would I? I'd still be waiting.'

'What do you think of it?'

'I am glad I advertised in the *Sheffield Telegraph*.' She laid the newspaper on the table beside her armchair.

'Advertised?'

'I believe the *Telegraph* attracts a better class of reader.'

Daniel frowned. 'You haven't taken out another advertisement, have you?'

His mother had form in this regard. Admittedly, the most recent advert she had placed had been to secure the services of a live-in companion. Mabel had been the successful applicant. She was also widowed, was around the same age as his mother, had the patience of a saint, and had settled in very well. Daniel decided he would speak to Mabel about keeping a closer eye on his mother. In her previous adventures in publication, she had advertised the pianoforte, the mirror that hung above the fireplace, and even her own bed for sale.

'Here she is.' His mother smiled imperiously at Mabel as she backed into the room carrying a tray with a teapot, three cups on saucers and a plate of sandwiches balanced on it. Then she turned her attention back to Daniel. 'You might say, my dear, that I'm advertising something of great value, the very survival of the Housley name.'

'Mother, you're not making sense.' He glanced at the grandfather clock in the corner of the room, wondering how soon he could escape to the comfort of the lounge at the Golden Ball and find somebody willing to have a game of backgammon. 'Mabel, what do you know of this?'

Mabel gave him a sideways look and folded her lips together.

'Mother, how many times must I reassure you that you are comfortably off? There's no need to sell your possessions.'

'Oh, she's not tried sellin' the furniture off again,' said Mabel. 'She's marketing summat else entirely.'

A secretive smile played on his mother's lips. 'Let's consider the subject closed, for now, my handsome boy.'

'As you wish. Mabel, you must call on me if my mother's eccentricities become overwhelming.'

'Do not talk about me as if I am not here. I must admit, these sandwiches are delicious, Mabel.'

Mabel patted her hand. 'You can safely leave her in my care, lad.'

Daniel was happy to acquiesce. He could admit to himself that he hadn't the patience for his mother's little dramas. Worse, she reminded him of his own weakness. No doubt another man now shared Louisa's life, where Daniel ought to be. Another man basked in the glow of her dimpled smile across the breakfast table. Daniel hated that man, and wondered how it was possible to harbour such a strong antipathy towards someone who might not even exist. Daniel had eventually rebelled against his parents and his church, but it had been too late. She had turned him away. He wasn't prone to melodrama but losing Louisa still felt like he had lost his one great chance at happiness. No one else would do, not that he had ladies knocking down his door.

'I had hoped to see grandchildren before I depart this earthly plane,' his mother said wistfully.

It was as if she had read his mind. Mabel saved her from the retort that was on Daniel's lips – *You're not dead yet* – by expressing the same sentiment in a more kindly manner.

'Why, Mrs Housley, you're hale and hearty.'

His mother wasn't having any of it. Her mouth twisted. 'You miss the point, Mabel. You'll be thirty, Daniel...'

'I'm twenty-eight.'

'...before you know it, and how many times since that unfortunate escapade' – she cut her eyes at Mabel, wordlessly telling Daniel that the woman did not know about Louisa, and he should not raise the subject – 'have you brought home a young lady to be introduced to us?'

Mabel raised her eyebrows enquiringly and looked disappointed when neither mother nor son spoke.

'I had my child too late in life,' his mother said sadly, 'and I am becoming resigned to the fact I may never see grandchildren. I should have had a girl child, and got her married off quick-sharp.'

This led to a discussion between his mother and Mabel about the young and comely daughters who lived in the house next door, and how they delighted in running errands for Mrs Housley and her companion. Why, nothing was too much trouble for them. Mabel had stepped outside the other day and, goodness me, there they were helping the gardener pull up the beets and onions and pick the last of the plums from the tree.

'I must admit, the plums are still sweet as anything,' his mother said. 'There's a bowlful in the kitchen, Daniel.

Take it with you. I'm sure you're not eating enough fruit and vegetables.'

When he felt enough time had elapsed to avoid protest, Daniel pushed his fingers through his hair and rose to his feet, running his finger along his collar and adjusting his necktie. In a moment, his mother would admonish him for fidgeting. 'Well, ladies, I think it's time I wandered home. It was pleasant to see you, Mother. Good evening, Mabel.'

Once on the pavement, clutching the bowl that Mabel had covered with a piece of muslin and tied with string, he reconsidered his decision to return immediately to the Golden Ball. He could turn his feet in that direction or he could stroll around the corner and pay a visit on his former employer and old friend. He wasn't empty-handed; he would arrive bearing the gift of plums. And there was something that he needed to know. He stood on the pavement, arms crossed and shoulders hunched. From the corner of his eye, he saw the curtain of his mother's parlour twitch. Daniel made his decision, turned on his heel and set off towards the Wellington Street home of Silas and Harriet Hinchcliffe.

Silas answered the door in britches and a shirt with the sleeves rolled up. His dark hair was peppered with dust from the factory yard. Daniel felt he could draw a line in the dust on the man's cheek.

'Dan!' Silas was gratifyingly pleased to see him. 'Tha's caught me just in from work. Gi' me a minute to go an' get mesen washed. Harriet! Come an' see who's called on us.'

As Silas pounded up the stairs in his stockinged feet, Harriet came out of the drawing room, leaning on a stick, her thick red hair loose on her shoulders. 'Daniel!' He removed the muslin from the bowl and held it out for her inspection. 'Plums? How lovely.' She took it from him and rested it on the sideboard. 'Thank you.' Their embrace reminded him of how long it had been since he was affectionately handled, and he scoffed at himself. He should return as a pampered lapdog in his next life and spend all his time being petted and fed.

'I wondered when you'd call on us. Isaac will be pleased to see you.' She pulled back, concern in her eyes. 'I hope everything is all right?'

Daniel followed her down the hall. 'I'm very well. But how are you, Harriet?'

'Oh, this.' She lifted the stick. 'My foot plagues me more when the colder weather arrives. Come and sit by the fire.'

Silas's wife had been born with a deformed foot that, she had once told him, was made worse by crude attempts to fix it. It was not often he saw her use a stick, but then he hadn't visited for many months, not since he took the job at Bright's. He bit his lip and rubbed his arms. He had neglected his friends, and now here he was under false pretences.

'Are you feeling cold, Dan? Come closer to the fire.'

The drawing room was made cosy by the light from the lamps and the coals that glowed in the hearth. The room was cluttered, half of it taken up by a mahogany dining table and chairs. There was a pink chaise longue and a tall potted plant in the corner; they were new, he thought. He hadn't seen the card table before either. A half-finished game of chess sat on it, a handful of rosewood pieces standing either side of the board like actors waiting to go back on stage. Books and periodicals balanced precariously on an ornate sideboard under the large bay window that was covered by heavy green velvet drapes. Daniel stepped over the family dog to sit in one of the two large, deep armchairs that flanked the fireplace. The collie lifted her nose a fraction of an inch and managed a feeble wag of her tail when Daniel spoke.

'Getting some warmth in those old bones, Shandy?' He patted her flank. 'Getting skinny in your old age, eh?'

Silas came in with a glass of whisky in each hand. 'Here tha goes, Dan.'

Dan took a glass. 'Thanks, Silas. I need this. I've just been to visit my mother.'

'How is she?' said Harriet.

'Bane of tha life still? Bossin' thee about?'

'Silas!' Harriet frowned. 'I should hope Isaac won't ever say that of me.'

'He's eleven, love. He still thinks the sun shines out tha—'

'Silas, stop it! How are you getting on at Bright's, Dan?'

Daniel laughed. Being in the company of these convivial people was a balm for the soul. 'I thought I'd bitten off more than I could chew but I'm finding my feet now. There are some lively characters on the factory floor; some of the women are more ribald than the men.'

'We were sorry to lose thee,' said Silas, 'but I see the attraction o' more money and a fancy title.'

'How's the forge?'

'Good, good. Still a small operation, tha knows.'

'Don't listen to him,' said Harriet. 'He's still determined to be bigger than Atlas Works one day.'

'Yeah, we'll need a bigger 'ouse to put all this lot in,' said Silas, gesturing around the room. 'Can't hardly move in 'ere.'

Harriet shrugged. 'After my aunt moved to the coast, my cousins decided I should have some of her furniture. I'm hardly going to turn them down, am I?'

Silas elaborately mimed sewing up his lips.

'Fetch Isaac down, love?' said Harriet. 'I thought his nosiness would have got the better of him by now.'

'I told 'im to finish 'is sums,' said Silas. He cleared his throat and, from where he sat, bellowed their son's name.

'I could have done that myself,' Harriet muttered.

'How's old Bright doin', Dan? How many have you got at the wire mills now?'

'Hundred and twenty, give or take. He's got his son selling for him but we had a big order fall through. I don't think I'm giving any company secrets away by telling you that. We had to lay a few of the warehouse women off but I think we'll be re-employing them soon.' Rose Butterfield's serious gaze filled his mind. 'I'm looking forward to delivering a bit of good news, especially after having been handed the job of letting them go.' He stared glumly at the fire.

'Is that why you seem a little out of sorts?' said Harriet.

Daniel fastened his gaze on the contents of his whisky glass. 'No, no, that's not it.' He paused to bring his stutter under control. 'I saw Louisa.'

His friends exchanged a glance. It was Harriet who spoke. 'When was this, if I can ask?'

'A few weeks ago.' He gulped. 'Longer. I can't seem to... Anyway, I took a ride on one of the new town trams. She was with her daughter. I think it must have been Alice, a little girl of six or so.'

Harriet nodded.

'She didn't see me,' said Daniel.

'No,' said Harriet, 'Louisa would have told me, if she had.'

'I've not been able to stop thinking about her. I know I'm being foolish.' He searched Harriet's eyes. 'I needed to tell somebody – to tell you, even though I know your loyalties lie with Louisa. And I wanted to know...' He shook his head. 'I don't know.'

Silas got to his feet and held out his hand for Daniel's whisky glass. Daniel couldn't meet his eye. He drained his whisky and gave the glass to Silas, who splashed another measure into it and handed it back.

'She's just about runnin' that hansom cab company now, tha knows. She's made a life for hersen and little Alice. An' it is just the two o' them, if that answers a particular question tha might have.'

Silas might have said more but Isaac burst into the room, a broad grin on his face. 'Uncle Dan!'

'Isaac! You have grown into a handsome young man,' said Daniel, mustering a heartiness he had not thought was in him.

'Spit o' his dad,' said Silas.

He wasn't talking about himself, although Isaac was as broad and tall as Silas and there was, naturally, a strong family resemblance. Isaac was Silas's late brother's child, taken in by Harriet when his mother disappeared. He'd been five when she had abandoned him and was now a strapping lad of eleven.

'I'm sure you've grown a foot since last Christmas.'

'He's playing football in a boys' team now,' said Harriet.

'An' I play rounders too, an' I'm helpin' Dad in the yard.' Isaac flexed his arm and Daniel dutifully pressed on his bicep.

'Very impressive indeed.'

'Can tha brew us a pot o' tea wi' them strong arms?' said Silas. 'An' then tha can impress our old accountant here wi' thee numeracy skills.'

Isaac bent to kiss Harriet on the cheek. 'Will we have the pikelets, an' all?'

'Yes, why not?' Her voice was artificially bright and Daniel was the cause of it. Harriet and Louisa were close friends and he had made her uncomfortable. But there was another question he needed an answer to, and he must ask it now, while Isaac was out of the room.

'Does she ever mention me?'

Silas shook his head. 'Dan, tha knows better than anyone that she's a proud lass.'

Harriet didn't speak but her kind smile told him more than words ever could.

Chapter 7

Archie sat with a group of men around a card table in the Q on the Corner on Paradise Square. He was facing her but had dipped his head to listen to something the man next to him was saying, and had not noticed her waiting in the doorway of the tavern. When he laughed and mock-punched the other man on the arm, she was filled with a yearning so deep and sudden it took her breath away. She moved forward but could not seem to get any nearer to him. *Archie!* He looked up from the cards he was holding, a slight frown clouding his face, then his brow cleared and he raised a hand in greeting to the man brushing past her.

She was invisible.

She was pushed again from behind, more roughly, and unseen hands wrapped themselves around her waist, preventing her from moving towards her husband. She watched Archie throw in his hand, smiling and shrugging as he did so. It was not a large loss, then. He could not see her. She was not there.

Rose moaned in fear and briefly closed her eyes. Now she was sitting on a bench on an empty omnibus that was travelling too quickly down a steep cobbled road, the motion flinging her from side to side.

'Ma!'

Rose woke with a start. She was half-slumped on the settee, Jane's anxious face inches from hers.

'Ma, you were makin' a noise.'

'Don't be daft.' She shrugged off Jane's hand, still clamped on her shoulder. 'Where are the lads?'

'Sittin' in the kitchen, havin' the tea I made them. I called you, but you were fast on.'

'I only closed me eyes for a minute.'

The flame of the oil lamp illuminated the sideboard Jane had placed it on and picked out the different shades of colour of the pegged rug on the floor, but the corners of the room were fading and the fireplace's cold black grate made Rose shudder. It had been light when she had dozed off and she had slept for an hour or more, and was groggy from it ahead of a night when she'd need all her wits about her.

It amused her to see Jane standing above her, hands on hips – a mother in the making – but Rose's overriding emotion was one of sadness. She wished that Archie had seen her, in her dream. His smile had been free from care, untroubled and innocent; it lingered like the taste of something sweet.

'Are ya comin', then?'

'Hush, Jane. Gi' me a minute.' She rose to her feet and shook out her skirt. 'Early night for the three o' thee. I want thee out o' the way.'

Her daughter pouted but knew better than to continue the argument started earlier that day. She would have her curiosity satisfied soon enough.

'This came.' Jane handed over an envelope. 'It were shoved under the door while you were asleep. Feels like there's money in it.'

Rose took the envelope from her. 'Did you open the door to see who had delivered it?'

'No, were I supposed to?'

Rose shook her head. She left the room quickly, before her daughter could question her further, and hurried upstairs. The envelope, and the handwriting on it, was the same as all the others. This time, a solitary sovereign fell into her palm. She wondered briefly why her mysterious benefactor did not simply send a larger amount less frequently, for all the cloak and dagger they must endure to deliver these small white envelopes. Ever since the previous donation was brazenly deposited on the mantlepiece, Rose had kept the front and back doors locked and the windows fastened. There were other reasons for a woman living alone with her children to exercise caution. Her next-door neighbour, Nellie Bore, had been jailed for stealing a pair of gloves from Cole's and sentenced to twelve months' hard labour. This seemed a harsh punishment until her neighbours learned she had no fewer than seventeen previous convictions for incidents of light-fingeredness in shops and markets all over the town. Still, she was in her fifties and not quite right in the head and shouldn't be locked away, not in Rose's opinion. Others were less sympathetic but it was acknowledged a spell of hard labour would no doubt finish her off. Soon after Nellie vacated the house, and to Rose's consternation, new tenants had moved in, a cocksure little man and his surly wife who fought a lot and let their large brood run wild. Late last night, Rose had lain awake listening to the couple hurl insults and, by the sound of it, pieces of furniture at each other. When the noise died down, and a rhythmical thudding set up, she had crept downstairs to check the doors and windows. *We're all safe and sound, Archie.* But she had found sleep difficult to find.

Tonight, she'd be locking up the house with a stranger inside it.

The twins were sound asleep, top to tail in the bed they were sharing. But, on the other side of the room, Jane's eyes glittered in the shaft of moonlight that fell across her pillow.

'Get to sleep, love.'

'Is she 'ere yet?'

'No, not yet. You'll see 'er tomorra. Go to sleep now.'

The knock on the door came at half past ten, when Rose was beginning to wonder if her temporary guest would be arriving at all. She had kept the fire in the hearth going; the girl might appreciate sitting by it after her journey. The autumn nip had developed into a bite earlier than expected. The elderly man who lodged in the house on the other side of Nellie Bore's had declared, with a wearying predictability, that a long and freezing winter was on the cards and he would not see it through to the end.

Rose eased the door open and held the lamp high, casting light onto the face of the unpleasant man she had met at her employer's home. She lowered the lamp to look at the girl beside him. She was bareheaded and barely reached the man's shoulder. Her thin white fingers were clutching a scarf that covered the lower half of her face. The girl glanced at Rose with large, frightened eyes before lowering her gaze back to the ground.

'Might we come in?' Albert Boothby already had one foot over the threshold.

Rose stood back. 'Aye, come into the front room. I've managed to keep the fire goin'. Lucky I 'ave no work to get up for in the mornin'.'

If Mr Boothby heard her reference to the lateness of the hour he made no acknowledgement of it. He strode in, the girl following in his wake. Rose hung back so she could observe her.

The girl's thick dark hair was woven into an untidy plait that reached all the way down her back. Her jacket had seen better days and mud was crusted on the hem of her skirt. She carried a small and beautifully embroidered valise that she set down on the floor. Rose gestured to the armchair she had just vacated and the girl walked quickly over and sat in it. She didn't speak and the face covering meant Rose could not tell whether the girl was returning her encouraging smile. Her forehead gleamed pale and smooth over delicately curved eyebrows but there were dark hollows under eyes that were as wary as a trapped animal.

'I won't stay,' said Mr Boothby. He pointed at the valise. 'I will require that back.'

The girl sprang to her feet. She spoke in a muffled whisper, and as if she was talking around stones in her mouth, but Rose detected an accent. 'I'll unpack, if you'll show me where I'm to sleep.' She sounded like one of the warehouse women at Bright's, a softly spoken Irish girl.

'I've no bedroom to spare so I've put thee in the cellar. It's big enough. The coal 'ole is separate.' Rose hesitated. 'Me an' my girl — Jane, you'll meet her tomorra — put one of the boys' cots down there, an' a comfy chair an' stool, but you have the run o' the house. I've borrowed a book from the library for you, if you read?' The girl didn't respond. 'But not late. I won't have a flame turned up in the night, not in the cellar.'

Albert Boothby tutted impatiently. 'I'm sure it's fine, Mrs Butterfield. Oonagh, you might empty the valise here and carry your possessions down. Mrs Butterfield will help.' He made a point of consulting his pocket watch. 'My housekeeper will be wondering where I am.'

'I'd almost given up on you mesen,' said Rose.

He smiled thinly. 'We stopped along the way, didn't we, my dear, for rest and refreshment at a little roadside inn I often frequent.' He turned to Rose. 'You will find Oonagh a most accommodating young lady.'

The girl coughed, a wet and rattling sound that went on for some moments. 'Thank you for looking after me, Mr Boothby.' She bent to unload her meagre possessions. This didn't take long, even with one hand holding the scarf firmly in place around the lower half of her face. Rose wondered what injury or disfigurement she was so desperate to conceal. Finally, the girl produced a purse that she held out as if she was unsure to whom she should hand it.

Mr Boothby indicated that Rose should take the purse.

'First month's rent,' he said. 'Oonagh has an appointment with a dentist-surgeon next week. Mr Bright will be in touch.' He picked up the valise and tipped his hat. 'Good evening, ladies.'

Left with the girl, Rose was momentarily at a loss. She scooped up Oonagh's belongings – a skirt that was no cleaner than the one the girl was wearing, two blouses, a framed print of a coastal scene and a bundle of letters – and straightened with a sigh. The girl had no change of petticoats, stockings or stays.

'Are you hungry?'

Oonagh shook her head. Her eyelids drooped.

'Follow me, then, love.'

In the cellar, Rose turned up the wick on the lamp. She had made the space as cosy as possible, with a rug on the floor and her best candlewick cover, which had been a wedding gift, on the bed. On the table, alongside the oil lamp, she had left a copy of *The Mill on the Floss*, borrowed from the free library on Upperthorpe. The girl set up her framed print on top of the book and looked around, her gaze settling on the shelves at the end of the room that Archie had built. She would just have to put up with Rose or Jane tramping through when flour, potatoes or preserves were required, or it was necessary to fetch coal from the chute that was behind the door near the stairs.

Rose said good night, reminded the girl to turn down her lamp and climbed the stairs to bed, where she lay awake, staring into the dark. She tried to reassure herself that she would become accustomed to having Oonagh in the house. And now she had a purse containing more than twenty shillings, coins that she had come by legitimately and felt free to spend. She wondered why so much money was being forked out for an immigrant worker, not to mention an escort all the way from York. Rose turned to face the wall, pulled up her blanket and closed her eyes. It was none of her concern. Still, a thought nagged her as she surrendered to sleep.

What lay under that scarf?

-

'So, what's wrong with her?'

Annie Whittaker pulled out a chair at Rose's kitchen table, unfastened the button of the black jacket she wore over a white high-necked blouse, and sat down. She reminded Rose of a magpie in those colours, with those sharp and eager eyes.

'Shush,' said Rose. 'She's sittin' in the front room. I gave her some knittin' to do.'

'There's nothing wrong with her hands, then, or her eyes.'

'She told Jane it's her jaw. That it pains her.'

'Her jaw?'

'Aye. I've not seen it, though.'

'What do you mean?'

'She keeps her face covered wi' a scarf. She's got a reight bad cough, an' all.'

Oonagh had been in the house for three days, the object of fierce curiosity from Jane and the twins, whose questions she had tolerated gracefully, answering them in a soft but somehow obstructed brogue. Thanks to her children, Rose had learned that Oonagh was from Galway in Ireland and had travelled to York with a friend to work in a match factory. Rose had not wanted to pry but Jane had been relentless.

'How old are you?'

'Nineteen. We got the boat over when I was fourteen, me and Molly.' More coughing. 'We lodged together.'

'And where's Molly now?'

'At the factory, still, in York.'

'Do you miss her?'

'Sure, I do.'

'What's wrong with you?'

'Jane!'

'Sorry, Ma.'

Oonagh had touched the scarf and for an awful moment Rose was convinced she would whip it away and show them a gaping maw where the lower half of her face should be. She didn't. 'I've a problem with my teeth. I'm to see a surgeon-dentist.'

Oonagh had politely thanked Rose for her dinner and taken it to eat in the cellar; she hadn't drunk so much as a cup of tea in the presence of Rose or the children.

Now, Rose poured more tea into Annie's cup. 'An' that's all I know.'

'Haven't you questioned her yourself?'

'Annie, we're not all reporters for the *Sheffield Tribune*. I'd rather leave her be.'

'I'm not a reporter either, much to my chagrin.'

'He's still not lettin' you near, then?'

'Rob is wearing my patience thin. He has published a couple of pieces that Jem has written on my behalf.' Annie cleared her throat. 'By the way, Jem had hoped to come along with me this morning but he's got so much on, and so he sends his apologies.'

Rose was mystified as to why Jem would want to drink tea with two women. 'All right.'

'He's fallen on his feet, at last,' said Annie. 'Jem, I mean.'

'Oh aye?'

'He has a scandalous past, you know.' Annie's eyes sparkled, making Rose laugh.

'Bit of a rogue, is he?'

'No.' Annie leaned forward. 'But his father was. He seduced my aunt, my mother's sister, and left her carrying his child. She was sent away, I don't know where, but she died when Jem was eight or nine years old and my father took him in.'

'That was kind of him.'

'Hmm, well. He wasn't too enamoured by the idea. My mother insisted.'

'You and Jem seem very close.'

Annie smiled. 'We are. We share the same rebellious streak that so infuriates my father. He made sure Jem was properly educated and had the rough edges knocked off. But Jem couldn't forgive the family for sending his mother away, so he made trouble. He was turfed out of the house as soon as he turned sixteen.'

'Oh dear. The poor lad. I can see how he would struggle to forgive the family, though.'

'Jem's own father would have said, "Turn the other cheek." Do you know why?'

'No?'

'Because' – Annie pressed the palms of her hands against her cheeks – 'the real scandal is that Jem's father was the local vicar.'

Rose burst out laughing. 'Never!'

'Yes, and Jem's mother wasn't his only conquest. There are little Reverend Martins all over Yorkshire.'

'Oh dear.' Rose dabbed at her eyes with the edge of her apron. 'We shouldn't be gossipin' about Jem like this. It's not right.'

Annie shook her head. 'He wouldn't mind it. In fact, I'm sure he'd be gratified to hear you stick up for him. You know, he likes you. I wonder if the feeling is reciprocated?'

'No,' said Rose, too quickly. She sat back and folded her arms. 'Don't go gettin' any ideas, Annie. I'm happy the way I am.'

Annie sipped her tea. 'Anyway, he's a sweet boy, with an aversion to going to church. Oh, that reminds me, I've brought sugar. Do you have a bowl?' She shook lumps of white sugar from a paper bag into the bowl Rose provided. 'Tongs? No? Fingers are fine. Tell me this, Rose. Who are the experts on conditions on the factory floor?' She didn't wait for an answer. 'The workers!'

'You won't get any joy there, love. Speakin' out can cost your job and nob'dy can afford that, however noble the cause is.'

'What price on a life? Do you know in the first six months of this year over a hundred and sixty died in factory accidents, over three *thousand* were injured and there were five hundred limb amputations.'

'Aye, an' grinders can expect to pop their clogs before they get to the age o' forty, an' miners live wi' the fear of bein' buried alive. There's danger everywhere.'

Annie put down her cup triumphantly. 'And so we need reforms that make all these places safer to work in. We need to convince the people before we can convince our leaders.'

'An' your husband before that.'

Annie sat back. She looked deflated. 'Yes, I suppose so.'

Then she leaned forward again, that irrepressible glint in her eye that Rose would come to know so well. 'He won't publish my articles, but there is another way I can employ his services, through you, Rose, and I can guarantee he won't be turning me down this time.'

Chapter 8

A cast-iron and glass canopy extended the length of the Georgian building that housed the Theatre Royal on the corner of Tudor Street and Arundel Street, and, thankfully, provided shelter to the very edge of the pavement. Rose seemed daunted and said something Annie couldn't catch. Annie didn't know which was louder, the rain drumming on the canopy or the noise from the people crowding the main entrance.

Rose had flattened herself against the damp brick wall of the building to allow a finely dressed couple who had descended from a carriage to sashay by. They would have seats for the circle and, Annie considered, were here to be viewed as much as they were here to view the entertainment. She took Rose's hand, intending to reassure her, but before she could speak Jem reappeared, moving against the tide of people pouring into the theatre.

Annie handed back his umbrella.

'We're in the gods,' he said, 'with the best view in the house.'

Rose raised her voice to be heard. 'It's all a bit fancy.'

'Not in the gods or the pit, it's not,' said Jem. 'We'll have the same experience as the ladies and gentlemen in the circle but without the bore of spending hours getting all dolled up.'

Annie took her hand. 'Wait until you get inside. You'll love it, Rose.'

'Round the back for us, ladies.'

Jem led them around the side of the building to a meaner entrance where less finely dressed people were congregated, queuing to get out of the rain. There was no canopy over this side of the building. Inside, a doorway framed a view of a set of eight broad stairs, carpeted in a rich red wool, that branched off to left and right. A huge gold-framed mirror hung at the top, with those approaching and passing by maintaining the pretence of not trying to catch a glimpse of themselves.

'Make haste,' Jem said, bounding up a narrow, uncarpeted and dimly lit set of stairs. Rose followed him, Annie bringing up the rear.

'Here we are!' said Annie when they emerged onto the gallery, the theatre laid out below them. 'From up here, you can see the musicians. Look!'

'What are we here to see?' asked Rose, finding her seat.

'There's no need to follow the story,' Jem said. 'Just enjoy the ballads, and soak in the atmosphere.'

Rose narrowed her eyes. 'I'd like to know what's happenin'. Do you know the story?'

He laughed. 'I have to admit, no, I don't. I'm just trying to impress you but you have found me out.'

'Jem, you've met your match.' Annie turned to Rose. 'It's a new production by Carl Rosa's English Opera Company. *The Bohemian Girl*. It's based on my life.'

Rose gave her a sceptical look.

'She's joking,' said Jem.

'Aye, I guessed that.' She squeezed Annie's hand. 'Just don't lose me in this lot.'

Annie beamed. 'I'm glad we could persuade you to come.'

She had turned up at Rose's cottage with Jem in tow and free tickets to see *The Bohemian Girl* at the Royal. The tickets had been provided by the theatre management in return for a review in the *Tribune*. Rob had jibbed at the last moment – he was tearing his hair out over a problem with his printing machine – and Annie thought Rose might enjoy a night out. She was quickly disabused of that notion.

'Oh no,' Rose had said, her voice full of dismay. 'I've got mendin' to do.' She'd sat down at the kitchen table, where a tin box of needles, thread and thimbles was partially obscured by a sprawling pile of skirts, stockings and britches. Annie had lifted up a small, worn shirt that was as shredded as if the most recent wearer had fallen foul of the bears in the pit in the Botanical Gardens.

'Bobby's,' Rose explained. 'Fell out o' a tree. Well, I say fell. He were left hangin' an' Jane had to pull him down. They weren't goin' to say owt but...' She took the shirt from Annie's hands. 'They couldn't really argue wi' the evidence. Beyond repair but it'll make dishcloths.'

'There seems to be a lot to get through.'

'Oh, it's not all ours. I take some in for extra money. An' I don't go out, not at night. An', anyhow, look at me. I've nowt to wear. An' Oonagh's due back any minute from the doctor's and I've not made any tea.'

It was Jem who convinced Rose, by appealing to her sense of *waste not want not*, lamenting that a ticket would now go to waste. 'And what excuse should I give the theatre manager when he sees the empty seat?'

'The one Rob should've 'ad?' said Rose, but she relented to Jem's cajoling.

Jane had promised to do the mending, after Jem appealed to her to help her mother out; Rose had taken off her apron and replaced it with Annie's jacket, on Annie's insistence. Annie borrowed a shawl to cover her dress and, when Rose said she hadn't a decent hat to wear, took hers off and gave it to her, telling Rose the combs and pins in her own hair would suffice and praying that would be the case. Rose reminded Jane several times to lock the door behind them and only open it for Oonagh. The heavens opened as soon as the door had closed behind them, a blustery squall that would surely strip the trees of their few remaining leaves. The two women walked either side of Jem, sheltering under the large black umbrella he carried. Annie was aware that while her hand was tucked in the crook of his arm, Rose kept herself a little apart. She was also aware that Jem favoured Rose, so that the walk was made more uncomfortable by fat drops of water falling from the umbrella spokes onto Annie's head, when she wasn't being prodded by the spokes themselves.

It was worth a damp head of hair to see the expression on Rose's face when they found three seats together in the front row of the vertiginous gallery. Annie explained that the theatre had recently been redecorated and boasted a new colourful act drop and stage curtains. The chandelier had been replaced to improve the view and additional gas lamps brightened the walls. A new ventilation system had been installed, although the air remained stuffy and Annie wished she were able to remove the shawl that covered her dress.

'What do you think?' Jem made a point of leaning forward over the drop to ask this question of Rose as Annie had seated herself between them.

'You're makin' me dizzy,' said Rose. She clutched the velvet-covered rail.

A sense of anticipation rose in Annie's chest as the orchestra took their seats and the lamps were turned down. The buzz from the audience faded as the first notes were played, bar the occasional catcall from the pit. The house was so packed that chairs had been set out in the passages. When the curtain began to rise, Rose touched her arm.

'Thank you for bringin' me.' Her eyes glowed in the dim light. 'This 'as been lovely.'

Annie smiled. 'If I were you, I'd reserve judgement until after the show.'

'I already know I've had a wonderful time. I just din't want to forget to say.'

–

Annie took the liberty of booking a hansom cab for midnight, to collect her from Rose's cottage and carry her home to Walkley. Rose agreed she would not sleep after so much excitement and Jem declared their evening out would be topped off nicely with a pot of tea, but did Rose have anything stronger in the house, like whisky or rum?

It had stopped raining when they joined the crowd streaming out of the theatre. Jem found a beer house after a few hundred yards and slipped inside, returning with a bottle of whisky that he tucked inside his jacket.

'What'll you write?' said Rose.

'That the opera was a splendid success, a spectacle of sound and colour that I predict will run for many months, if not years.' He executed a bow, almost losing the whisky bottle. 'Or was it the company that made it shine so?'

'Carl Rosa's Company? That seems to be rather stating the obvious,' said Annie.

'You know very well I mean your company, and Rose's in particular,' he said.

Rose laughed. 'You're a charmer, Jem.'

'Yes, but I fear it doesn't seem to be working on you.'

There was a glow in the front-room window of Rose's cottage and the door opened before the three of them had got through the gate. A woman stood on the threshold, holding up a lamp. Her lower face was covered with a scarf.

'The children are asleep,' she whispered in a voice that sounded slurred to Annie. 'I thought I'd wait up. Did you enjoy yourselves?'

'Aye,' Rose answered. 'Thank you.'

Annie was curious. 'Are you Rose's lodger?'

'Yes.'

'I'm Annie. This is my cousin Jem.'

'I'm Oonagh.'

'Would you like to share a pot of tea with us?'

'Ah, no thank you. I'll be off to bed now.'

Her voice, even allowing for the scarf, was faint. When Rose took the lamp from her, and it swung near Oonagh's face, Annie thought the girl's eyes looked strange, the pupils shrunk down to pinpricks. She waited until they were sitting at the kitchen table with cups of tea.

'What's the matter with her?' Annie said. 'Did you see her eyes?'

'Aye. Am not sure,' said Rose. 'She's been to the dentist-surgeon three times now, collected in a gig an' brought back in a subdued state. She dun't talk much but she's happy to play cards wi' the children. She's no trouble.'

'She looks like she's on something, for the pain perhaps.' Jem poured a generous slug of whisky into his cup and Annie grimaced.

'You've got a walk home ahead of you, Jem.'

Rose's eyes twinkled. 'Don't go fallin' in the gutter. Don't want a watchman stumblin' over thee.'

A shadow crossed her face. Annie reached across the table and took her hand. 'He'll be careful. Won't you, Jem?'

It was after Jem had left, and with only minutes to spare before Annie's cab arrived, that Rose haltingly began to talk about the night her husband had been killed. Annie was surprised, and wondered whether the theatrical ballads had awoken emotions long buried. She had noticed Rose's eyes fill with tears several times during the performance.

Rose told her that Archie's body had been lifted from the pavement and carried on a stretcher to his father's house. As day broke, she was fetched from her bed and taken there.

'He were laid out on the kitchen table,' she said, 'an' his skin were as waxy as a tallow candle. His lips were white.' She paused. 'I've never told anybody about this before. I don't know why I'm tellin' thee now.'

Annie remained silent.

'I din't want to leave his side. Silly, in't it? He weren't there. His skin were as cold as snow.'

'It's not silly,' said Annie.

'It were just that, once I walked away, well, that'd be it, wun't it?'

'Oh dear, Rose.' She cast about for something to say, some words of reassurance. 'You have your children, and must put it behind you—' And stopped when anger flashed in the other woman's eyes.

'Easier said than done,' said Rose, ''specially as them that took his life were never brought to book.'

'I'm sorry.'

'Me an' all. An' ever since then, I've had summat else to contend wi' – summat I find unsettling, a mystery I can't solve – and on top o' *that* I've now got this lass livin' wi' us.' Rose sighed. 'I've still not seen her face,' she said, almost ruminatively.

'If she has a wound, it might not be something you'd want to see,' said Annie. 'Have you talked to her, about her circumstances? What brought her here, to you?'

'Nah.' Rose stood up, startling Annie. 'Is that your carriage outside?'

Annie cursed the immaculate timekeeping of the Greaves hansom cab company.

'What was the other thing?' she said. 'You said you had something to contend with, a mystery. What is it?'

'I'll tell thee another day. You need to go.'

'The cab will wait for me.' And if it didn't, she would bed down for the night on the settee. She felt a pang of guilt, then dismissed it. Rob wouldn't wait up for her. He'd been so busy lately he always fell into a stupor immediately after supper.

'Are you sure?'

'Yes,' said Annie firmly.

'All right, then. It's summat I 'ave to show you, though.'

Rose took a lamp and led Annie upstairs and into her bedroom. Annie could hear the children snoring gently in the next room. She watched as Rose got on her knees and pulled a chest from under the bed. She lifted the lid, and for one horrible moment Annie was convinced she had the remains of her husband in there, a jumble of bones and an empty-eyed skull, and the skin on the back of her neck prickled.

'I haven't long after all,' she said, and her voice shook.

But Rose wordlessly lifted a black cloak out of the chest and Annie saw that there was nothing more than paper scattered underneath. She looked more closely. Not paper: small white packets – envelopes, like the ones Rob sold – all bearing, in careful lettering, the name *Rose Butterfield*.

'What are they?' she said.

Rose picked one up and shook out the contents, holding up her palm towards Annie.

'Coins?'

'Aye. Coins. I've been gettin' these envelopes for years now, sometimes every few weeks; sometimes months'll pass and I'll think they've stopped comin'. I don't know what to do wi' 'em.'

Annie bent to sift through the envelopes. She thought there must be two dozen or more of them.

'How much money in total?'

'A lot,' said Rose flatly. 'A lot to the likes o' me, anyway. An' I've got no idea who's givin' it me. Or why.'

'It has to be something to do with Archie.'

'Well, he saved some people from the great flood, but then why all this pretence?'

Annie frowned. 'It's very curious.'

A series of sharp knocks on the front door startled them both.

'Oh dear, that will wake the household. I should go,' said Annie. 'Perhaps I could return tomorrow, and we can talk more, if you'd like.'

'I'd like it,' said Rose.

On the garden path, Annie gave her address to the driver and turned to wave to Rose, who stood on the doorstep. She was stepping into the cab when Rose called her name, and there was lightness in her voice again.

'Annie! Thank you for me night out. I told thee I'd forget!'

Chapter 9

Standing at the end of the bar in the Golden Ball, Daniel drained his glass and set it down gently. The Saturday lunchtime trade was brisk. As well as the regulars propping up the counter, a party from Doncaster had stopped for refreshments and were loudly demanding the landlord's attention. They were on their way to the Bramall Lane cricket ground where a county match was due to be played that afternoon. The omnibus they had hired had shaken their bones like dice in a bag and they had mutinied, demanding the driver stop at the next hostelry.

Daniel nodded genially to the gentleman imparting this information to him; the man's breath betrayed he'd already had a skinful before stepping foot inside the Golden Ball.

'And how many times have you stopped on the road from Doncaster, so far?' Daniel said, when a response seemed to be required.

The man seemed to find this uproariously funny.

Leonard, the landlord, winked at Daniel. 'Another, lad?'

'Please.'

'On't house. Tha looks like all tha troubles have come to haunt thee at once.'

The man had no idea.

Daniel supped his second pint of ale more slowly. He couldn't tell Leonard what ailed him; he'd be a laughing stock forever more. *Eligible bachelor. Wishes to make the acquaintance of an accomplished young woman, age twenty-five or thereabouts, with whom to establish a comfortable home and embark on family life.*

It hadn't been furniture his mother was selling via the pages of the *Sheffield Telegraph*. It had been him.

The specified age wasn't an arbitrary choice. He knew how his mother's mind worked. By the age of twenty-five, a woman should have put frivolity behind her and be actively seeking a husband. Over that age, she was potentially defective, left on the shelf, and the chances of her bearing the grandchildren his mother so desired obviously lessened with age. Had his mother received help in composing the advertisement? Mabel would surely be party to her shenanigans. Had the typesetter who'd filed it under *Wanted* snickered to himself as he set the page? *Please reply to Mr D. W. Housley at the following address with a view to embarking on a correspondence.*

Daniel's face burned anew with shame.

The maid of the house, Lucy, brought him the hotpot he had ordered, neatly avoiding with a swing of her hips a pat on the backside from one of the Doncaster party. Daniel thanked her and dipped the accompanying crust of bread into the stew morosely. Leonard left his wife to field the customers and came to lean on the end on the bar, mopping his forehead with a grubby flannel.

'What news, Dan?'

'N-news?' he said, swallowing the small bite he had taken and finding it had miraculously swollen to the size of a boulder. He washed it down with a hard swallow of ale. Did the landlord know what his mother had done? Was he teasing Daniel? There were no *Telegraph*s to be seen in the tavern. Leonard favoured the *Sheffield Independent* and had also begun taking the new title, the *Tribune*, which he said contained more of the salacious gossip he enjoyed and less of the boring politics.

'Young buck like thee. Are tha courtin'? Found a place to live? Not that I'm not enjoyin' having thee here. Stay as long as tha likes, so long as tha pays thee way, eh?'

He didn't know. Daniel relaxed his shoulders.

'No, I'm not courting.' *A correspondence with a view to matrimony.* 'I'm still looking for more permanent lodgings and, yes, I'm enjoying staying here. Never a dull moment.'

'And what will tha do wi' theesen on this fine afternoon?'

Daniel turned to look outside. A thick fog had rendered the window pane greyly opaque. 'I hope the visibility is better in Bramall Lane.'

'If the fog lifts, this lot will be seeing twice the number of cricketers on the field by the time they get there.' Leonard wheezed with laughter.

'I'm going on an errand that I think I'll enjoy,' Daniel said, in answer to the landlord's question. The thought of delivering good news lifted his spirits a little and he mustered a smile.

'That's more like it,' said Leonard's wife from the other end of the bar. 'Hate to see thee lookin' so miserable, Dan.'

Several faces turned inquisitively in his direction. Daniel grimaced and bent to his bowl. 'Lovely hotpot, Mrs Archibald.'

'Goes wi'out saying,' said Leonard. 'Get theesen a wife like mine, son, and tha won't go far wrong.'

This set Daniel fretting, again, that the landlord *had* seen the advertisement. He silently cursed his mother and bit off more of the crust of bread so that, mouth full, he was not required to do more than smile and nod at the landlord. It occurred to him that his mother had meant for him to find the letters when she asked him to fetch her shawl from the bedroom. She had shown not the slightest contrition when he confronted her.

The correspondence had been stacked neatly on her dressing table, four piles of differently coloured and sized envelopes, some with wax seals of green or blue, but all with one thing in common. They bore his name above his mother's address. *Mr D. W. Housley*. Daniel had leafed through them. None had been opened. With a certain suspicion already forming in his mind, he took them downstairs and laid them on the table that Mabel had just lifted his mother's breakfast tray from. She had fixed him with a challenging glare. 'Sometimes a boy needs his mother's help in finding the correct match.'

Daniel had shaken his head in disbelief. 'You've gone too far, Mother.' He was aware of Mabel quietly leaving the room with the tray. 'I had found somebody. It was you who decided she was not the *correct match*.'

His mother had been unperturbed, and merely nodded sagely. 'Will you spend all your days alone and unloved, mooning over that vulgar girl? I'm only thinking of you, my only and beloved child. I believe I explained to you that I was advertising a precious item, the continuation of your father's good name!'

Mabel had returned with a copy of the *Telegraph* that she handed to Daniel without speaking. He found the advertisement, ripped out the page and stuffed it in the pocket of his waistcoat, recognising the futility of such an act when thousands of copies had been distributed all over town, his shame folded inside every single one of them. 'I thought,' said his mother calmly, 'that we might open them together, and decide which to discard and which has potential.' He'd given her such a look of incredulity that even she seemed slightly abashed. He'd left her without another word and stalked back to the Golden Ball, where he had gone straight to the bar.

Two pints of ale too quickly downed had left him slightly light-headed. If he had a third, he might find himself confiding in the landlady. Instead, he would run that errand. Daniel said his farewells and walked out to greet the gloomy afternoon. The fog had thickened and, mingled with factory fumes, gave off an acrid stench. He hunched his shoulders and set off towards the middle of town. The road he took was busy but the thick air lent a ghostly, otherworldly cast to the pedestrians he passed and the horses pulling wagons, carriages and omnibuses through the streets. One of the new horse-pulled trams loomed out of nowhere as Daniel crossed the tracks on Broad Street and he hurried to the other side, his heart in his mouth. The fog made the town alien to him; he might be wandering around in a dream, and never find his destination.

And then he turned a corner and found himself at the bottom of a steep road lined by terraced cottages. His spirits rose. He had found her.

–

Daniel knocked on the door, and waited, and after a few moments knocked again, unwilling to accept that she was not at home.

He was turning away when the door was flung open and Rose Butterfield stood there, wiping her hands on her apron. There was a smudge of flour on her flushed cheek and what looked like egg yolk on the sleeve of her dress. Fine strands of hair escaped from her dark braid. He thought she looked exceptionally pretty.

'Jane said she could hear somebody knockin' – I weren't expectin' to see thee, Mr Housley.'

'I'm so sorry. I think I've called at an inconvenient time.' He backed away and reached for the gate, finding the latch and lifting it.

'No, we're only bakin'.' She peered past him. 'I din't realise the fog were this thick. Can't even see across the road.'

He stumbled over his words. 'I wanted to deliver... I have some good news and—'

'Come in, then, come in. Let's keep the cold out. You can mither me as much as you like if you're bringin' me good news.'

Daniel followed her into the house and through the short hallway. The door to the front room stood ajar. It was dim inside but he glimpsed glowing coals in the fireplace. A brighter light came from the room on the other side of the hall. Rose led him that way, into the kitchen, where a fire crackled in the grate. The air was filled with the aroma of baking bread. Daniel inhaled. The smell alone could warm him through.

A young girl stood at the table, and next to her two boys knelt on wooden stools. They were fighting over a large spoon, their hands sticky with cake mixture.

'Excuse the mess,' said Rose. 'The kids are bakin' a cake for Jane's birthday tomorra an' as you can see the flour's gone everywhere but in the panshon, and now they're arguing o'er who gets to lick the bowl out' – she raised her voice – 'an' I'll be tannin' some hides shortly!'

The spoon clattered into the mixing bowl.

'It were my turn,' whispered Bobby.

'Your kitchen is delightfully cosy,' said Daniel. 'How old will you be tomorrow, Jane?'

'Eleven,' she said proudly. 'I'll be gettin' a proper job so as I can help Ma.'

'Let's not put the cart before the horse,' said Rose. 'You won't be workin' for a couple o' years yet, at least. You've still got learnin' to do.'

'Oonagh started workin' when she were twelve,' said Jane. 'She told me. She were sweepin' an office at the docks. That's how she found out about the boat to England.'

Rose sighed. 'An' look at the depredations she's suffered. Anyhow, Mr Housley isn't here to listen to you gabbing on. Bring us a cup o' tea into the front room and we'll finish the cake later. Make sure you grease that tin, Jane, an'' – she held up a finger to forestall the protests already forthcoming – 'you can all have a turn with the bowl later. Don't touch it 'til I say. Or else.'

Daniel followed Rose into the front room. 'You have a lot on your plate.'

'Aye, well.'

He was surprised to see a girl sleeping in an armchair in one corner, a pile of knitting held loosely in her lap. A thin woollen scarf, knotted behind one ear, covered her mouth and lower jaw, the material darker where some liquid had seeped into it.

'Have a seat,' said Rose. She went over to the fireplace and picked up a poker to stoke the coals.

Daniel took off his coat and carefully folded it over the back of the settee before sitting down. He coughed gently to clear his throat, afraid of waking the girl. Her forehead gleamed palely in the dim light.

'Oonagh's my tenant,' said Rose. She gently disengaged the girl's thin fingers from the knitting and put the needles and the ball of yarn on the carpet beside the chair. 'Vests for winter, although it'll be the followin' winter at this rate. She's had an operation and taken a draught the doctor gave her. She'll sleep on for a bit. The stuff makes her groggy.'

'What is it that ails her?'

Rose frowned. 'I don't like to pry. It's summat to do with her teeth, I think.'

She looked at Daniel expectantly. He hesitated. 'Will we disturb her?'

'Not likely.'

'Then, I hope you don't mind my turning up like this. I wanted to deliver the news personally. Mrs Butterfield, you can have your job back.'

It suddenly occurred to him she might not *want* to return to Bright's. He frowned and twisted his hands together. 'If you're agreeable, of course. We have won a big order from our American cousins and need workers across every area that we can rely on. You're a valued member of staff.'

'Not that valued,' said Rose, 'or I wouldn't 'ave been let go. Oh, don't look like that. Let me put you out o' your misery. A'course I want me job back.'

Daniel looked relieved. 'I'm glad to hear it, Mrs Butterfield.'

Jane entered, carrying a pot of tea and a jug of milk. The boys followed, each cradling a teacup. They put the cups down gently on the hearth tiles.

'Thank you,' said Daniel. 'You're very kind.'

One of the boys addressed him directly. 'Can we lick the bowl out now?'

'Um…'

'Don't bother Mr Housley,' said Rose. 'And the answer's no. Make theesens scarce for a bit. Jane, you can take the bread out and put the cake in. Would you like summat to eat, Mr Housley?'

'No, but thank you for offering.' He cleared his throat. 'I would be pleased if you called me Daniel, outside the workplace.'

'Aye, a'course. I'm Rose.'

She poured the tea, added a splash of milk and handed him a cup. Daniel took a sip and nodded appreciatively. It was a strong brew.

'How have you been keeping, Rose?'

'I've been makin' ends meet by takin' in a tenant.' She nodded at the sleeping girl. 'But I don't know how much longer she'll be 'ere. I'll just be glad to get back to work, if I'm honest.'

'Can you start next Monday?'

'Aye, I can. Better the devil you know, an' all that. How are you findin' Bright's yourself?'

Daniel coughed self-consciously. 'My biggest challenge at the moment is persuading Mr Bright to change working practices so that we may adhere to the new health and safety rules.'

'Is that because of that lad whose mother embarrassed him?'

'Not just that, but it has a bearing, yes.'

Daniel was aware of the boys lingering in the doorway. He stood up and rummaged in his waistcoat jacket for any loose coins he might give them. They hopped up and down in excitement as he handed them each a shilling and advised them to spend it wisely. He was aware of Rose out of the corner of his eye, bending to retrieve something from the carpet. The twins raced into the kitchen to show Jane their treasure. 'Here!' Daniel called. 'Take a coin to your sister.' One of them returned, took another shilling, and scooted off again.

Daniel turned to see Rose reading his mother's advertisement.

She looked up at him and frowned. 'Sorry. I weren't intendin' to pry into your personal business.' Her mouth twitched in amusement. 'It were on the floor.'

He took the fragment of newspaper from her, his cheeks burning, and crumpled it in his fist. 'Please don't apologise. It must have fallen from my pocket.'

Rose nodded sympathetically but there was merriness in her eyes. 'We'll say no more about it. It's none o' my business.'

'My mother,' he said. His fist clenched around the newsprint. 'She did this in my name and I was not privy to it.' *With honour and in strictest secrecy.* That had been another carefully phrased inclusion in the accursed advertisement. 'I discovered it this morning. She already has a stack of responses.'

'Oh dear.' Rose laughed, a lovely sound that acted like a balm on the anxiety that knotted his stomach and clouded his mind. 'I can't help thinkin'…'

'What is it?'

'Well, you're obviously summat of a catch, to get all them replies.'

Daniel grimaced. 'She wants grandchildren and is prepared to embarrass me to achieve them.'

'In that case, I sharn't be writin' to thee. Think I've got enough kids,' Rose said, and broke into fresh gales of laughter.

Daniel had never heard her laugh so freely. He smiled, although he felt, ridiculously, a little hurt. 'You are so forthright, Rose. I think you'd be more than a match for my mother.'

'I'm sorry. It's tickled me. How many letters 'ave you had?'

'Forty.'

'Forty!'

He smiled wryly, and could see she was about to set off again but then there were three sharp raps on the front door and Rose sighed instead, and got to her feet.

'It'll be the man that's lookin' after Oonagh,' she said. 'Mr Boothby. D'you know 'im?'

Daniel shook his head.

'He's overdue a visit.'

'I'll leave you in peace,' said Daniel, getting to his feet.

'Oh no, it'd be better if you stayed,' she said. 'Unless you've got more calls to make, bearin' good news.'

'This was the only call I wanted to make today, Rose.'

She smiled distantly, her merriness so quickly dissolved. Daniel accompanied her to the door and hung back as she greeted the man and woman standing on the threshold. She introduced them to him as Mrs Annie Whittaker and Mr James Martin. Not the Mr Boothby she was anticipating, then, but friends come to call. Daniel made his excuses and said his farewells. He was sure he had never met Mr James Martin before and couldn't account for the narrow-eyed look of suspicion the man gave him.

The air had cleared, of fog at least. Smoke in shades of white, yellow and black lifted ponderously from the stacks in the bottom of the valley and the clouds were dark over the higher ground. Daniel turned up his collar and set off for home, thinking of Rose's unself-conscious laughter. It reminded him of Louisa. Since he had glimpsed her from the tram, everything did.

Chapter 10

Annie and Jem turned up at Rose's cottage just as the company secretary of Bright's was leaving. Rose waved Daniel off and ushered the other two inside.

'This door'll be comin' off its hinges, at this rate.'

'A day for visitors,' said Jem. He seemed oddly put out.

'Indeed,' said Annie. 'I hope we're not disturbing you, Rose. I wanted to talk some more about your factory life.'

'She's not a specimen to be dissected,' said Jem, waspishly.

'What's got into you?' said Annie.

Rose took them into the kitchen.

'I've this cake to finish decorating,' she said. 'Annie, it's lovely to see you, both of you, but I've told you before, I haven't time for all that nonsense. I'm too busy livin' it to agitate about it.'

While Annie chatted, undaunted, about her political group, Rose and Jane finished the cake. Jem had brought a bag of marbles and stretched out on the kitchen rug with the twins, firing the little glass balls in all directions, ignoring the dire warnings from Jane they'd run under the stove and be lost for good. Oonagh appeared, leaning on the doorframe of the kitchen, her large brown eyes taking in the scene. Rose thought Oonagh's eyes looked bright; if she was smiling, it was hidden beneath the scarf covering her jaw. Or perhaps it was another drug-induced glassiness.

'That looks grand,' Oonagh whispered, her voice soft and slurred.

Jack and Bobby jumped to their feet.

'Would you like some, Oonagh?'

'Ma, can we 'ave it early?'

'Can we 'ave it now?'

Rose nodded to Jane. 'Now then, it's up to the birthday girl.'

Jane's eyes lit up. 'Is it? Let's eat it, all of us together.'

'Hoorah,' said Jem. 'Annie, put the kettle on.' He got to his feet, dusted down his trousers and looked around the room. 'I'll get the plates and a knife.'

Rose pointed to the cupboard and drawer he'd find these in.

Jem saluted. 'Boys, collect those marbles up before somebody goes head over heels.' He directed a broad smile at Rose. 'I'm very glad we called on you.'

Rose looked away, a flutter in her belly belying her words. 'Let's not get carried away,' she said, 'it's only a cake.'

Jem divided the cake into eight pieces and declared that the birthday girl should have two. Rose had never seen Jane look at anybody so adoringly before, not since Archie had died. A brief silence fell when Oonagh took her plate and left the room, then Annie clapped her hands and said the children could have the run of the kitchen.

'Don't mess wi' owt, or go in the sugar jar!' said Rose.

She followed Annie and Jem into the front room, feeling some trepidation. The girl preferred to eat alone, and here were these two rambunctious characters destroying the peace. How had Rose's life become so suddenly complicated, so crowded with people wanting something from her? She wished them gone, and life restored to normal, and was surprised by the vehemence of her feelings. Perhaps Oonagh had escaped to the cellar. But Rose entered the front room to find her sitting in her usual corner. Jem and Annie crowded together on the settee and Rose pulled a chair towards the door and perched on it. 'So I can hear what that lot are up to in the kitchen.'

Jem attacked his cake and Annie turned her attention to Oonagh and, typically, launched straight in.

'So tell us, what's brought you here?'

'Oh no, you don't 'ave to,' said Rose, and to the others. 'She's shy.'

'I don't mind,' the girl said, in her soft, slurred lilt. 'I came on the boat with Molly, my friend, a while back. Five years ago.' She sounded surprised. 'There was no work where we lived.' She looked down at the uneaten cake on her plate. 'We were surprised,' she whispered, 'to get jobs straight away, though we had been told there was plenty of work for those that were willing. They were looking for girls. They paid our coach fare to York and we moved into a room together, me and Molly. It was grand.'

'What do you do?' said Annie.

'I work in a match factory,' said Oonagh. 'Making and packing lucifer matches. I'm hoping they'll send me back, once my teeth are fixed. I've not been able to send any money home, while I'm here.'

'You must be missing your friend,' said Annie.

'I do, yes.' She looked up at Rose, her eyes dull. 'I might go down and take another draught of medicine.'

Rose folded her arms. 'I think we should leave Oonagh in peace now.'

'Of course,' said Annie. She was frowning. 'Do you think the work made you ill, the job you were doing?'

'No, I'm told it's a problem with my teeth. Or with my jawbone.' She shrugged. 'We were warned about the white phosphorus by the other lasses. That it was...'

'Toxic,' said Jem. He laid down his fork, leaving his slice of cake half-eaten.

'Yes.' She swallowed, and mumbled something Rose didn't hear, then said, 'The foreman said we should wash our hands whenever we got the chance. Some of the mixers wore masks, even after the new ventilation was put in, and they got looks, I can tell you that.'

'Looks?' said Annie.

'Yes, for making too much fuss about it all, and they would've been teased but we weren't allowed to talk while working, in case anything got spilled. I saw one girl get sacked on the spot for dropping a rack of matches.'

'What do the mixers do?' said Annie.

'They stir the phosphorus with glue to make a paste.' Oonagh shuddered and the uneaten cake almost tipped off her plate. 'I'm sorry, I can't eat this.'

Rose went over and took the plate from Oonagh's hand – her skin was clammy to the touch – and put it on the floor. Then she sat on the arm of the girl's chair as if she could protect her from questions that seemed dangerous, somehow. 'I think she's gettin' tired.'

Jem put his plate on the rug by his feet. 'What ails you, Oonagh?'

She looked at him, then looked away. 'I was sent here to see a dentist-surgeon. My teeth, my gums. The bone. I don't know.'

Jem glanced at Rose before he spoke. 'Are there no dentist-surgeons in York?'

Oonagh shrugged again. 'I was brought here.'

'Are you a mixer, Oonagh?' said Annie.

'Oh no. It was my job to dip the sticks into the paste.' She looked at Annie with pride in her eyes. 'Hundreds and thousands at a time and I never dropped a single one.'

'What does Molly do?'

'She's a packer. We've got a room in a boarding house near the factory, and we get Sunday afternoons off, but...' She shrugged. 'I miss the fresh air of home. We just walk through the mucky streets, breathing in dust. So we stay in, mostly. It's strange, though...' She trailed off.

'What is?' said Jem, gently.

'Now' – she was suddenly more animated – 'we both thought there was a funny smell and a taste in the air, at the factory. Our lodgings started smelling the same.' She brushed at the smock of her apron. 'It was on us.'

'What do you mean?' said Annie. She looked at Jem.

Oonagh's eyes were far away again. Rose wasn't even sure she'd heard Annie's question. She patted the girl's arm. 'D'you want to go an' rest now, love?'

Rose turned to the others. 'She's tired and it pains her to talk too much. I think we've heard enough...' She felt Oonagh's hand squeeze her arm and looked into the girl's feverish eyes.

'There was a glimmer,' Oonagh said, 'in the air and on the factory walls. We glowed too.'

'Glowed?' said Annie. 'What do you mean?'

'It was on our clothes, at night, when we were in bed. We'd put our clothes on the chair.' Oonagh held out her arms, her fingers pinched, mimicking the movement, and Rose shivered. There was something ghostlike about it, imaginary clothes going over the back of an imaginary chair.

Jem rubbed the back of his neck. 'And then what?'

'Well, this glow, this light, came off them. Fairy light. That's what Molly named it.'

She coughed, bending forwards with the effort, and her voice cracked when she spoke again. 'Sorry. I've a terrible cough lately. We made wishes on it, on the fairy light.'

'You need to rest now,' said Rose. She wanted Oonagh out of the room. She was afraid of the horrors that lurked under the girl's scarf.

'Was it a white glow?' said Annie.

Oonagh shook her head slowly. 'More greenish.'

Annie had a grim look on her face. 'I've heard of this.'

'It was in our mouths too, and on our hands' – she ran her fingers along her forearm as far as her elbow – 'all the way up to here.'

Jem nodded. 'Yes, I know of it too. Phosphorus jaw. Here's your example, Annie, of factory exploitation. Here she sits in flesh and blood. Oonagh, do you have phossy jaw?'

Rose and Oonagh spoke in unison, Rose challengingly, Oonagh in a whisper: 'What's phossy jaw?'

Jem looked at Rose when he answered. 'A disease of the bone, caused by the white phosphorus.' It seemed as though he was going to say more but changed his mind.

'No, I'm certain it's my teeth,' Oonagh said. 'I had a few taken out, at the back. I paid for that. But it didn't help, with the pain. Then one day we were told there was to be an inspection of the factory and to be on best behaviour, but the foreman pulled me off the line. I have abscesses on my face. They've told me the badness needs to be cut out.'

'Abscesses?' said Annie faintly.

'In my cheek, near my mouth. I was told there was a dentist here who could fix it, and my accommodation and my treatment would be given freely. And that man who brought me here—'

'Albert Boothby,' said Rose quietly.

'Yes. He told me not to tell anybody that they didn't want me at the factory, or even in the town, in case I had a poison in the blood that was catching. There was a death, you see. Something had got in a mixer's brain. The girls talked about her. Then we weren't allowed to mention her. I know that sounds terrible. But I don't have that.'

She looked at each of them in turn, fearfully. Rose couldn't think of anything to say.

Oonagh continued. 'Mr Boothby said he'd employ me as a scullery maid but when he saw me – when he said he needed to get a good look at me – he told me my face would frighten his staff and visitors to the house. That's why I keep this' – she touched the scarf – 'around my face. I don't want to frighten you, Mrs Butterfield, or the little ones.'

Rose's eyes filled with tears. 'Does it hurt?'

'All day long. I'm glad of that draught I'm given. It takes some of the worry, I mean to say, some of the pain away.'

'You shouldn't take too much of that,' said Jem. 'Sounds like you're being dosed up with poppy.'

The girl shrugged. 'It helps.'

Jem shook his head. 'It's been banned, white phosphorus, in some countries. Not here, though.'

'How terrible,' said Annie.

Oonagh's eyes were hooded. Rose thought she looked exhausted. 'I'm getting cured, though. I keep telling you, I don't have that.'

'Can we see?' said Annie. She gestured to Rose, to stay the protest on her lips, but kept her eyes on the girl. 'I promise you won't surprise us.'

Oonagh sighed and closed her eyes, and for a moment Rose thought she had fallen asleep. Then she lifted her hand and began to unravel her scarf. Rose slowly put her hand to her mouth, pressing her fingertips against her lips. She could see from their expressions that Annie and Jem were as horrified as she was. The girl kept her eyes downcast, which was a mercy, for Rose could not have returned her gaze and did not want Oonagh to see the shock that belied Annie's words.

It was difficult to take in, at first. The right side of Oonagh's face appeared undamaged, although her complexion had an unhealthy sheen, but on the left the girl's jaw was misshapen, as if it had been smashed and put back together wrongly. The symmetry was odd, a caved-in absence above the neck where a smooth jawline should be. Three open, weeping sores, each about the size of an old half-farthing, punctured her skin from her earlobe to her chin. The sight made Rose's stomach quail.

Annie inhaled sharply but nobody spoke until Oonagh had finished rewrapping her scarf around her face.

'How many operations have you had?' said Jem.

'A few,' said Oonagh tiredly. 'I don't know. The bone broke on its own because it had died, that's what they told me, so they took it off. Now they're saying I've still got more than half my lower jaw, and it's not in the upper jaw or... higher up.'

'Not yet,' said Annie. Rose threw her a warning look.

'I'm nearly cured. The gentleman who owns the factory is helping me as much as he is able to,' said Oonagh. 'He'll pay for my boat fare home. I'm looking forward to going home, soon as I'm well, for a visit. I miss the sea.'

'Where is your friend?' said Annie. 'The girl you came with?'

'Ah, she's still there, at the factory. She seemed all right, last I saw of her. I'll see her again.' She stood up. 'I'll eat this downstairs if you don't mind. Your Jane made a grand cake, Mrs Butterfield.'

Rose couldn't trust herself to reply. It was Annie who broke the silence that followed Oonagh's departure. 'I can't bear it. Her whole face has been destroyed. It's just such a terrible thing. And she thinks it's because of bad teeth.'

Jem let out a breath. 'No, she doesn't. Not really.'

Rose briefly closed her eyes. 'What'll her mother think when she sees 'er? What'll she think o' the people sendin' Oonagh home like that? An' here we sit, gawpin' at her.'

Annie shook her head. 'It's not your fault, Rose. You gave her somewhere safe to stay.'

'In my cellar, for a princely sum. I'm moving 'er upstairs. She should've never been down there.' She put her fingers to her lips again, determined not to break down in tears.

'No,' said Annie. 'It's this match factory owner – and his friend who has covered up for him – that should be brought to account. We should see to it that they are!'

'They never will be,' said Rose. 'These people never are.'

'This won't go on forever,' said Jem. 'The tide is turning.'

'And what's done is done,' said Rose.

Annie snorted. 'Listen to the pair of you, reciting homilies.'

'I think we've all had a shock,' said Jem. 'We ought to be going, Annie.' He turned to Rose. 'I had come here to ask you whether you would like to attend the theatre again, with me? I have two free tickets to see a play this evening. But I'm no longer in the mood for it, and I'm sure that neither are you.' He paused for breath. He had a look on his face Rose had never seen before. She realised it was uncertainty. 'So perhaps I could call on you again' – he gave Annie an exasperated look – 'without Annie here as chaperone.'

Rose frowned. 'What do you—'

'Ma! Ma!'

It was Jane, calling from the kitchen, her voice high with excitement, or fear. 'Now what?'

She rushed through, aware of Jem and Annie on her heels, and found her daughter and the boys standing on the back doorstep, peering down the narrow path between the cottage and the privies.

'Too late. She's gone,' said Jane.

'Who's gone?' said Rose. 'What are you talkin' about?'

Jane handed her a small white envelope. 'We saw her puttin' it on the ledge and then she scarpered.'

'Is it another one?' said Annie excitedly. 'What did the woman look like? Or was it a child?'

'Hush.' Rose threw Annie a warning glance. 'I think we've all had enough excitement for one day. You three can clean up the kitchen before teatime. Thank you,' she said to Annie and Jem, 'for callin'. I don't know about visiting the theatre again. Goodness knows there's enough drama goin' on here.'

Rose struck a match to light the wick of the oil lamp. She extinguished the flame on a quick outbreath and closed the lantern. She checked there was no smoke in the chamber and the lamp was well lit, before lifting it to carry to the privy and thence to bed. It was an action she had carried out a hundred, a thousand, times but now, for the first time, she stopped to examine the spent head on the slender stick of wood she held between thumb and index finger.

Eventually, she flicked it onto the hearth, an involuntary shudder twitching her shoulders. She would be sleeping in the small cot in the cellar tonight; Oonagh was already in Rose's bed. Rose had tucked the bedsheets up to Oonagh's disfigured chin as if she was one of her own children. She had kept her eyes averted from the lower half of the girl's face.

In the cellar, she checked that the latch on the door to the coal chute was fastened, put the lamp on the table and quickly undressed and pulled on a nightgown, shawl and bed-socks. When she finally snuffed out the lamp, the cellar was pitch dark. Rose curled up in bed, warming her hands between her thighs and staring into the blackness.

The cellar smelled of root vegetables and damp earth and even though her eyes had now adjusted to the dark, the blackness was absolute. She wondered what Archie would have made of Jem, and decided against pursuing that thought. She had resisted the attentions of other men and Jem was no different, despite his fancy talk of theatre trips and chaperones. Archie would be more interested in what Annie had to say about how Rose might make use of the money donated by her mysterious benefactor. The suggestion she had made was better grist for the mill. She turned over, pulling the blankets over her head.

But her final thought before sleep took her was of Oonagh's mother, of the impotent fury she would surely feel when her damaged daughter was returned to her, and of Jane, turning eleven tomorrow in a dangerous world not made for women.

Chapter 11

It was a curious thing. The more his business thrived, the less patience Rob seemed to display towards his *shrewish wife*. Sitting on the omnibus, her spine held stiff against the rocking and swaying, Annie tightened her hand around the pamphlets she had rolled tight like a baton, a weapon to wield. He had called her *shrewish* and *reckless* and *self-regarding*. He had stopped short of forbidding her to help organise the march – his print shop was making money from the production of the pamphlets, after all – but told her she must not attend.

She had been determined not to lose her temper but her voice had grown louder with every word she uttered, a sliding scale of outraged disbelief. 'What am I to say? How do I encourage others to make a stand if I am not to stand with them?'

'It's simple. You tell them your husband forbade it,' said Rob. 'You tell them that as the wife of a newspaper proprietor you can't be seen marching with a rabble or making a nuisance of yourself in Paradise Square.'

Annie had gasped. 'A rabble? Don't you support our cause?'

He'd looked momentarily confused. 'Of course I do, Annie. But I don't want you caught up in it. What if you were injured, or arrested?'

'You're treating me like a child.'

'You're behaving like one. The matter is closed.' He threw her an exasperated look. 'I'm late for an appointment. Where's my wallet?'

'How should I know?'

'If this house were not so untidy...'

He had closed the front door so hard the knocker rattled on its hinge, leaving Annie stewing with resentment. Snatching up a handful of the pamphlets Rob had brought home from the shop, she had stamped out of the house. She'd intended to walk to Rose's street, to stroll down through the leafy district towards the smoky bowl of the town, and in doing so gradually restore her equilibrium. But she had taken only a few steps along the pavement when the horse pulling the Walkley bus that would stop outside the town's central church came clopping along. The shops and houses on Trippet Lane were close to the high street, among them the Seven Stars public house at number thirty-six. She would visit there first.

A flatbed cart stood outside the tavern, a pair of horses yoked to it. The cart was piled with furniture. A long, upturned table sat on top of two wardrobes, its underside crammed with chairs, stools and crates. The ends of three rolled-up carpets flopped out as though they had expired under the weight. A stout bowler-hatted man was walking around the precarious stack, testing the ropes that held it in place. 'Ey up, Annie,' he said. 'What does tha think? Will we make it to Port Mahon?'

Annie pretended to examine the load. 'Looks sturdy enough to me, Charlie. So today's the day?'

'Aye. Tha'll find the wife upstairs, sayin' her final farewells.'

There were a handful of men drinking in the gloomy interior of the Seven Stars. She hurried past, gathering up the hem of her skirt to climb the narrow staircase that led to the landlord and landlady's accommodation, rooms that would soon be occupied by new tenants of the brewery. Her footsteps echoed off the bare floorboards of the upstairs hallway, so that when she found Mary Pearson standing by the window in one of the empty rooms, the older woman was already turning her head inquisitively.

Mary was a tall woman in her vigorous late fifties, handsomely high-cheekboned with a wide generous mouth. She had been Mary Holberry before she married the landlord of the Seven Stars, and had been involved in the Chartist movement as a young woman, fighting alongside her husband, the martyr Samuel Holberry. She had, thrillingly, been thrown into jail for agitating for workers' rights – *while up the duff an' all, Annie!* In the archives of the female political association, Annie had found an old Chartist newspaper describing Mary Holberry as *possessing an excellent temper and, considering the defects of education, a mind of no mean order.*

Annie adored her.

'Ey up,' said Mary. Her eyes were wet. She turned back to gaze out of the window. 'Tha'll have to indulge me. I'll miss this little street, miss bein' at the heart o' town.'

Annie was glad she had acted on the spur of the moment and come to Trippet Lane first. She walked over to Mary and touched her hand. 'You're not going far, and the surroundings will be much more pleasant on the edge of town.'

'When 'ave I ever sought out *pleasant*?' Mary laughed. 'The children are grown an' Charlie's of an age to retire but I won't enjoy being put out to pasture. Nowt to see but fields an' a view of the general infirmary.' She folded her arms and raised her eyes to the ceiling before casting an impatient glance in Annie's direction. 'What's that you've got?'

Annie unfurled the pamphlets and handed one to Mary. 'We're getting the meeting captured for posterity.' She couldn't keep the triumph from her voice. 'My cousin Jem has arranged to have a daguerreotype made when everyone is gathered in the square, so we'll have a lasting record of our petition being presented to Mundella.'

'Let's 'ope we achieve sufficient numbers, then.' Mary scanned the leaflet. 'Who's payin' for that picture to be taken, by the way?'

Annie frowned. 'I will meet the cost, if the association can't.'

'Good for thee, then,' said Mary. 'Allus plottin', is our Annie.' She waved the piece of paper. 'I'll put this up in't downstairs window before we go, shall I? My final task as landlady of the Seven Stars.'

'Please.' Annie hesitated. 'There's something else you could do for me, today. Now, in fact, if you can spare an hour.'

'Sounds intriguin'.'

'It's a clement day for a short stroll.'

She marched purposefully from the room and was gratified to hear Mary's slower tread behind her, amusement in her voice. 'What plan are you hatchin' now, Annie?'

—

Rose greeted the additional visitor with equanimity, as Annie had known she would. What did surprise her was that Rose had never heard of Mary Pearson – or Holberry, as she had been – or the Chartist movement, or the Sheffield Female Political Association that arose from it, created to win the vote for women and the first organisation of its kind in the country. Annie had learned the rousing declaration by heart. *Would you have woman enjoy all the political rights of men? To this we emphatically answer: Yes! For does she not toil early and late in the factory, and in every department of life subject to the despotism of men? And we ask in the name of justice, must we continue ever the silent and servile victims of this injustice? Perform all the drudgery of his political societies and never possess a single political right? Is the oppression to last forever? We, the women of the democracy of Sheffield, answer, No!*

Their petition to the House of Lords was roundly defeated. That had been in 1851. Only three years ago, a suffrage bill failed to gain support. But perseverance was Annie's watchword.

She was eager to tell Rose about Samuel Holberry, the leader jailed for his part in a famous uprising, who was mistreated in prison and died there, leaving Mary a young widow, a young widow with small children, and all alone, just like Rose. She wanted to talk about the night-time demonstrations in Paradise Square – conducted in silence so that no one could be accused of seditious talk – that were nevertheless broken up by troops from the Hillsborough barracks. On further consideration, that might deter Rose from supporting the cause, where less cautious souls might find the story exhilarating, as Annie herself did. This latest protest carried on a fine tradition – a march from Attercliffe to the square, where a petition would be presented, calling for improvements in factory conditions, to the local member of parliament, Mr A. J. Mundella.

He had agreed to attend, which Annie was treating as a personal victory.

But she didn't get the opportunity to educate Rose. Mary got there first.

'It were all long before your time, love,' she said.

Rose made a pot of tea and the three women sat in the kitchen, which was warmly scented by just-baked bread. Annie laid the pamphlets on the table and Rose put a saucepan on top to flatten them out. The children, Rose said in answer to Annie's query, had gone to play in the fields off Jericho after spending half the day at Sunday school learning to read from the Bible. They would return in a fractious mood if Rose didn't allow them some time to run about. Oonagh was resting, she said, although she didn't answer when Annie asked where the girl was. She had popped her head into the front room when Rose let them into the house and the girl hadn't been reclining on the settee or sleeping in an armchair. She must be upstairs, in Rose's bed.

'I've been telling Mary about Oonagh on our way here,' she said, 'and the conditions she was being forced to work under. I mentioned the troubles at your factory too.'

'No different to any other,' said Rose.

'Of course. But the mother who complained about lack of safety clothing – I'm glad to say she's coming on the march.'

Rose nodded. 'Oh aye?' She gathered up a smock that had been folded on the kitchen table. 'Look at the state o' this,' she said, shaking it out. 'Threadbare. I bought it for Jane from that new clothes store at the market, only the other day. It's not survived one wash.'

'You get what you pay for,' said Mary.

'True enough.'

Annie pulled a pamphlet from under the saucepan and slid it towards Rose. 'We've had these printed. I hope you'll come along. Oonagh should come too, if she's up to it.'

Rose picked it up and glanced at the text. 'Hmm. Anyhow, Jane's growin' so fast I can't waste the coin on anythin' finer.'

'There's a good second-hand shop on South Street,' said Mary. 'I'll think o' the name o' it in a minute.'

Annie tried and failed to hide her impatience. 'Why not buy a sewing machine, then?' She tried for a more reasonable tone. 'I've got a Singer and I purchase the better-quality fabric already cut out and sew it together. It's quite straightforward.' She turned to Mary. 'Rose was laid off with no notice, on the whim of a factory owner who cares about nothing but his own purse, and her lodger, who comes from a match factory, is in a terrible state. Women are being exploited left, right and centre, and—'

'So 'ow much does a Singer sewing machine cost?' said Rose.

'I don't know.' Annie threw up her hands. 'I think they sell new for about seven pounds.'

Mary laughed. 'Buying cut-outs is all well and good so long as you can afford the seven sovereign for a sewing machine, or you'll spend all your waking hours wi' needle an' thread.'

Annie gritted her teeth. 'It's a worthwhile investment that saves money in the long run.'

'That's true, that's true,' said Rose, 'so long as you've got the luxury of gettin' a long run at summat in the first place.'

She poured more tea into Annie's cup and offered the sugar bowl. 'I can't put one o' these posters in my window, or join in your march, however much I might agree wi' thee. I'm back at work tomorra, back at Bright's. Oonagh will be goin' soon. I've got to think about me an' the kids.'

'Of course. I hadn't realised you had been given back your job.' Annie swallowed. She fanned her face with a pamphlet. 'I get carried away sometimes, with what my husband likes to call my little campaigns. He cares more about his precious publication than—' She stopped. 'I'm sorry.'

'Nowt wrong wi' what you're doin', Annie, and no need to apologise,' said Mary. 'Us women are the majority of the nation an' yet we get no say in owt. But who has the time, these days? Like Rose here, we're all too busy looking out for oursens.'

'And our children,' said Rose pointedly.

Perhaps a change in subject was required. Annie put down her teacup. 'Rose, I wondered whether you had thought about my suggestion regarding your late husband. May I elicit Mary's opinion on it, and tell her about the anonymous donations you've been receiving?'

'Why not?' said Rose. 'If I'm to take your advice, I'll 'ave to get used to all and sundry knowin' about what happened to Archie.'

Annie explained to Mary her idea, a way in which Rose might finally get some answers, and how it might be funded through the treasury she was concealing under her bed. It was a long shot, Annie acknowledged, but worth a try.

Eventually Mary interrupted her, and addressed Rose directly. 'I can't understand why tha's hoarding the money, let alone gettin' caught up in one o' Annie's schemes.

Tha's got enough to buy a cartload o' Singer sewing machines!' She snorted with laughter and Annie was surprised to see Rose join in.

She was about to argue her case, again, when the children burst in through the back door. The boys were soaked through and Jane's skirt and sleeves were wet. She was brought up short by the sight of the visitors, then turned to her mother to explain that she'd shoved Bobby and Jack under the tap at the end of the road as they were covered in the sort of muck that Rose would not want trampled through the house.

'Upstairs an' towel theesens off,' said Rose, fending the boys off. 'I'll gi' thee a hug after. Go on now. Follow Jane.'

The girl had already stamped out of the room.

Mary rested her chin in her cupped hand. 'Little darlin's,' she said. 'They grow up too quick, don't they?'

'Not quick enough,' said Rose. She shook her head. 'I don't mean that. Archie never got the chance to meet his boys, tha knows.'

'I know. I remember readin' about it, at the time,' said Mary. 'He got in the way of a union matter, din't he? Got himself blown up. Wrong place at the wrong time.'

Rose bristled at this. 'The police-detective said the same, an' seemed not interested in finding them that'd killed my husband, the father of my three. I can't get past it.'

She looked at Annie, her eyes dry and angry. 'An' now I'm finally goin' to do summat about it.'

Chapter 12

Daniel ate a late supper alone at a table in the corner of the Golden Ball, sitting beneath a haze of clay pipe smoke. The saloon area was stuffy and smelled of wet wool, thanks to the party of men who had hurried inside to dry their backsides as close to the roaring fire as they could get. Nevertheless, it was pleasantly cosy, and when he had finished his meat and potato pie, and the maid had taken his empty plate away, Daniel decided to linger rather than retire to his room for the night. At least if he remained in the saloon he would not see his cold breath misting about his face. The flue of the chimney that served the fireplace in his room was blocked, he'd been informed apologetically by the landlady, and they were waiting on the sweep to come and sort it out. She'd given Daniel an extra blanket for his bed and been worryingly vague about when the problem would be fixed.

He joined the regulars at the bar and braced himself for the inevitable ribbing about the lack of a good woman in his life. His romantic status seemed uncommonly popular as a topic for discussion. He counted himself lucky that nobody was party to his humiliation at his mother's hands, or if they were – if they had read the offending advertisement and deduced the truth – they had decided to keep their counsel. He looked at their faces. This was unlikely.

'Here's our Mr Housley,' declared the landlord.

Daniel paid for his meal. 'I'll take a pint of porter from you, Leonard, before I go up.'

One of the locals nudged him in the ribs. 'Got a young lady warmin' tha bed for thee?'

Mrs Archibald's voice carried clearly from the other end of the bar. 'I'll have no strumpets in my establishment!'

'That woman of thine, Len, has got ears like a bat's.'

The landlord tapped his arm. 'Tha should be married off, lad, and miserable as the rest o' us.'

'I heard that, an' all, Mr Archibald.'

'Sorry, love.'

'What's that you have?' said Daniel, indicating the sheet of paper in Leonard's hand. He wasn't remotely curious, only desperate to change the subject.

'This 'ere?' Leonard looked down at the paper. Daniel could see the page was headed APPEAL FOR INFORMATION. The text beneath, contained within a black border, was too small to read. There was a post box address in a larger font at the bottom of the sheet, below another line of bolder type: TWENTY SOVEREIGN REWARD.

'It's a sad tale, really,' said Leonard. 'Six year since a watchman got himsen killed walkin' down Change Alley. I remember it well. Some stupid sod had set a pipe bomb. Police never found out who.' The landlord put the sheet on the counter, face up. 'Hence this.'

'It's bin a long while,' said one of the men at the bar.

'Aye,' said another, 'an' people have short mem'ries over this sort o' thing. Wonder why it's bein' raked up now?'

'Am told these are in all the town's taverns.'

Daniel's face had begun to burn as soon as Leonard mentioned the location. Change Alley was where Rose Butterfield's husband had lost his life.

'Can I see?' he said.

Leonard handed over the sheet and Daniel quickly scanned the text, trying to keep his expression free of the conflicting emotions that assailed him. If he indicated he knew the widow he would be teased mercilessly, and he hadn't the patience for it. No doubt Rose had received help from her friends in the printing trade. The police would not take kindly to this.

Nor would Archie's killer or killers if they were still around.

Daniel rubbed his hand over his face. This was completely out of character. Rose was not reckless; she had been cajoled into taking this action, and as her friend he was obliged to warn her, and offer to retrieve as many copies as possible if need be.

–

The window of the company secretary's office at Bright's wire mills was no larger than one of the ledgers balanced on the bookshelf alongside it. It was a poor relative of the tall arched windows of the polishing and finishing rooms, where good light was crucial. But it did provide a cobwebbed and soot-stained view over the factory's central courtyard.

Daniel repositioned his chair so that he could sit and look at the comings and goings around the warehouse entrance, a book of accounts open on his crossed legs. If Mr Bright or one of the clerks popped their head in, he would say that he was making the most of the after-noon light. Or perhaps, for once, he might overcome this propensity to justify his actions, and simply not say anything at all about why he'd moved so far from his desk. There was no fireplace in this office – it was really little more than a glorified cupboard – and his intertwined fingers were as cold as the air that blew through the rattling frame. When he saw a group of women enter the yard from the side door in Otter Street, he couldn't untangle his limbs quickly enough to get a closer look. How ridiculous he would appear if anybody gazed upward, his nose pressed like a pig's snout against the pane. He came away from the window, absent-mindedly brushed a tendril of cobweb from his cheek, and walked as quickly as possible out of his office, along the corridor and down the stairs without quite breaking into a run.

'Rose!' He remembered where he was, and saw that the other women were staring at him. One of them laughed and elbowed Rose and said something he didn't catch. 'Mrs Butterfield! Can I have a moment of your time?'

Rose broke away from the women, who continued on to the warehouse entrance, and walked towards Daniel with a quizzical expression on her face. He waited for her to reach him.

'What's up, Daniel?'

He held up one finger to forestall her and with his other hand dug around in his waistcoat pocket.

Rose folded her arms, an amused smile on her face. 'You've not been in the newspaper again, have you, love?'

'Ha ha. No.' He produced and unfolded the poster and showed it to Rose. She gazed steadily into his eyes, refusing to look at it. 'This was left in the tavern I'm staying at. It's circulating around the town.'

A small frown creased her brow. 'Aye. Jem agreed to distribute 'em around the public houses. He's done the shops an' houses on Change Alley an' all the surrounding streets too. I'm not doing owt illegal, if that's what you're worried about.'

'I'm just wondering, why now, Rose? After all this time, and when you've just got your job back? And you have your children to consider.'

'An' one day, they might want to know who took their father off them.' Her eyes flashed. 'I don't see what business it is o' yours, Daniel.'

'I'm your friend, I hope. I'm concerned about you. What will you do with any information you get, assuming you get any at all?'

'I'll take it to the police, a'course. What did you think I'd do, go after whoever killed Archie, packin' a gun?' She rubbed her arms. 'I wun't even know how to go about buyin' a gun nor gunpowder.'

'Well, that's certainly good to hear.' He laughed. 'What an absurd conversation we're having.'

Rose smiled. 'Tha started it.'

'You wouldn't consider withdrawing the posters?'

'Bit late for that, love.'

Daniel searched her eyes. 'Can I ask, what if you are disappointed? What if you never find the culprits?'

'Then at least I'll know I tried.'

She nodded at the poster that Daniel had screwed up in his hand. 'Be careful wi' that. I had to pay to get them printed, though Annie got me a discount.'

'Was it your friend Annie who suggested this?'

Rose ignored the question. 'I have to get to work now.' She began to walk away, then turned back. 'I don't know why I'm telling thee this, because I'm not one for signs or portents—'

She stopped to allow a delivery boy to weave a heavily laden barrow between them, in no more control of it than he was his oversized clogs. A piece of coal rolled from the mountainous stack, setting off a mini-avalanche. The boy wavered, on the verge of setting down the handles of the barrow.

'Come back for 'em,' said Rose.

He nodded gratefully and set off again, disappearing through the open door of the boiler-house.

'Tell me what?' said Daniel. He was afraid she would take advantage of the interruption and leave him standing in the yard.

'The print shop I used for the poster. It's the very same place Archie were killed.'

He couldn't work out the expression on her face. It looked like embarrassment. 'I know,' he said.

She shrugged. 'It means nowt, I suppose.'

'Listen.' He hesitated. 'There are some rough sorts out there. Don't put yourself in danger, Rose.'

'I won't.' She smiled. 'Thanks for the concern, Daniel. I mean it. Now, I've got a night shift to get on wi' and you'll be wantin' to get home.'

'My mother has summoned me to supper.' He pulled a face that made Rose laugh.

'P'raps she's found thee a wife at last.'

'God forbid.'

'Sithee soon, Daniel.'

He watched her walk away. Then blurred movement caught his eye and he turned to see the boy dart from the boiler-house, this time barrow-less, and run around the yard retrieving the coal he'd lost, shoving it into a burlap bag. Daniel returned to the factory and climbed the stairs to his office, which was now full of shadows as the day darkened into early evening. A sliver of unease ran up his spine. He had laughed at Rose's remark but perhaps his mother *was* laying a trap for him. He had instructed her to destroy all the correspondence – and any that might arrive in the future. What if she hadn't done so? What if, instead, she had taken it upon herself to reply to those candidates who, in her opinion, might make a suitable match? What if at this very moment she was taking tea with one of them, awaiting his arrival?

He picked up his hat and his coat and the paper bag of sugared jellies he had purchased from a confectionery stall earlier that day; his mother had a sweet tooth. Daniel opened the bag and popped one in his mouth, and chewed ruminatively. She wouldn't dare.

–

If they all ignored the fact that it was conducted without him, then Daniel would say that the conversation flowed. His stutter got the better of him as soon as he entered his mother's parlour, his greeting dying on his lips. He had mustered a smile for the girl who sat opposite his mother, her hands resting demurely on the reticule on her lap. He handed his mother the bag of jellies, and sat on the chair a smirking Mabel indicated, arranging and re-arranging his limbs stiffly.

His mother thanked him effusively for the confectionery, offered one to the girl, who demurred, and made the introductions. The sharp glance she had given him when he entered had been a mixture of triumph and warning. Daniel wanted to throttle her.

Miss Abigail Baker was the daughter of the recently deceased vicar of Ecclesfield parish. Daniel might have read about it in the newspaper, his mother suggested. He had made a non-committal noise and, through strangled vowels, expressed sorrow for Miss Baker's loss. She responded with a high-pitched nervous titter. Miss Baker was nineteen years old, the youngest of eight children, and doted on her nieces and nephews. Daniel was a company secretary and a devoted son to a mother who wanted nothing more than to have grandchildren running about the place. This elicited another high-pitched trill. He hoped it was a result of a temporary case of nerves and not an affectation or tic of some kind. It was like being in the company of a budgerigar. He immediately felt ashamed of this uncharitable thought and attempted to widen the polite smile he was maintaining.

His mother told him she had already explained to Miss Baker the slightly unconventional way in which she had contrived to bring two delightful young people together, and told Miss Baker that Daniel had quickly accepted that his mother wanted only the best for him. Perhaps, if this introduction was successful, they might arrange to meet again, at a future date. There was no hurry, she said in a voice that unmistakably inferred there was.

Daniel's throat closed every time he attempted more than a few words. He felt desperately sorry for this girl, in whom he had no interest, and for himself. He sipped the tea Mabel brought him and listened to the three women speculate over the new horse-pulled trams – 'Rails on the streets!' said Mabel. 'Mixing wi' carts and cabs and people in their fancy carriages demanding right o' way as they do. Bedlam! I can't see it catchin' on.' – and Daniel considered telling Miss Baker he had taken a ride on the new tram, but that reminded him of catching sight of Louisa on the street, and he swallowed painfully and kept silent.

After half an hour had passed, Miss Baker said she would take her leave. Her brother had arranged to collect her from the end of the road. She hoped that did not seem rude, but it seemed inappropriate to be effecting introductions with members of her family, at this point.

Daniel also rose to his feet and straightened his jacket. 'I'll accompany you out,' he said, ignoring the beaming smile on his mother's face. He spoke without looking in her direction. 'I won't be back for supper, Mother. I think I may have forgotten to say, but I've made other plans.'

He knew she would not argue with him in front of the young lady.

Outside, he felt able to breathe again. It was a still, quiet evening, the cold air clearing his nostrils. The street lamps gave off a foggy glow, silhouetting the bats that fluttered from treetop to treetop. He made some comment about the night creatures coming out to play and told her about the family of owls that lived in the tree behind his lodgings at the Golden Ball. As they neared the junction, a black shape solidified into a small carriage and they were hailed by the man holding the reins.

'My brother,' said Miss Baker. She giggled, a gentle trill, and his heart went out to her. 'I'm sorry you were surprised by my visit today.'

Daniel's gut squirmed. 'Not at all.'

'I know I seem very young and unsophisticated to you.'

He didn't have anything to say to that. 'It was a pleasure to meet you.'

'And you, Mr Housley.'

A silence stretched between them and then Miss Baker nodded and climbed into the buggy to sit alongside her brother. The man raised his hat to Daniel, who lifted his hand briefly in acknowledgement before allowing it to drop by his side. The brother must be in the know, and Miss Baker certainly had a tale to tell him. It didn't take long for the buggy to disappear into the mist; the echo of hooves lasted for a few moments longer. Daniel thought about turning on his heel and returning to his mother's house to have it out with her. How many more ambushes must he face? Over a few seconds of deliberation, he ran through the scenario in his mind, and decided he could not face an encounter. It had been his reluctance to stand up to his mother that had contributed to his losing Louisa. He'd behaved in a cowardly manner and got what he deserved.

Daniel lifted the collar of his coat, glanced up and down the deserted street, and set off to climb the hill that would take him back to Attercliffe.

Chapter 13

The night shift always seemed endless. Standing at her station in the long, low-ceilinged warehouse, Rose was aware of the furtive looks she was getting from the two dozen men and women – mostly women – working alongside her as she packaged rolls and coils of wire to be transported to the manufacturers of sprung furniture and crinolines. She was standing near the gas stove intended to warm the entire room and the heat of it was making her drowsy. Meanwhile, Ethel, standing near the other end of the same table, closer to the door that stood open, was complaining bitterly of the cold. If they had been carrying out the same task, Rose would have suggested they swap places, but Ethel had been given the job of noting the number and contents of each box as it was carried out to the waiting cart. She was leaning against the grimy whitewashed wall, her mittened hand clutching a clipboard, the stub of a pencil clenched in her fingers.

Rose worked on. Annie had told her that, once made up, some of the crinoline frames over which elaborately embroidered skirts were draped were more than six feet in diameter. How did these women go about their daily lives? Although if Rose had a skirt as wide as that, she'd have a bit more elbow room in the warehouse. She smiled to herself. If she had a skirt as wide as that, she wouldn't be standing here. Annie said the fashion was changing now to a less bell-like look, and that it would soon be all about the flat front and the high bustle at the back, though she was certain that crinolines would have their day again. It made no odds to Rose.

She yawned widely, her jaw cracking, and was reminded of Oonagh. The poor girl would have no face left if they kept scraping her bone away, the way they were going. It was enough to make you wonder whether these surgeons knew what they were doing.

'Keepin' thee up, are we?' Eben Goddard was a watery-eyed man with a neck like a plucked chicken.

He liked to stir the pot and, ordinarily, Rose would have paid him no attention but the retort was out before she knew it. 'You should be workin' twice as hard as me.'

He jerked his head back. 'How d'you reckon that?'

'Because I'm earning half as much for doin' the same job, an' doin' it better, an' all.'

He made a womanly moue of his mouth. 'Somebody rolled out o' bed on the wrong side.'

'Shut thee gob, Ebenezer,' said the woman on the other side of Rose. 'Here, Rose, come wi' me. I need a wee. Ask old Rat-face if we can take a break. He likes thee more than me. Let's bring Ethel wi' us, an' all.' Susie Shaw rarely bothered with Rose, but Rose could guess why she was so keen to share a break with her. No doubt she had seen the poster and wanted to find out more, so she could share the information with all their co-workers.

Outside, the blackness of the night beyond the factory lights made her feel the world had shrunk, reduced to the square footage of the wire mills and the frenzied production within its high brick walls. The cold air seeped through her clothes, making her shudder. There was no moon, no stars, the black dome obscured by smoke or clouds. She imagined that if she walked out of this noisy yard she would step into an endless void, and fall forever with nobody to catch her and set her back on her feet. She shivered again.

The three women huddled on an outcrop of stone behind the building that housed the boiler and engine rooms. Rose could feel in the ground the vibrations from the rhythmical clank and grind of the machine inside.

'Be lovely an' warm in there,' said Susie.

'Too hot for me,' said Rose. 'An' too loud. What's up? We've only got five minutes.'

'I could freeze to death in four,' said Ethel. 'I know why Susie's dragged us out, though. She told me before. Tell Rose, quick.'

'It's about that poster tha's made,' said Susie.

'I guessed as much. I bet I'm the talk o' the place.'

'Well, aye, a'course,' said Ethel. 'What did tha expect?'

It was difficult to make out Susie's expression in the dark.

Rose was becoming impatient. 'So what is it, then? I don't need anyone else tellin' me I've done the wrong thing.' She thought about what Annie had said. 'What's wrong wi' wanting some justice?'

'Get off thee box,' said Ethel, 'an' listen.'

Susie lowered her voice. 'Me husband were in the Blue Pig an' this fella 'ad hold of your poster an' were tellin' all and sundry he knew who'd killed Archie. He were adamant about it.'

Rose's stomach clenched and for an awful moment she thought she was going to be sick. She gulped.

'He reckons he deserves that reward.'

Ethel patted her hand. 'A lot o' people talk rubbish to get seen. Or to get their filthy hands on someone else's coin.'

'Who's the fella?' It came out in a whisper. Rose cleared her throat. 'Does your husband know him?'

'Aye,' said Susie, 'he's allus in there. He reckons he's waitin' on his brother to turn up wi' the money he stole off 'im. Been waitin' years.'

'See?' said Ethel. 'Obsessed wi' money.'

'Aren't we all, love?'

Rose didn't respond. She was beginning to regret going along with Annie's suggestion she use some of the money she'd stored under Archie's cloak to offer a sizeable reward for information that would lead to her husband's killer or killers. *Don't put yourself in danger*, Daniel had told her. Before that, Jem had questioned why she wanted to stir up the past, but was sympathetic and had eventually agreed to distribute the posters around town on her behalf. She realised now that she had not been expecting anything to come of it. She'd been carried along on the wave of Annie's enthusiasm. Now, she had to deal with the consequences of her uncharacteristic boldness.

The Blue Pig. She'd never heard of it.

'Whereabouts is the—'

'You lot!' The warehouse gaffer had come outside to find them. 'We're not payin' thee to sit and scheme like the three witches o' *Macbeth*.'

'Come on,' said Ethel, leaning heavily on Rose's shoulder to haul herself to her feet. 'Can't afford to get laid off again, can we?'

Back at her station, Rose lifted a coiled wire snake and held the thin metal in her hands for a moment. Her mind was on Susie's revelation, and whether there was any truth in the man's claims, when a loud bang, followed by the sound of breaking glass and a high-pitched scream pierced the night air. It had come from close by, in the yard. She looked up, and met Eben's alarmed eyes. 'What were…?'

A man's shout for help carried clearly across the yard, his voice cracked with fear. Rose's first thought was of a blaze somewhere in the factory. She knew she wouldn't be the only one. For one taut moment, the tableau in the warehouse was frozen, then everybody moved at once, a tide of people pouring from the building, Rose among them. She came to a gasping halt when she saw the twitching body of a man lying face down, half in and half outside the boiler-house. Another man stood over him and shouted a warning to those approaching. 'There's glass all o'er!' The windows of the boiler-house had been shattered. Only moments ago, she had been sitting where shards of glass now stuck out of the dirt. The man they called Mr Ollerenshaw to his face and Rat-face behind his back had saved the three women from serious injury, or worse.

Something else was wrong, something so fundamental that Rose could not at first comprehend what her ears were telling her. Then she realised. She could hear clearly the excited conversation between two men who pushed past her. The factory engine had stopped.

'It must 'ave been that leak in the pipe they were talkin' about patchin' up the other day?'

'There's some pressure in that!'

'Aye, that there is. It'd account for the engine stallin'.'

'Tha wunt want to be in the path o' that.'

Rose hugged her elbows and turned away when the man lying on the ground was rolled over by two others. A collective sigh rose into the sky, and then somebody cried out, 'It's Harold.' Harold Cousins was the engine tenter.

'He's not breathin'.'

'Get a cart an' get 'im to the infirmary.'

'Fetch a doctor.'

'Bit late for that, fella.'

'Did tha hear me? He's not breathin'.'

'He only lives next door. We can carry 'im there easy enough.'

'Harold! Harold!'

'I don't think shakin' him'll do any good.'

'He's scalded to death. If he's still alive now he won't be by tomorra.'

Several men squatted down to lift him from the ground. His body sagged like a sack of potatoes. Another voice overrode the general clamour. Rose looked in that direction. It was Eben, supporting a strapping youth against his scrawny body. 'Get this one to the infirmary. He's burned his arm to buggery.'

The lad's face was a white disc in the dark and his eyes were wild with fear.

A woman called from the crowd. 'What 'appened?'

'Leave 'im be,' snarled Eben.

Rose was close enough to hear him speak. 'I told 'im it were goin',' he said. 'An' I ran out. Where's Jim? He were there an' all. He were closer to it than I were. Where is he? Where's Jim?'

A horse and cart were driven into the yard and the boy propped up in it, fielding questions from the men who had gathered around him. There were calls to fetch Mr Bright, and to search for Jim and not let the cart leave for the infirmary without him on board. 'What about Harold?'

143

'Harold's dead. He's bein' took 'ome.' Words that were spat out harshly, from the shock of it. Rose retreated back towards the warehouse, shivering uncontrollably. She wanted nothing more than to run home and embrace her children, but nobody seemed to be in charge, and everyone continued to mill about, some calling Jim's name, some speculating about what had happened.

'Boy said it were a faulty joint, that Harold were tryin' to tighten the bolt and it went and he got the brunt o' it.'

'Wi' the pressure o' that…'

'No wonder the windows blew.'

'Like a bomb goin' off.'

'It's a bugger. If tha dun't die o' shock then tha'll suffocate o'er a day or so.'

Rose caught the fleeting scent of dried blood and knew she was reliving a memory. She had put her lips to Archie's cold cheek when they brought him away from Change Alley and laid him on his father's table. She had inhaled the blood drying on his clothes, saw it congealed around the gaping wound in his chest. Now, she put her hand to her mouth, sickened.

As she backed away from the scene, she stood on something that yielded softly, someone's foot, and turned to mutter an apology. There was nobody there. Rose looked down, puzzled, and at first saw only a bundle of clothes. Her eyes widened when she saw that it was a man, hunched into a ball on the muddy earth near the horses' trough. She dropped to her knees and fearfully rested a hand on his shoulder. If this was Jim, he had crawled some distance before collapsing. She felt quite calm, speculating on this, but then the blood roared in her ears and she was seized with the horrifying thought that she would collapse in a faint on top of him. She opened her mouth to shout out, to tell the others she had found Jim before the cart left, but her voice had deserted her. Finally, she summoned up the strength to yell for help, cries that became sobs when a handful of people came running.

One thought circled and circled in her mind. He had been crawling to the animal trough thinking that the water might ease his pain.

–

The next afternoon, she woke from another dream about Archie. He was walking away from her, deaf to her pleas to turn around, his cloak whipped by a howling gale, his retreating back soon swallowed up in a swirling mist. Then the mist cleared and she saw he now had Jack on his shoulders and was clutching the hands of Bobby and Jane, and it was she who was being left behind, and the mist now clung to her, wrapped her in a scalding hot embrace and poured up her nostrils and down her throat.

Rose hung over the bowl in the kitchen, splashing cold water onto her face, the nightmare clinging to her still. It had to do with the terrible accident. She had been determined not to think about what she had witnessed, and had fallen asleep while composing a list for the grocer, but the mind was not so easily fooled.

The factory would be closed until the following day so that the pipe could be repaired and normal operations resume. Mr Bright had asked some of the workforce to do double shifts to make up for the break in production. Tomorrow, she would ask Susie Shaw if her husband had a name for the man who reckoned he knew who had killed Archie, and find out where in town the Blue Pig was located.

Chapter 14

'Goodness me, are you the man of the house now?'

Daniel Housley had opened the door to let Annie and Jem in, and blinked in confusion.

'I came to see how Rose is,' he said. 'You heard about the incident?'

'I covered the opening of the inquest,' said Jem. 'Your place is looking at a big compensation pay-out.'

Annie manoeuvred between them and into the hallway. 'You gentlemen might spend all day standing here. I'm going in search of Rose.'

She found her in the front room, holding mending in her lap, but gazing out of the window where slow coils of grey smoke rose from the stacks to mingle with whiter, scudding clouds. Rose smiled when Annie entered. She had dark shadows under her eyes. Oonagh was dozing in the armchair, looking like the ghost of the girl Annie had last seen, her skin milk-white. The scarf she wore to hide her jaw was the silk one Annie had given her when she'd overheard Oonagh complaining to Rose that the wool irritated her skin.

Oonagh opened her eyes and gazed at Annie.

'How are you today, Oonagh?'

Rose answered for her, standing and stretching, and laying down her mending. 'It pains her to talk. She's had some more bone scraped off. We're hopin' that's the last of it.' She helped Oonagh to her feet. 'Come on, you've been restin' there for hours. Shall we all go in the kitchen? There's more room. I'll brush your hair, Oonagh.'

'And are *you* all right?' Annie asked Rose.

She nodded, her eyes sliding away from Annie's frank gaze. 'Accidents happen.'

In the kitchen, Jem sat at the table and stretched his legs before him. 'Not so long ago, a skilled man would be responsible for every part of his work, in his own workshop or smithy. Now he's herded into a factory along with hundreds — thousands — of others, by the likes of Bright, who imagines himself to be a captain of industry but in reality isn't fit to run a tap.'

Daniel shook his head. 'But we have to adapt to keep up with the overwhelming demand for Sheffield product. The days of sole operators in riverside cottages and the little mesters in their workshops will soon be a thing of the past.'

'Spoken like a company secretary who oversees a thousand-strong workforce.'

Daniel looked stung.

'Oh, now, that's unfair,' said Annie. 'I don't know what's got into you today, Jem.'

'Nothing at all.' He glowered at her. 'Rose, can I fill the kettle for you?'

Rose nodded. She was standing behind Oonagh's chair, gently untangling the knots from her hair with her fingers.

'Aye, an' I've got scones ready to come out. They're hot,' she said as Jem jumped to his feet and bent to peer into the stove. 'Use a towel.'

'I'll make the tea,' said Annie.

Rose reached into a kitchen drawer for a hairbrush and stroked it through Oonagh's hair in long steady sweeps. It looked to Annie like part of a regular routine. Rose might have been the girl's older sister, helping her to get ready for church. It would be a comforting, familiar scene, were it not for the scarf and what lay under it.

'You've lovely hair,' Annie said to Oonagh. The girl's eyes crinkled in pleasure. Annie wondered whether they had always been this expressive, or whether Oonagh had learned to speak with her eyes when her mouth was permanently covered.

Daniel looked uncomfortable. He fidgeted with his collar. 'Mr Bright sends his best wishes to you, Oonagh. He's sorry he's not been able to visit but he is relaying back to your employer the progress you are making.' He addressed Rose. 'He tells me the dentist-surgeon believes a cure has been effected.'

'It's a shame it requires so brutal a method,' said Jem. He raised his hands. 'It's what we're all thinking.'

Oonagh turned her head in Jem's direction and slowly nodded. Rose gently moved her to face forward again and continued to brush and braid her hair.

Annie clapped her hands together lightly. It was an involuntary movement. An idea had come to her in an instant and she knew it would work. She was aware that Rose was regarding her suspiciously.

'What're you plottin' now, Annie?'

'It's not a plot.' Annie considered not saying anything, instead waiting until she had time to mull it over. But the idea was fully formed. She could visualise the scene, and she could not resist explaining herself. 'It's not a plot,' she repeated. 'It's a plan. Our protest march takes place in seven days—'

Jem interrupted her. 'I thought Rob had forbidden your attendance.'

Rose raised her eyebrows in surprise but didn't comment.

'I will be at the march,' said Annie quietly. 'I will be handing our petition to Mr Mundella.' She could not believe Jem had made such a remark, and so flippantly, in front of the others. She glared at him, and glanced quickly at Daniel and Rose. Daniel looked suitably embarrassed. Rose had returned her gaze to the braid she was threading around Oonagh's head. 'I don't wish to discuss that further, cousin, not in company.'

Jem sat back and smiled, trying to pass off his gaffe as a trifle, but he had the grace to look abashed.

'I did offer to cover the protest,' he said, 'but Rob in his wisdom has decided I am needed elsewhere. I shall remain alongside him all day, selling freshly published editions of the *Tribune* over the shop counter and greeting customers. Then in the evening, wonder of wonders, your father has invited me to his club, Annie, and I have managed to extend that invitation to Rob.'

What Jem was really telling her was that Rob would be otherwise engaged all day and all evening, and if her husband felt the need to check on Annie's whereabouts, Jem could alert her to the fact. She'd already decided she would not be hurrying home on Rob's command.

'I've often wondered what goes on in these gentlemen's clubs,' said Rose, a hint of a smile on her face. 'I bet it's full o' these so-called captains of industry.'

Jem beamed at her. 'It's not that fancy. There's a smoking room, a billiards room and a room in which to dine, used largely by those gentlemen not lucky enough to have a wife at home, or experience home baking such as here in your lovely kitchen, Rose.' A slight blush coloured his cheeks. He cleared his throat. 'I'm hoping Rob will be impressed by the news room, where the *Tribune* has its place amongst the local and national titles.'

'What does the news room look like?' said Rose.

'Well, um.' Jem frowned. 'I'd say it's the largest room in the club. There are scores of newspapers and periodicals to read and the walls and bookshelves are decorated with reference material. Volumes of encyclopedia, maps, portraits of important people…'

'All men,' said Annie.

Jem made his eyes round and innocent. 'I wasn't aware you had visited.'

'You know I haven't. I would bet on it, though.'

He turned back to Rose. 'It's frequently noisy. There will be men arguing over the topics of the day, someone deciding to take it upon himself to read aloud an article that has tickled him or carries some import. I hope one day my words will be worthy of being read aloud.'

'You should visit the Q on a Saturday teatime,' said Daniel. 'The landlord there regularly regales his patrons with the news of the day, and they carry the *Tribune* too. You might have already had your articles memorialised in the spoken word. The Golden Ball, where I'm lodging, advertises its own news room too, although obviously not on as grand a scale as your club.'

'It sounds very convivial,' said Annie.

'Do either of you ever go into the Blue Pig?' said Rose.

Both Daniel and Jem looked at her with puzzled expressions on their faces.

'The Blue Pig?' said Daniel. 'I don't know that establishment.'

'I do,' said Jem. 'There's a tavern called the Blue Pig near the railway station, if that's the place you're thinking of.' He looked from Rose to Annie, his eyes widening. 'I visited it on your behalf, Rose.'

Annie realised the importance of Rose's question a second later and put her hands to her face. 'The posters,' she whispered.

'It's a rough sort of place,' said Jem.

'Rose, has someone approached you?' said Daniel. He twisted his hands together. 'I have to admit I was hoping nothing would come of this scheme. There are ne'er-do-wells who will probably do anything to get their hands on that reward.'

'Tell us, Rose,' said Annie. 'I don't know how you manage to stay so composed.'

'Well, I've 'ad a little bit of time to think on it. Just gi' me a minute.'

Infuriatingly, Rose went to the stove, picked up the iron kettle and poured water into the teapot. She gave the contents a good stir. Annie automatically held out her cup and Rose refilled it.

'Still nice an' strong. D'you want some more sugar in it?'

'No, no. Oh, go on, then. What I want to know is why you're so interested in this tavern.'

Rose got up and closed the kitchen door. 'I don't want the kids hearin' this. They'll be back in a bit. I sent 'em to the shop round the corner for porridge oats.'

'All the more reason to hurry up and tell us,' said Annie.

Rose frowned. 'All right. Like I say, I've been mullin' it over and it's probably nothin', but a woman I work wi' told me her husband told her' – she paused for breath – 'that a man was mouthin' off about the poster, reckoned he knew...' Her face crumpled. '...he knew who killed Archie.'

Annie jumped up to guide her to a chair and Oonagh moved her chair closer, touching Rose on the arm. Rose shook her head impatiently.

'I'll be reight. Just gi' me a minute.'

'I've upset you, I'm sorry,' said Annie.

'Bull in a china shop,' said Jem.

Rose laughed shakily. 'I've never 'eard that expression before. I want to find this man and ask him what he knows. I want to go mesen, but I can't go on me own.'

'I can accompany you,' said Daniel.

'I'd be glad to take you, Rose,' said Jem.

Annie laughed. 'No shortage of volunteers.'

'P'raps,' said Rose hesitantly, 'if Daniel stays outside wi' me and Jem goes into the Blue Pig and asks around, and if the man is there, brings him out?'

The men nodded in agreement.

'Then it's settled,' said Annie. 'When?'

'After your march?' said Rose. 'I've asked the woman I work wi' to see if she can find owt else out, so I'd like to leave it a few days at least.'

'We'll follow your lead,' said Jem.

Daniel was biting his lip.

'Daniel doesn't agree wi' any o' this,' said Rose.

'Why not inform the local constable?' he said. 'Let the police investigate this.'

Rose shook her head. 'They did nowt at the time, did they?' She let out a shuddering sigh. 'Anyhow, enough o' that.' She gave Annie a weak smile. 'We were talkin' about how Annie's plot is really a plan.'

'Yes,' said Jem. 'I think I derailed that conversation. Sorry, cousin. What's the plan?'

Annie had forgotten all about her grand idea. She wanted to learn more about the man in the Blue Pig, and get the specifics from Rose about what her work colleague had told her. But she did have some groundwork to lay, and the march was only a week away. She felt a moment of uncharacteristic doubt. She was going to have to be crafty, and Rose might be cross with her afterwards – would undoubtedly be cross with her – but what she intended would catch the attention of the town's dignitaries, and ultimately benefit the working man and woman, and that included Rose.

Annie pushed her doubts aside.

'Well,' she said. 'We're meeting on Burgess Road, near Zion Lane.'

'That's around the corner from Bright's,' said Daniel. He sounded alarmed.

'Several of the employees who aren't working on Saturday afternoon will be taking part,' said Annie, 'along with the ladies of the association and a goodish number of our supporters. I thought you might come too, Rose, especially considering what you witnessed the other night.'

'I'd advise against it,' said Daniel, 'for any of Bright's employees. He can be a bitter man.'

'Daniel's right,' said Rose. 'I'm sorry, Annie, but I won't be joinin' in.'

Annie pretended to ponder this. 'Then perhaps Oonagh might come along,' she said eventually, as if the idea had just occurred to her. 'Provided she has recovered some of her strength by then, of course. She's the perfect example of how workers must suffer in order for their masters to reap their vast profits.'

Rose shook her head. 'I don't think she'll be reight. She's been through such a lot.'

Oonagh put her hand over Rose's and leaned close to whisper in her ear. Annie couldn't hear what was said but could see how it pained the girl to speak, how she stopped once or twice, dipping her chin and squeezing her eyes closed. When she had finished, Rose looked at Annie, a defeated expression on her face. 'All right, then. Annie, it looks like you might get your way. Oonagh wants to come, and I can tell you I'll be tryin' to talk her out o' it, but if she's adamant, I'm not lettin' her go wi'out me. So that's settled.'

Annie couldn't hide her delight. 'You'll both join in?'

'Aye, provided she doesn't change her mind in the meantime, or has any kind of setback.' Rose looked at Daniel and shrugged. 'If we do end up goin', I'll make sure we keep oursens in the background. I don't go lookin' for trouble.'

Annie nodded. She decided she would not push the point, not today.

It was her intention to have Oonagh stand alongside her on the steps of the Freemasons' Hall when she handed over the petition to the member of parliament, and for the girl to reveal her ravaged face to the assembled crowd.

Chapter 15

Tons of molten steel cascaded from the lip of the giant egg-shaped container in a shower of sparks that sounded like thunderous applause. Daniel could just make out the tiny silhouettes of men scurrying about behind the beast that was Hinchcliffe & Son's new Bessemer converter.

'Breathtaking!' he shouted to Silas, who stood alongside Daniel on a second-storey platform at the far end of the factory floor.

The grey metal orb squatted on the ground over a shallow pit, supported on both sides and encircled by the struts, girders and wheels that made up the tilting mechanism.

'Less than an hour it's took to magic thirty tons of pig iron into pure steel,' Silas shouted back.

Daniel nodded enthusiastically, unable to tear his eyes away from the enormous liquid steel-filled ladle now being swung on a gantry, its contents to be teemed into moulds of various shapes and sizes. He had watched the pig iron being poured into the converter before the machine was swung back to the vertical and oxygen blasted through the base to create a white-hot spear of fire, a ten-foot-tall column of ignited gas. It was left to the skilled operator to decide when the temperature was right and how long the burn would last, and to do this he had to get as close as possible to the mouth of the converter when it was tipped forward, towards the ground. Daniel was just starting to become accustomed to the metallic smell that had overwhelmed him when he first set foot inside the factory, choking his senses as if he was drowning in a burning sea. This was as close as he wanted to get to the superheated guts of this mighty machine. For the man supervising the burn, it must be like staring into the mouth of hell.

'Time for grub, I reckon,' said Silas, clapping him on the back.

Daniel followed Silas out of the chamber, down two flights of stairs and along a narrow corridor, eventually emerging onto the street, where he craned his neck to look back at the dense smoke billowing from the stacks. The steelworks was enclosed by a high wall, a blank stretch of bricks giving no clue to the alchemy taking place within. Daniel blew into his hands, suddenly chilled. The last of the light was leaking out of the sky.

'My ears are ringing,' he said. 'I've never seen it up close before.'

Silas laughed. 'It's a reight sight for sore eyes, in't it? Makin' steel were too expensive before Bessemer refined his machine. Now we're tekkin' orders for new railroads as well as plate for navy warships.' He buttoned up his coat. 'Feelin' the cold after bein' in there. I reckon we've got time for a jar or two before Harriet sends out the search party. There's a nice little hostelry in Campo Lane. What d'you think?'

'I think that's an excellent idea.'

The public house had a small snug containing two round wooden tables, a weakly burning gas lamp on the wall and an empty hearth. It was warm enough from the heat of the fire in the main saloon, and they had it to themselves. Silas returned from the bar with pints of porter and began to explain in earnest his latest venture. Daniel was glad of the respite; the whole town knew about the fatalities at Bright's and Silas had been wise enough not to mention the incident, but wait for Daniel to speak of it. It meant he could relax in Silas's company – which reminded him he was in the company of the owner of a foundry at twenty-seven years of age, only nine years after arriving in town as a penniless youth.

'You make me feel quite unambitious,' Daniel said.

'I've been lucky,' said Silas, 'reight from the start.' His smile had a grim set. 'Give or take.'

'An understatement,' said Daniel. Silas had almost drowned in the great flood of 1864 and had subsequently been flogged for an offence he hadn't committed. Daniel had once glimpsed the criss-cross of scar tissue on his back. Silas never spoke about it. 'Tell me how you've achieved' – he waved his arms around – 'all this?'

'I couldn't 'ave done it without this silent partner that's put up most o' the capital,' Silas said. 'He'll take a share o' the profits, a'course, an' is in charge of the purse strings, but has no say in how I run the business. It's my name above the door, an' Isaac will be apprenticed to Hinchcliffes when he gets to the age o' thirteen, after he's finished his schoolin'. This silent partner's existence won't ever be publicly disclosed, that's what the bank told me. Harriet were wary, at first, but we 'ad legal advice and it's all above board, apparently.'

'Who is this wonderful benefactor?' said Daniel.

Silas laughed. 'Buggered if I know. One thing I was told is he's helpin' a few factories get a foothold in the steel industry an' none o' 'em are bein' told his name. An' nobody I know has got wind of it.'

'How curious.'

'I suppose. Don't look a gift horse in the mouth, that's what I said to Harriet.' Silas peered at Daniel over the rim of his pint pot, then set it down carefully. 'If tha were ever lookin' for another job, Dan, I'll be after a right-hand man, somebody I can rely on who'd end up a director o' the company. Tha knows already we work well together.'

Daniel was touched. 'Be careful, Silas, or I just might take you up on that.'

Silas shrugged. 'I'm just sayin' the offer's there. Have a think on it.'

–

Daniel took a second marzipan slice from the shallow glass bowl in the middle of the dining table.

Harriet smiled. 'I'd forgotten what a sweet tooth you have. No, don't be silly.'

Shamefaced, he had gone to put it back.

'Tha'll need it, Dan, as a consolation when I win this game,' said Silas, holding up the two cards in his hand. 'Fifty-fifty chance.' Daniel wavered, and eventually plucked one of the cards and turned it to face him. It was the Queen of Hearts. Silas clapped his hands together. 'Beat thee again!'

The three of them were playing Old Maid around the table, which had been cleared of dinner plates, cutlery and wine glasses. Isaac had gone up to his bedroom with his arithmetic book and a promise from Daniel that he would be up to test him later. The boy was being home-schooled by Harriet, who wanted him as numerate and literate as possible before joining the family firm. Silas, who had not learned to read or write until the age of eighteen, was even more zealous than his wife in ensuring Isaac got a rounded education.

'Shall we have another game?' said Harriet.

'Only one more,' said Daniel, 'if I'm to test Isaac on his numbers and then walk back to the Ball. Thank you for dinner, Harriet, it was lovely.'

She dealt out the cards. 'Haven't you found a house yet, Daniel?'

'Not yet.' He wondered how much he should reveal of his reluctance to search for more permanent diggings. 'I'm fond of my accommodation, actually, because of the company I can enjoy after a day at work. A home-cooked meal whenever I want one. If I lived alone, I shouldn't see anybody once I closed the front door behind me.' He regretted speaking. They were both looking at him with pity in their eyes.

'Still not found a lass willin' to put up wi' thee, then?' said Silas.

'Ha.' A wave of sorrow came over him. 'I did, once, didn't I? And I might have gone against my parents, were it not for… you know. Although I think my mother was more concerned about her social status than anything else.'

Silas snorted. 'I'd have never ended up wi' Harriet if I'd paid attention to that sort o' thing.'

'Or, indeed, if I had,' said Harriet.

'Aye, that's true,' said Silas. They smiled across the table at each other affectionately, as if they were the only people in the room.

This was what Daniel yearned for, what he could have had with Louisa, had he had more courage. They might all be sitting here, now, the four of them enjoying each other's company once again, with no stilted talk, no prescribed manners to negotiate, no forced and inane tittering.

'Look how wonderfully your rebellion ended,' said Daniel. He hoped he didn't sound bitter.

'Harriet 'ad more to lose,' said Silas, 'bein' already engaged to be wed to a man o' means.'

Harriet arched an eyebrow. 'Enough of that. I hear from Silas you've made the acquaintance of a newspaperman. I imagine you must be in the know about all the town's gossip.'

'A journalist and the proprietor's wife,' said Daniel. 'They're interesting people. I met them through one of the factory workers who has become a friend. A good friend. I hope she feels the same.'

'Oh aye?' said Silas. 'A woman friend, eh? Does she have a name, this friend?'

Daniel laughed. 'Don't give me that look. Genuinely, a friend. Rose. I feel brotherly towards her. No more than that.' He took a card from Harriet. The queen, again. He kept his face straight and presented his hand to Silas. 'She's got a lodger who was made poorly working in a match factory. A young girl. It's a sad situation.'

Silas took the queen. 'Hmm.'

'What's wrong with her?' said Harriet, plucking a card from Silas's hand.

'Something to do with the stuff used to make lucifers, some wasting disease. Annie wants her to go on a protest march.'

'Dan, tha's surrounded by women. Who's Annie?'

'She is the proprietor's wife, and something of an activist.'

'Goodness me,' said Harriet. She held out her two remaining cards and Daniel took one. He'd got the queen back. 'And the journalist?'

'Jem. James Martin. Annie's cousin. I'm going to lose again, aren't I?'

'Looks that way,' said Silas. He put the last pair down on the table and Daniel threw the queen down on top.

'I don't really have any town gossip to share,' he said, 'though you might be interested to know that Rose is the widow of the watchman killed in Change Alley six years ago. Do you remember it?'

'Why, yes,' said Harriet. 'It had to do with the union trouble. I do remember it.'

'Well, it was never solved and Annie had the idea of putting up posters, offering a reward for information.' Daniel picked up the cards and shuffled them lazily. 'Rose went along with it.'

'This Annie sounds like a bit o' a firecracker,' said Silas.

Daniel tapped the cards to straighten the edges and laid them carefully on the table. 'I should go and visit with Isaac before I leave.'

Harriet put her hand over his. 'Something is troubling you. What is it?'

'I'm wondering,' he said, trying to keep his voice steady, though his heart had begun to race, 'how is Louisa?'

He had become obsessed with the idea he would see her again every time he ventured into town, while telling himself that he was merely taking in the street scene, so that he would not feel disappointed when none of the faces he saw belonged to her. The self-deception wasn't working.

'She's very well,' said Harriet. 'I sometimes look after Alice for her, when she's busy at work. Which she often is. Alice is six now and like a little sister to Isaac.' Her eyes filled with tears. 'He dotes on her. We all do.'

Silas got up and wrapped his arms around Harriet. She relaxed her head against his torso. Her cousin, another Alice, had been swept away in the great flood at the age of six. She'd been sleeping in Harriet's bed that fateful night. Louisa's daughter was named for the lost child. Daniel didn't know what to say and the silence swelled.

Harriet broke it, pulling away from Silas, who kissed her cheek and sat back down. 'I didn't tell Louisa that you'd seen her on the street, Daniel. I thought there would be no point in bringing it up.'

'No, no,' he said, 'of course not.'

Silas frowned and began to speak but Harriet shook her head and he subsided. Daniel got to his feet. 'I'll go and see how Isaac is getting on with his arithmetic.' He took another slice of marzipan from the bowl and smiled at Harriet. 'Not for me. For Isaac, if he's permitted.'

—

Daniel descended the steps to the cold pool of light the street lamp cast on the pavement and looked back at Silas, who raised his hand in farewell.

'Don't leave it so long next time, Dan. Isaac loves to see thee, an' Harriet an' all.' He moved back into the shadow of the hall, then seemed to change his mind and trotted down the steps. 'I shun't say owt.' He looked back at the house. 'Harriet's told me to keep me nose out, but I don't get why tha can't make amends wi' Louisa. I've already told thee she's on her own. An' here's thee, moonin' about the place...'

Daniel was affronted. 'No, I'm not!'

'...an' a lot o' water's passed under the bridge. She might be glad to see thee.'

'If only it were that simple.'

Silas shrugged. 'I don't know, Dan,' he said. 'Some o' the time it is.'

Chapter 16

Saturday dawned bright and dry but cold enough to have numbed her nose and ears in the night. Returning to the cellar from waking the children, Rose made the most of the residual warmth of her bed, getting back under the covers to put on her clothes. It was a day to wrap up warm, which meant that Oonagh would not look out of place stepping out of the cottage swathed in a thick scarf that not only covered her hair but could be wound tight around her face.

Rose sat the boys at the kitchen table with crumpets and jam and went to find Jane. Her daughter was in the front room and had lifted the net to stare out of the window. A magpie sat on the low wall that separated the garden from the street, grooming its white chest feathers with a sharp black beak.

Jane turned to look at her mother. 'One for sorrow,' she said.

Rose rubbed her arms. 'I'll light a fire in 'ere before we go if you can keep an eye on it. You'll need to bring some coal up, an' make sure the lads don't get in the chute again.'

'Is Oonagh gettin' worse?'

'Why d'you ask?'

Jane glanced behind her mother at the front room door, which stood open. In a flurry of squawks, a second magpie landed on the wall.

'There,' said Rose, pointing. 'That's better. Two for mirth.' The strutting birds reminded Rose of the gentlemen she had seen at the theatre in their starched shirts and tailcoats.

'I can't make her out, when she tries to talk. She's not eatin' owt neither.' Jane pointed as a third bird landed alongside the other two. 'Oh, look. Oh dear. Three for a funeral. What's the next one?'

'It's a nice one again. Four for a birth.'

'An' she smells funny, like a... like a dead mouse.'

'Jane!'

'But she does.'

It was true. Rose hadn't been allowed to see Oonagh's face lately but a sweetly rotting odour followed the girl around. The silken scarf donated by Annie had been ruined by the pus that soaked it through. Rose had tried to scrub the scarf clean through gritted teeth, fighting biliousness, and had unexpectedly become tearful with rage. She thought she understood, in that moment, Annie's zealotry, her passion for her cause.

Rose studied her daughter's profile, her gently curving jaw and rounded chin.

'There's still only three magpies,' Jane said. She turned to her mother, frowning.

'It's a silly rhyme and you're a silly billy.' Rose stroked Jane's hair from her forehead. 'Go an' brush that hair. Them birds'll be mistaking it for a nest when you go outside. I'll be back in time for tea, all right?'

Oonagh shook her head when Rose offered her something to eat before they left but accepted a cup of hot, sweet tea that she carried into the back lane to drink. Both women wore heavy shawls, thick woollen stockings under their dresses and pinafores, fingerless gloves and lace-up boots. Oonagh's boots were new, another gift from Annie, and she complained in a faltering, congested voice that they pinched her toes. Rose made a sympathetic face but decided there was nothing to be done; it was too cold for clogs, and if a person was lucky enough to have boots they should wear them.

Ordinarily, Rose would maintain a fast walking pace up the steep incline of her street and into the middle of town, but this was impossible with Oonagh in tow. She realised, as they set off, that she and Oonagh had never been out together. The girl was collected by a gig for her surgical appointments and returned home in no fit state to do anything other than go to bed or recline in a chair, her eyes squeezed shut or – even worse – glazed over as if she was half-dead.

The magpies took off messily as she closed the gate, like dead leaves being thrown in the air. There were several birds wheeling in the sky now. *Five for heaven. Six for hell.* She inspected the small front garden but could see no tell-tale flash of white, no envelope stuffed in the window frame or half-hidden under the bush. She took Oonagh's hand – the girl's fingers were a bundle of fragile twigs – and they made slow progress towards the part of town that would be thronged with market stalls this morning.

'P'raps we should go straight to Paradise Square,' she said.

Oonagh shook her head and gently tugged Rose's hand. Her eyes burned in her skull. Rose could hardly bear to meet her gaze. The girl had been brought to realise how seriously damaged she was, and how her terrible pain was caused by men who did not care about her fate, and her anger came off her like flames.

'Aye, all right. It'll be cold waitin' around.' Rose smiled as encouragingly as she could. 'Better to be marchin' wi' the rest.'

They threaded their way through the densely packed stalls of the sprawling farmers' market off Castle Street, Oonagh turning her head this way and that. Regret washed over Rose, leaving her close to tears. In all the time Oonagh had been in the town, she had never walked through these bustling streets, and her eyes were wide and bright, drinking in the scene. Rose should have taken her out, but she had always seemed too frail, too sick to do anything other than sit in a chair. It was Annie who had galvanised the girl.

'Watch out!' Rose pulled Oonagh to a halt to allow a barrow laden with toppling pyramids of carrots, potatoes and beetroot to wheel past. The boy behind it, whose head barely cleared the top of the pile, was whistling loudly in an attempt to clear his way, a piercing sound that drilled into Rose's head. It was a relief to get through the market and onto the high street. Rose nodded to the passers-by she recognised but most of the people crowding the pavements were strangers from the surrounding villages, flocking in to stock up at the ironmonger, chandler and grocer, bartering over those items they couldn't grow or rear themselves, candles, saws and rope, boots and hats and winter oilskins.

A shiver ran up Rose's spine when they passed the end of Change Alley. Somebody in this town knew who had killed Archie. It might be this man here, shoving past Rose and pushing open the door to the wine and spirits shop, or this man, trying to catch her eye, selling pocketknives on the corner, his gnarled fingers purple with poor circulation and the cold. 'Come on, love, no time to tarry.' She squeezed Oonagh's hand and they walked on.

Fargate, where they would take the omnibus to Attercliffe, was only marginally less crowded. Here were the finely dressed ladies and gentlemen, come to town to browse the fancy items in Cole's department store, the leather-upholstered home furnishings, elaborately fashioned gowns and waistcoats embroidered in brilliant colours. Oonagh stared at the items displayed behind large plate-glass windows, her awed gaze taking in the fringed lamps and Persian rugs and gilded picture frames. Rose pulled her onwards. When they reached the Attercliffe bus stop, the passengers had already boarded and the driver was on his box, holding the reins, his face hidden in a muffler, while another man fed the two harnessed horses from a nosebag.

Rose clutched the rail at the back of the bus and ushered Oonagh ahead of her into the musty-smelling interior, praying they would find seats and not have to travel on the exposed top deck. There were a dozen people, mostly women and a couple of elderly men, inside the carriage. Two of the women shuffled about to make room, elbowing their neighbours, and Rose made sure Oonagh was safely seated on the opposite bench before sitting down herself to face the girl.

Away from the distractions of the street, Oonagh seemed to give in to the pain in her jaw, her eyebrows drawn together, her head bent and tilted so that she stared at the damp rushes on the floor of the bus. Looking at her gave Rose a hollow feeling in her chest. Whatever Annie was setting out to achieve, it would be too late for this poor creature. Her disfigurement was permanent, and Rose wondered what sort of life she would have.

When they alighted on Baker Street to walk the short distance to the church at the end of Zion Lane, a barefoot boy clutching a loaf of bread scooted to a halt in front of them, making Oonagh exclaim in surprise. He dodged around them and continued running, his shirt-tails flapping.

'He stole it?' Oonagh whispered.

'Looks that way, an' he'll get locked away for that if he's caught,' said Rose. 'I just 'ope my three will never have to resort to nickin' bread.'

She wondered, not for the first time, what she was doing joining a protest, potentially jeopardising the carefully ordered life she had built since Archie died. He would never have believed his Rose would do something so foolhardy. She could hardly believe it herself.

She led Oonagh towards a one-storey building that adjoined the church. The noisy chatter that came from within increased in volume as she opened the door. Inside the room, pans of soup were being warmed on a large stove beneath a stone chimney breast. There were about thirty people sitting at the longer of one of two oak trestle tables. The smaller table held stacks of plates and bowls, a pile of spoons, several loaves of bread and a bowl of dripping. A man stood behind the table, gripping a loaf with one hand and slicing through it with the breadknife he held in the other.

'Nah then,' he said, 'see owt o' that little thief on tha way in?'

Rose nodded. 'I don't think you'll see that loaf again.'

'I would'a fed him, an' all. Little varmint.'

'Rose!' Annie strode towards them, wielding a large metal ladle and trying to take off her apron at the same time. Some of her braid had come unfastened and tendrils of hair were stuck to her cheeks and forehead. 'And Oonagh, too! Thank you for coming. I was so worried you'd change your mind.'

'I tried to persuade 'er,' said Rose. 'She were havin' none of it.'

Annie laughed, as if Rose had been joking. 'You are a one.' She turned to the man with the knife. 'I'll leave you to it. I think we're almost finished.'

'It does smell lovely,' said Rose.

'Chicken broth,' said Annie. 'Would you like a taste? Would Oonagh? We haven't long. I could bring a cup with us.'

Oonagh shook her head.

Rose said: 'Let's get this o'er with.'

'One moment.' Annie was busy replacing her apron with a dark grey jacket and matching hat. She added a white sash, tied at one hip, and opened the drawer of a small table by the door, taking out a stack of pamphlets. She handed some to Rose and some to Oonagh. 'To distribute to onlookers as we march along, tell them what we're about.'

Rose quailed at the idea of shoving unwanted bits of paper into people's faces. Oonagh tapped her arm and pointed at the text contained within an illustration of blue and white intertwined ribbons. Rose spent a few moments reading. There were several words she couldn't interpret but she had the gist of it.

'All right, they're sayin' women and children shouldn't be workin' more than ten hours a day in factories, and there's summat about improvin' inspections o' machinery and workin' methods. It's all in this petition they're handin' to Mr Mundella, who is one o' our members of parliament.'

Annie finished fiddling with her hat and took a deep breath. '*We* are handing a petition to Mr Mundella.' She hugged Rose and Oonagh in turn. 'It's very important to me that you are here. Let's not keep the gentleman waiting. We're due in the square at two o'clock.'

The allotted meeting point was too close to Bright's wire mills for Rose's liking. A crowd was milling about on the junction where she could see the end of the factory wall and the top of the main stack. Smoke rose implacably from it, straight up in the still, cold air, to mingle with the residue from other factories nearby. Rose took a deep, comforting breath of the familiar and unchanging air of the town as Annie introduced her to her friends from the political group she was involved in. They were all wearing similar jackets and hats to Annie's, and matching sashes. Like Annie, they all wore dusky pink skirts, trimmed in grey velvet. It was a uniform. There were around thirty of these women and Rose was relieved Annie introduced her to only four – Sophia, Susannah, Esther and Rebecca – who circled around Oonagh like bees on lavender. Oonagh looked at Rose, consternation in her eyes.

Rose whispered in her ear. 'I've forgot their names already. Let's just call 'em the sash women.'

The corners of Oonagh's eyes crinkled.

Rose was startled when Annie blew on a whistle and began to herd the crowd into a rough semblance of a line. A couple of the sash women were encouraging bystanders to join the back of the parade, the rest lined up three abreast. A young police constable stood off to the side, a nervous look on his face. Rose spotted Ethel standing behind the officer and crossed over to her, clutching Oonagh's hand.

'Ethel, what're you doin' here?'

'I could say the same to thee.' Ethel looked at Oonagh and then over Rose's shoulder. 'I come for a look. There's a few 'ere from Bright's, tha knows.'

Rose turned to follow her gaze. 'Not that I can see.'

'Family members o' the workers, then. Them that's deceased.' Ethel pointed to a woman who was standing on the pavement near the front of the line, with five or six small children hanging off her skirts. 'That's Harold's widow an' kids. An' young Jim's mother an' father are linin' up for the procession, look.'

Harold Cousins, the engine tenter, had died instantly in the blowout, but Jim had been alive when he was transported to the infirmary. He was a strapping lad and it had taken two agonising days for his lungs to give up on him.

'Bright shoulda replaced that pipe. Joint were worn out,' said Ethel. 'There's got to be some sort o' account-ability when tha's got half a dozen children orphaned and an apprentice lad who never hurt nob'dy.' She peered at Oonagh again. 'But what are you doin' 'ere, Rose? This in't tha sort o' thing, is it?'

'Am 'ere for Oonagh, who's lodgin' wi' me.'

Ethel looked the girl up and down. 'What's tha story, then?'

Rose answered. 'She wanted to come an' support the parade. An' it'll be a calm an' orderly procession to the square, where Mundella is meetin' us. Nowt scandalous, though am a bit apprehensive about bein' so close to Bright's.' She looked for Annie in the crowd. 'I'd like to get goin'.'

Ethel folded her arms, and scowled at Oonagh. 'Why's tha all wrapped up like we're in Siberia?'

Oonagh began to cough, doubling over and turning away, pulling on Rose's hand.

'What's up wi' her?'

'She's got phossy jaw from workin' wi' poison in a match factory.' Rose could see that Ethel had no idea what phossy jaw was. She didn't want to enlighten the woman; for Ethel, it was a morsel of gossip to barter. 'She wanted to come.'

'What factory?'

'Not in Sheffield. Elsewhere.' Even to Rose's ears this sounded unnecessarily mysterious. 'We'd better go. Oonagh, can you manage it? Looks like we're off.'

'All right, enjoy tha *procession*.'

One of the sash women shouted out that the march to Paradise Square was underway and there was some scattered applause from those taking part and from the handful of people watching from the pavement. A second constable had joined the first. They separated so that they were on either side of the procession, about halfway down. Annie guided Rose and Oonagh to the front and placed herself between them. After walking a few yards, Rose gently detached her hand from Annie's. 'Can't hand these things out wi' only one hand,' she muttered, shaking the pamphlets. She hoped there'd be a roadside bush or tree she could drop them behind and rid herself of the embarrassment of foisting them onto anybody.

Marching along Effingham Road, they passed the high brick walls, wrought-iron gates and wooden side doors of the steel forges and factories that lay between the River Don and the canal. Shift workers leaving a large mill joined them for a short distance, and Rose divested herself of all of her pamphlets, which were taken eagerly from her hands. A group of dockers working on the banks of the canal where it ran close to the road offered catcalls, whistles and cheers. Annie waved happily to them. The procession was making faster progress than Rose had anticipated but she knew the terrain would steepen once they reached Furnival Road and it would be a hike up through Haymarket towards the high street and Church Street. She glanced worriedly at Oonagh. The girl's face was pale but she seemed to still have strength in her legs. Her eyes were bright, once again taking in her surroundings keenly.

They attracted more attention in the centre of town, not all of it welcome. A man loomed out of nowhere, right in front of Rose, and spat brown-coloured phlegm on the ground. She stepped over it.

'Bunch o' daft women makin' fools o' theesens.'

'Pay him no heed,' said Annie, unnecessarily.

A gentleman approached and doffed his hat to Rose. Annie offered him a pamphlet but Rose put her hand on Annie's arm. She didn't like the look of the sneer on the man's face. Then she recognised him. It was Mr Boothby, the man who was paying her to keep Oonagh safe. And here she was, on a march, with Oonagh, and leading the procession to boot.

'Mrs Butterfield,' he called, as Rose picked up her pace, her stomach knotted in fear. 'I hope you're not leading this poor girl astray. She's in no fit state to be out.' To Rose's horror, he reached out to tug Oonagh's scarf. The girl cried out, a rattling, anguished sound. Rose was terrified he would pull the scarf off Oonagh's face completely and expose her terrible injuries but she couldn't get to the girl to help her. Annie stood between them, her mouth hanging open in shock. Suddenly, or so it seemed to Rose, there were half a dozen of the sash women surrounding him, and then one of the constables was pushing through and calling for calm. Boothby held up his hands in a gesture of innocence, although a smile played on his lips. Rose turned away from him and re-adjusted Oonagh's scarf with trembling fingers before putting her arm around the girl's shoulders and guiding her away from the procession. She should not have listened to Annie. She should have forbidden Oonagh from joining in. The girl was shaking. Rose hugged Oonagh's body against hers and turned the corner of the street, where she halted, a gasp forcing its way from her throat.

They had arrived in Paradise Square.

Chapter 17

She gazed on the scene before them. Oonagh was crying softly but had stopped shaking. Rose's first thought was that the square was not as tightly packed with bodies as it had been when she had stumbled upon the political rally months earlier. But there were a few hundred people standing on the cobbles and the hum of conversation rose into the air like a cloud of bees. Rose didn't think she'd ever seen so many women crowded in one spot. Many of them were working women, like Rose. There were some who were more finely dressed too, and a group of top-hatted men who gave off an air of self-importance and untouchability. There were other men, some gathered around a coffee stall at the foot of the square, others standing outside the Q, pint pots in hand, observing the scene. Annie had done well. Rose felt a rush of pride and was, for the first time, glad she had come along.

'What does tha think, Oonagh? Was it worth the walk, then?'

The girl used a corner of her scarf to dry her eyes and laughed gently. 'Sure, Annie will make an agitator out of you,' she whispered.

'Not I,' said Rose. 'I just want a quiet life, no palaver.'

She looked around the edges of the square and her eyes fastened on a familiar face. The last time Rose had seen A. J. Mundella, he had been addressing the crowd from a balcony, canvassing for votes, while she had simply been trying to cut across the square to the grocer's shop. Today, he stood on the steps of the Freemasons' Hall, and she was here as an active participant. The thought sent a thrill through her body.

Mundella was chatting to the man who stood beside him, a man with high, chiselled cheekbones and a shock of unruly dark hair. This man turned to look out over the square, his narrowed eyes sweeping the crowd. Rose looked away from him quickly, glancing at Oonagh and frowning to hide the curious mix of emotions she felt, emotions she could not name. He should not be here today but she was not mistaken. The man was Jem. She had never thought him handsome before. Seeing him unexpectedly, she had looked at him with fresh eyes. She risked another look but his eyes moved over her and away; he hadn't seen her. Rose shook her head and smiled. She was acting like a lovesick girl. But she was surprised by how uplifted she was, seeing him there. Jem had said Rob would keep him busy today, away from his cousin's *little march*, but nevertheless here he was. Rose dropped her arm from Oonagh's shoulders and took the girl's hands in hers, searching her eyes. The girl was her responsibility, and she had had a fright.

'D'you want to stay or shall we go? Nob'dy would think badly of thee if we went home.' She realised as she spoke that she didn't want to leave. She wanted to make it Oonagh's choice. 'I could do wi' a cup o' tea, an' I've got some carrots and celery I can make into soup to warm us up?'

Relief flooded through her when Oonagh shook her head and whispered that she would like to stay. Rose glanced across the square. Jem was looking directly at her, waving his arm, a wide grin on his face. She waved back. 'All right then, love. I suppose we've not paraded all the way from Attercliffe to slink off now. Keep by me.'

They set off towards the Freemasons' Hall. Rose glimpsed Annie leading her party out of an alleyway towards them. A ragged cheer rose up when Annie's brigade entered the square and unexpected joy swelled in Rose's heart. This was her friend, her good-hearted friend who got things done and was afraid of nobody. She should try to be more like Annie, less like a mouse. They met at the foot of the steps.

'I thought I'd lost you!' said Annie, hugging the two women in turn. She stepped back, and almost toppled a tall tripod on which sat a box the size of a man's head. A circular tube protruded from one side of the box.

A man reached out to steady the device. 'Look out, madam,' he said.

'Oh, I'm so sorry. Excuse me please.'

'Is Annie causing chaos?' called Jem. Annie nodded enthusiastically and ran up the steps to shake Mundella's hand. They began an urgent conversation, their heads together, obscuring Jem, who hung back in the doorway. He leaned sideways and winked at Rose. She shook her head in admonishment, her heart pounding, wondering how Annie had the nerve to act so casually with a member of parliament. Eventually, Annie trotted back down to Rose and Oonagh.

'Mr Mundella is going to address the gathering,' she said, 'and then accept the petition from us. We'll pose for a daguerreotype, which might take a few minutes. Jem will write something and hopefully Rob will print it. Jem tells me there's a man here from the *Sheffield*

Independent, and a reporter has come all the way from Doncaster, so there'll be coverage of some sort.'

She turned to Oonagh, her face alight. 'Would you step up with me, to stand alongside us? You'll have your picture taken with Mr Mundella. What do you think of that?'

Rose shook her head. 'Best not,' she said. 'All o' this is a lot for a young girl to cope wi' an' she's exhausted. Just look at her.'

Despite the chill of the day, sweat beaded Oonagh's forehead and the shadows under her eyes were dark smudges against her white complexion.

Oonagh turned away to cough, then looked at Rose. Her cracked voice was almost inaudible. 'I will go,' she said. 'I want to.'

'Are you sure?'

She nodded.

Rose sighed but didn't object when Annie took Oonagh's elbow and led her to the top of the steps, where introductions were made. Then the member of parliament turned to face his audience and raised his hand for quiet. The chatter faded as he began to speak.

He reminded his audience that during his time in office he had introduced several bills relating to dangerous working conditions in factories, beginning with the textile mills, and further amending the law to include any establishment employing fifty or more people.

His voice rang out across the square. 'The ladies gathered here today have my sincere sympathy and my solemn pledge to help eradicate dangerous working practices by improving the system of factory inspection. It will be enshrined in law that no child or young person should be set on the cleaning of machinery that is in motion.' He paused to allow a smatter of applause to die down. 'I am determined to shorten the hours that children and women spend labouring alongside male workers.'

A customer of the Q, next door to the Freemasons' Hall, smacked his hands together, booed and lifted his leg in a mock-fart before retrieving a tankard that had been balancing precariously on the window-ledge. 'No voters 'ere, love, just a load o' women. Get on wi' it, will tha?'

There was laughter as well as voices raised in complaint and Rose was jostled from behind as those standing closest to her surged forward. She was reminded of the last time she had been caught up in a crowd in Paradise Square and a wave of dizziness passed over her, with nothing to hold on to as the world tilted. She tensed the muscles of her legs and looked at the ground she stood on in an attempt to steady herself, remaining rooted to the spot as bodies heaved around her. When she had gathered her senses, she found herself standing behind a crowd that was six-deep, far too distant from Oonagh for comfort. She could see the girl searching for her and waved from where she stood, plastering what she hoped was an encouraging smile to her face. Perhaps she had made a mistake, after all, bringing the girl here, allowing Annie, who had nothing to lose, to infect them with her enthusiasm. Life was precarious enough, without going looking for trouble.

Mundella talked on, and finally got to the point. 'I accept this petition with gratitude in my heart, as the sentiments expressed endorse my own campaign for better rights for the working man, and woman.'

'And child!' A shout from the crowd.

'Of course, young people too,' said Mundella.

He turned to Annie, nodded gravely, and held out his hands for the petition. Rose saw an arm shoot up, a hand with one finger extended to the sky, and bit back a cry of alarm. It was the man operating the daguerreotype. Polite applause rippled through the square as Mundella and Annie, her chin raised, held the petition between them. Oonagh stood alongside Annie, part of the frozen tableau. Rose inhaled raggedly, relieved, when the man dropped his hand, the image finally captured. It was over, and they could all go home now.

She rubbed her forehead where a fat drop of rain had fallen on it and glanced up. Black clouds were gobbling up the overcast sky in the east. Rose didn't know which way the wind was blowing, but she knew Oonagh should not be caught in a downpour. She reckoned they could walk home in ten minutes, even at a stately pace. Jane would have put the pie in the oven by now and made gravy from the meat juices and flour as Rose had taught her. The boys had been taken by a neighbour to Port Mahon to practise their football skills – they were clamouring to join one of the youth teams that had sprung up recently – and would soon be returned to the doorstep, dirty and hungry. Rose would make the soup and might invite Annie and Jem to have some tea. There wasn't time to bake a loaf so she'd buy breadcakes on the way home.

But something was wrong. The sash women were standing arm in arm near the steps the politician was now turning to descend. Rose's heart began to hammer when Annie started to speak in a high, reedy voice that betrayed her nervousness. Mundella stopped, one hand on the iron rail, and craned his neck, a confused look on his face. The crowd had begun to disperse, but now paused to stare at the two women – Annie and Oonagh – who remained in position at the top of the steps. There was a whistle from outside the Q and a rough voice invited *the lovely ladies* to join him for a jug of ale. Oonagh looked at Rose. It was impossible to read the expression in her eyes. Rose could see Annie had hold of the girl's hand again. Jem, standing behind them, had a puzzled look on his face.

A terrible sense of foreboding drove Rose to move forward as quickly as she could, shouldering her way through in an attempt to reach the steps. It was like the worst kind of dream, where she moved as if she was up to her waist in black mud, yearning for something always just out of reach, or, worse, trying to escape from whatever grisly fiend chased her, and making no progress, and knowing she could not halt the train of events. Somehow, she already knew it was too late.

And she couldn't catch Oonagh's eye.

'We have the evidence,' Annie said loudly, her voice carrying clearly across the square. Another drop of rain fell on Rose's face and the fringed edge of her shawl fluttered. There was pressure inside her skull. A storm was coming. She was almost at the foot of the steps.

'It has been proved,' Annie continued, 'that shorter hours lead to more productivity, and that advances in safety mean fewer deaths and cripplings. BUT.' The sudden, shouted word made Rose's flesh crawl. She knew Annie's intention. She tried to push the unwanted thought away, praying she was wrong, that her instincts had failed her. Let the dark cloud above break apart and drench the square. Let everybody run for cover.

Annie raised Oonagh's hand into the air.

'This girl has had the beauty of youth snatched from her. Mr Mundella!'

The member of parliament had continued his descent to street level and reached the pavement. He stopped and lifted his shoulders, a curiously defensive pose. He was close enough for Rose to touch. He turned and looked back at Annie. 'Mrs Whittaker? Let's not turn this into a circus.'

Annie wasn't paying attention. She whispered in Oonagh's ear and Rose saw fright on the girl's face, but she was nodding at Annie, nodding and nodding.

A cry of alarm pierced the air when Annie put her hand to the scarf that concealed Oonagh's face, twisting the wool on the side where her jaw remained intact, though already ulcerated. Oonagh had told Rose two days ago that eventually her entire lower jaw would have to be removed. She had sobbed in Rose's arms. How would she eat? How could she talk? She would starve. She might as well be dead. Now, Annie continued to pull on the scarf, drawing the material away from the other side of Oonagh's face. Rose realised that the cry of alarm had come from her own lips, and by some magic it had sucked all the sound out of the square, which seemed to Rose to tremble in anticipation.

She raised her hands to her face as if it was she who had a disfigurement to hide and watched helplessly as Oonagh turned to show her ravaged profile to the crowd. There was an intake of breath from those close enough to clearly see the damage, and murmurs from further away. Rose moaned. There was an angry red weal under Oonagh's eye. She had told Rose about it, and explained it was the early stage of a new ulcer and that there was no way to stop the march to putrefaction. Below the weal, a raw hole about the size of a half-crown exposed Oonagh's swollen and inflamed upper gum. And below that, her face simply caved inward, a line of angry stitching in the crease where the outline of her jaw should be.

The sadness in her gaze when she met Rose's eyes was unbearable, and overwhelming. Rose threw herself forward, determined to get to the girl, to gently wrap Oonagh's scarf around her face and give her back what dignity remained, and she got her foot on the first step but was prevented from climbing further and at first couldn't understand why. Her arm was in a vice-like grip. She looked over her shoulder. The same young constable who had overseen the march now had hold of her.

'What have you done?' she screamed at Annie.

Annie's face crumpled. 'She wanted to, she said she should do it, to show them.'

'You mean *you* wanted to. Gerroff me!'

She summoned all her strength and yanked her arm free but the constable wasn't giving up that easily. He got in front of her to block her way.

Rose changed tack. 'Please let me through, just let me get to 'er. Please.'

'Turn around and trot away,' he said. He poked her in the chest and his mouth curved into a smirk. 'Go on, your sort like a march. Think you're soldiers, don't you? Why don't you stamp your little feet up and down and march off home?'

Rose stared at him in disbelief. This young lad with bum-fluff on his chin was laughing. Laughing at her. At all of them. From the corner of her eye, she saw Mundella was being hurriedly led away by some of the gentlemen who had been in the crowd. The cobbles were wet now and the patrons of the Q had retreated inside. People were streaming out of the square. Annie was doing her best to support Oonagh but the girl was crumpling to the ground.

Rose screamed, 'Oonagh!' Jem darted forward and caught the girl in his arms, sinking down to cradle her head. He took off his jacket and placed it over her. Now all Rose could see of Oonagh was a lock of dark hair that had come loose and lay across Jem's hand like a question mark.

Annie was behind the constable, pushing on his back. He folded his arms, ignoring her completely. A fury Rose had never known she possessed took hold of her. She knew what to do. Archie had taught her, after a woman they knew had been set upon by a drunken youth. He wanted Rose to be able to defend herself. *Hit them where it hurts.* She moved in close, grabbed the constable's arms, barely registering the surprise on his face, and raised her knee hard and fast. He doubled over like a bedsheet being folded – and for a split second Rose saw her daughter, frowning with concentration as they tackled the four corners of a sheet, and wondered how she had ended up brawling with the authorities – then she pushed past him, towards Oonagh.

As she mounted the second step, a searing pain ripped through her skull. A hand had pulled off her scarf and grabbed a fistful of hair to pull her backwards. She landed in a sitting position on the pavement, jarring her back so hard it brought instant tears to her eyes, and hands were on her back, forcing her forward so that her forehead almost touched her knees. Her ears roared so loudly that Annie's shouts were muted, and other voices arrived in a whisper.

'These bleedin' women. I knew it'd end wi' hysterics.'

'Make an example o' this one. She got Charlie good an' proper, did tha see it?'

Rose closed her eyes, sickened with pain and shame, as her arms were pulled behind her and metal bracelets slotted around her wrists.

Chapter 18

The gig was waiting on the pavement near Lady's Bridge. Annie climbed inside and shrank back to shelter from the wind-driven rain. She was glad of the weather; it gave an excuse for the wetness on her cheeks. But her father didn't even spare her a glance. He made encouraging murmurs, intended for his horse, not for Annie, and flicked the reins. The gig jerked forward, setting off at a quickening pace.

By the time they'd travelled through the industrial district on the banks of the Don, where factories and mills chugged black smoke into the gloom, Annie could bear it no longer. In a moment, they would turn away from the river to begin their ascent towards the open fields of Walkley. Her father's silence all but drowned out the pounding rain and clatter of hooves.

'Thank you for collecting me.'

He continued to stare straight ahead, a study in grey, his mouth a bloodless line above his high, stiff collar. 'I hope you understand the extent to which you have embarrassed our family, Annabel.'

'What happened was never intended,' she said carefully. 'In my opinion, and in Jem's too, those police officers acted in an unnecessarily cruel way.'

'I don't want to hear about that reprobate of a cousin of yours. His mother will be turning in her grave.' He shook the reins to encourage the horse up an incline. 'It is a wonder that James has found himself a respectable job at last. The boy has cause to be grateful to your poor, mistreated husband.'

This was monstrously unfair. Annie looked away, focusing on the bedraggled hedgerow and the deserted upward sloping field behind it. She could not stop thinking about the moment when her hands had been grabbed, her fingers crushed in a steely grip. The shock of being so roughly handled for the first time in her life was worse than the pain itself. She had been forced to stumble quickly down the steps of the Freemasons' Hall, terrified of losing her footing and ending up in the dirt, like Rose. She closed her eyes. Poor Rose. Poor Oonagh.

Rain dripped and splashed onto the edge of Annie's seat but she didn't want to move any closer to her father. The waves of disapproval emanating from him were almost visible, a shimmer in the air between them. 'Oonagh was taken to the general infirmary. It's a minor detour. May we visit? I'll stay for a short time only.'

She flinched when he reached out and plucked at the sash she still wore. 'I suppose Oonagh is part of this brigade?'

'Yes. She suffered an injury in the... in the general melee.' It was a small lie. She hadn't the energy to explain further. Crucially, he hadn't rejected her request out of hand. She decided she would, as Jem might say, push her luck. 'And I'm afraid to have to report that another supporter was put in a cell, the only one to be locked up. She was treated roughly.'

'That would be the young woman who brought a constable to his knees. I am aware of it.'

'Rose was provoked,' said Annie. 'I saw it for myself. In fact, it was my fault. Father, the situation Rose is in –

that we're all in' – her breath hitched – 'it's entirely my doing.'

'And I find that entirely too easy to believe.' He glanced at her before returning his attention to the road. 'And *I'm* afraid to have to report that a long spell of hard labour stretches before a woman who commits that level of violence against a man whose job it is to uphold the law. I appreciate you wish to make amends but that woman is a heathen.'

Annie tried to keep her voice under control. 'She's a widow with a young family.'

'Then she ought to have taken that into consideration before involving herself in a brawl.'

Annie braced herself against the movement of the gig as her father steered the horse up a dirt road. 'My son-in-law is expecting his wife home before he attends my club with your cousin. I advise you, Annabel, to strive to be a more dutiful wife. Rob has been patient with you, more patient than many husbands would be.'

She bit her lip. Arguing about her marriage with her father would only lead to more calumny being heaped on her head.

'I shall take your silence as acquiescence. We'll go to the infirmary but you'll have five minutes with your friend. No more.'

She nodded. It would have to do.

As they drove through the gates and onto the road that led to the infirmary, the bare branches and thin twigs of the trees on the path seemed to reach out to her, as if to snare her. Annie's chest tightened. She could not tell her father that she was profoundly afraid of what she might find.

Rob paced the floor of the front parlour.

'You'll wear a hole in the carpet,' said Annie wearily.

Her hands trembled slightly as she unfastened her bonnet and set it down on the seat beside her. She wasn't sure whether her body was reacting to the sight of Oonagh lying half-conscious on a small hospital cot, the disfigurements she had tried so hard to conceal visible to all, or to Rob's anger. Her clothes were damp but she would have to have it out with Rob before she could escape upstairs and change. Rose hadn't that option. Rose was sitting in her filthy dress, torn open at the waist where she had been manhandled, locked in a meagre cell beneath the town hall. Away from her children. The thought of it was unbearable and Annie clenched her stomach against another stab of guilt.

'We can't leave Rose there,' she said, her voice shaking. It seemed that clasping her hands together to still the tremor merely transferred it to another part of her body. 'If she is locked up, then so should I be.'

Rob threw her a contemptuous glance. 'Jem and your father were whirlwinds of activity on your behalf, while you cooled your heels in the constable's office. Your cousin tried to get Rose free too, but all his wheedling – and then his cursing – was to no avail. Arrangements were made for Daniel Housley to stay at the house with her children. Lord knows what people will make of that.'

'Better than the workhouse,' said Annie.

Rob shook his head as if in disbelief. 'And the girl, who by all accounts is very sick, will be remaining in the infirmary until – well, until.'

'Yes,' said Annie. 'I saw her. She's very poorly.'

'This is the result when you put a bunch of misguided, silly women—'

Annie got to her feet. 'I'm not remaining here to listen to such nonsense.'

Rob stopped in front of her. 'How am I to face the gentlemen of your father's club tonight? It won't be the *Tribune* they'll want to talk to me about.' He reached out and shook her by the arm. 'It will be my errant wife!'

Annie remained limp in his grasp until he released her and resumed his pacing. 'Then don't go,' she whispered, and then more loudly: 'Where is Jem now?'

'Jem is at the shop, looking after our customers. Where he should have been all along but decided in his wisdom to chase after you. He's booked a cab and will be collecting me' – Rob glared at the grandfather clock that stood in the corner of the room – 'in precisely twenty minutes.'

'Then you must get dressed for your evening out,' said Annie. She walked to the door and stopped. 'You have never supported me in all the time I've been part of the women's association. You never really believed in our cause, did you? You'd have to be a woman or a working man to understand the struggle.'

Rob put his hands on his hips, an almost comical disbelief written on his face. 'I work from dawn to dusk and into the night to keep you in the luxury to which you've always been accustomed. Don't talk to me about the struggles of the poor or claim that being a woman has led to mistreatment. You're nothing but a spoilt brat.'

He clenched his fists in his hair, leaving it standing on end. Annie could guess what was coming next and a hopelessness settled on her chest. She took a step into the hallway.

'Wait!'

She stopped.

Rob spat out the words. 'You are forbidden from attending meetings of that group; you are certainly forbidden from taking part in marches and demonstrations. And you are to end your association with this Rose Butterfield woman, who is clearly exerting a bad influence on you. Look at me!'

She did. He ticked the points off on his fingers. 'You will focus on your housekeeping duties, which are sorely lacking of late, and on providing a welcoming home for your hard-working husband and you will grant me the marital rights to which I am entitled or we shall never have a child.' His face was bright red. 'You could be behind bars tonight. Am I to lock you up myself?'

Annie closed her eyes briefly. 'Rob...'

'Think of your father, of his standing in the community. You're the wife of a newspaper proprietor.'

'Yes.'

'Though I have to say that a rebellious wife is worse than no wife at all.'

'Rob, you have lost your temper, and I do understand why, but—'

'But me no buts!' He strode into the hall and for one awful moment Annie thought he would raise his hand against her. She had never seen him in such a fury.

She stumbled back until her hand found the stair bannister. 'My clothes are soaked through,' she said, 'and so I am going to change and perhaps we can speak again, in more rational terms, on your return later tonight. Invite Jem to stay the night.'

She left him standing at the foot of the stairs and hurried up, not to the bedroom they shared but to the smaller one that Jem used. She sat on the bed and listened to his heavy tread on the stairs. She got up to wedge a chair under the doorknob, and allowed herself to sob, finally. She listened to the sounds of the house, the creaks and rattles, and to Rob opening and closing doors. She heard the carriage arrive and Rob clatter downstairs and out of the door. He didn't say goodbye.

Annie sat in the dark for a few moments longer, then left the room. In the kitchen, she put together a light supper of cheese and apples and pickles, although she had no appetite at all. She lit the lamp that sat on a small table by the door of the front parlour, dragged a chair over to it and set out inkwell, pen and paper on a blotter.

There were letters to write, and her supper went uneaten.

It was close to midnight when she heard the clatter of hooves outside the house and that particular timbre of men's voices when they believe they are whispering only, but have had their senses dented by alcohol. Annie had been dozing in an armchair by the dying fire, under a blanket. She straightened, and waited, hoping Rob's anger had been blunted by the satisfying sight of the *Tribune* spread across the news desks in her father's club. She imagined these desks as sturdy, mahogany versions of the counter in the shop, where customers came to pore over the latest edition and were occasionally gently encouraged to get their purse out if it looked as though they intended to stand there and read the whole thing. 'Astonishing value for money at one penny,' Jem or the salesman, if he happened to be around, might comment, 'or free to read in various hostelries across the town. Sadly, we can't provide you with a jar of ale. That'll be one penny, please.'

Jem would have coaxed Rob out of his foul mood, she was sure of it. Her husband's tempers were like midsummer showers, intense but soon blown over and forgotten about. She would put the added element – her fear that he had been about to strike her – out of her mind, for now.

The two men entered the room on a breath of cold, brandy-scented air. Annie was gratified to see that Rob had the grace to look somewhat shamefaced.

'You're still up,' he said.

'I think she knows it,' said Jem. He leaned down to kiss the top of Annie's head. 'Troublemaker.'

Rob couldn't meet her eye. He sank into a chair.

'I'm going to write a comment piece about what happened in the square today,' said Jem. 'Rob has agreed to publish it.'

'How magnanimous of you,' said Annie.

He grunted. 'It's more than you deserve.'

'Stop it, you two,' said Jem. 'We're all feeling the effects of—'

'Too much brandy?' said Annie.

Rob unbuttoned his waistcoat. 'I spoke to your father. He's agreed to help secure Rose's release and, bearing in mind the circumstances at the time, he will endeavour to erase her name from the charge sheet.'

'I'm glad to hear it,' said Annie. 'I should like to go and visit her once she's returned home. Will they release her tonight? I need to apologise to her.'

'She ought to be grateful, not expecting apologies!' said Rob. 'And I haven't forgotten what I told you earlier. I don't want you associating with that woman.'

Annie saw Jem had clenched his fists, although he answered mildly enough. 'All Rose has tried to do is protect Oonagh. None of this is her doing.'

'I'm not a child to be told whom I should and should not see,' said Annie.

'You may do whatever you like,' said Rob. His shoulders slumped. 'I'm going to find my bed.'

'Tomorrow is Sunday. I'll visit after church.'

'I'll go,' said Jem quickly. He coughed. 'It's only that I have a feeling Rose might not be amenable to a visit from you, Annie, at least not yet.'

Bobby wriggled in Rose's lap, throwing himself forward against the bar of her arm. Annie had noticed her eyes following her other boy around the room as Jack kicked a ball of yarn about. It rolled under the settee and he flopped onto his belly to retrieve it. Jane's head was bent over her mending so she wasn't aware of Rose's gaze when it settled on her, nor her mother's eyes filling with tears.

It was Sunday evening, already dark, when Jem and Annie knocked on Rose's front door. Annie had insisted on coming along; her stomach churned when Rose let them inside without a word. They followed her into the front room where she sat, pulled Bobby onto her lap and looked up at them wordlessly. They'd hesitated – even insouciant Jem seemed uncomfortable – then sat in the chairs by the fire and Annie babbled about the encroaching winter and how she knew Rose's hands suffered in the cold, and here was a pair of fur-lined gloves to keep her fingers warm. She leaned forward and laid the gloves down next to Rose.

'I'm so sorry, Rose.' She didn't know what else to say and returned to her seat.

Bobby picked up the gloves and put them on, laughing and batting his mother in the face. She released him and he chased after Jack. 'Look, am a bear. Rowl!'

'Has tha seen Oonagh?' said Rose, at last turning her gaze on Annie, though her eyes were cold.

Jane's head jerked up at the mention of the girl's name.

'Yes,' Annie said hesitantly. She smiled at Jane.

Jem took the hint, jumping to his feet. 'Young lady, let's grab hold of these little rascals and go and have a game in the kitchen. Do you have a chess board?'

'No,' said Jane shyly, 'but we 'ave cards for playin' patience.'

'Perfect! Lads, come and learn some games where you can win all the pennies in my pocket.'

Annie waited until she heard the snick of the kitchen door closing. 'I went to see her after my father collected me' – she felt heat rise in her cheeks – 'but she was so poorly. I stayed only a few moments. I don't think she knew I was there at all. Rose, I'm sorry. I shouldn't have done it, and I wouldn't have, if she hadn't agreed. And I should have told you what I was intending.'

'But you knew that I'd never let 'er go on the march, or get anywhere near you on them steps,' said Rose. She shook her head. 'Daniel looked after the children, or they'd 'ave been put in a home, or taken to the workhouse an' separated, wi' no idea what were goin' on. He sat up all night, sat right here.' Her voice cracked. 'I were worried I'd never see 'em again.'

Annie felt Rose stiffen when she moved to sit next to her on the settee. What a mess she had created. She put her hand over Rose's and could have sobbed with relief when Rose didn't snatch it away.

'When did they… when did you get home?'

'Early this mornin'. It were still dark. I got a lecture.' Rose's mouth twisted. 'I were made to feel like the worst sort o' criminal, like the kind that get deported. An' then I 'ad to walk home in a torn dress. I've never been so ashamed in me whole life.'

'Oh, Rose. But it's all over now. My father will make sure that you won't be charged.'

'So I've been told. Yes, I've been told how lucky I am.' She laughed, a bitter sound. 'I weren't the only one on them steps. I seem to recall you havin' a good go at that constable. But I'm not the daughter o' the borough magistrate, am I?'

'I'm sorry. I made a mistake.' Annie was on the verge of tears but she would not give in to them. She did not want Rose to think they were manufactured to garner sympathy. She took a deep breath. 'I am sorry.'

'Bein' sorry won't change owt.'

'I know.'

Rose sighed. 'I'm goin' to see Oonagh tomorra and then I'm goin' to Bright's to see if I still have a job. No doubt the word'll be out.'

'I'll come with you,' said Annie, 'when you go to see Oonagh.'

'I'll get mesen there, if it's all the same to you. I'm runnin' the risk of bein' arrested in your company.'

Annie tried a tentative smile. 'Then I'll go later. Shall I take her something sweet to eat?'

Rose seemed to consider this. 'Summat soft, that won't hurt her mouth, that she won't 'ave to chew on.'

'I shall make it my mission.'

Annie was relieved to see a smile flicker at the corner of Rose's mouth.

'Heaven save us from your missions.'

Chapter 19

The office of the owner of Bright's wire mills contained a walnut desk, twice the size of the desk in Daniel's office, and armchairs arranged in front of a cosy fireplace. There was a mahogany escritoire in one corner, on which sat a neat stack of paper, an inkpot and pens. A framed sketch of Edgar Bright and his son hung on the wall above – a long-ago gift from a satisfied customer with an artistic bent. The office was only slightly larger than Daniel's but gave off an air of spaciousness. This was because all the company documents, the ledgers, the timesheets, wages envelopes, and every bit of related clutter, resided in Daniel's office.

There was only one chair at the desk – the one behind it – and that was the chair in which Mr Bright now sat. Visitors, even those of equal standing, might cast about for somewhere to sit – and throw a longing glance towards the armchairs around the fireplace, which were reserved for gentlemen from the upper echelon – but ended up like all the rest, standing before Mr Bright like penitents, while he settled back, folded his arms, tilted his head and looked down his nose at them. Daniel ran his hand over his hair, pulled at his waistcoat and told himself to stop fidgeting.

'You wanted to see me, Mr Bright?'

The man nodded but didn't speak. Instead, he screwed up into a tight ball the piece of paper in his hand and threw it towards the wicker basket beside his desk. He missed his target. Daniel fought the impulse to retrieve it and deposit it in the bin. He could hear the paper crackle as it partially unfolded itself. Edgar Bright shook his head sadly.

'I have spent all morning wasting paper, Mr Housley. Making lists, scoring through them, making new lists. The issue I have is that I can't make a gallon of work fit into a pint pot of a workforce.' He pulled a fresh piece of paper towards him. 'We shall need to place advertisements for additional warehouse staff, buffers and rollers, and increase production by some margin. We might just about have managed if I hadn't to let some of my best workers go. It's extremely vexatious.'

Daniel folded his arms and hunched his shoulders. He breathed out slowly. 'I see,' he said. 'Who are we letting go, and what is the reason?'

'Don't be disingenuous. You know very well or you wouldn't have that look on your face. That young woman, for one. You know who I'm talking about.' Bright waved his hand in the air. 'The polisher and packer. I heard about the mischief she got into. And she knows she's in trouble. That's why she hasn't shown up today.'

'I have the absence recorded,' said Daniel. He would have to tread carefully. 'Unfortunately, Mrs Butterfield has been indisposed.' He could not contemplate telling Rose she would be losing her job. Not again, so soon after she'd regained it. And not now, after all that had occurred.

'I know exactly where she's *been*,' said Bright. 'She was given the care of an extremely unwell young girl whose disfigurements are now the talk of the town. I was contacted by the reporter from the *Tribune*.'

'Jem?'

The man's eyes narrowed. 'You know him?'

'No. I mean, yes, in passing. He's an acquaintance.'

'Hmm. Well, he was asking all sorts of questions about this Irish girl so it's plain he has been told of my connection to her. My very tenuous connection, I might add. And who by, I wonder?'

Daniel tried again. 'Mrs Butterfield is a hard worker, a reliable girl who knows this place inside out and is popular with the others.'

'Yes, I know all that. This is why I have such a headache. But if I am to fire old Ethel and the rest of the malcontents who joined in that march then I can't very well allow the only employee who was arrested to keep her job. She attacked a police officer – it's all over the factory – and was let free the very next day. She must have friends in high places indeed.'

'Ethel has also only just returned to us,' said Daniel.

'She attended the march.'

'She told me she was an observer, that it started so close to her house she could hardly avoid it.' Daniel shook his head, impatient with himself. 'Is marching for better conditions a sackable offence? This will reflect badly on you, Mr Bright, and is illegal in the eyes of the unions.'

He was surprised by his own forcefulness but Bright seemed unaffected. He rested his elbows on the desk and steepled his fingers. 'The young woman has been absent without reason. The other one is too old to carry out her job effectively. I'm sure I can think of valid reasons for sacking the rest who marched.'

He gave Daniel his instructions and dismissed him. In the corridor, Daniel leaned against the wall and ran a hand over his face. He was to be the bringer of bad news again, so soon after helping Rose. He pushed himself away from the wall, retrieved his hat, coat and umbrella from his office and trotted down the stairs and into the yard. He would carry out these last tasks – he could not bear the thought of anybody else breaking the news to Rose – and then he would compose his letter of resignation and seek employment elsewhere.

He passed the engine house, barely aware of the earth-shaking rhythmical pound from within, and was reminded of the thrill of seeing the mighty cascade of molten metal at Silas Hinchcliffe's steel works, and the offer Silas had made. Would Louisa accuse him of encroaching on aspects of her life? She and Harriet were dear friends. The thought of encountering her – and not just a glimpse in the street but an actual meeting – thrilled and terrified him in equal measure.

'Mr Housley!' A woman's voice from behind him, where the warehouse lay. Not Ethel, thank goodness, but a younger woman, hurrying towards him, wiping her hands on her apron.

'Mrs Shaw, is everything all right?'

'Aye.' She gulped for breath. 'I saw thee leavin' an' I wondered if I could get thee to pass on a message to Rose?'

Daniel decided not to ask how Susie Shaw knew how friendly he had become with Rose. Factory workers talked and he was a natural source of gossip as a young company secretary, unmarried. The women in the ware-house speculated on a potentially melancholy past, a domineering mother, his eligibility. Rose had told him some of it. He smiled. He did not mind being associated with Rose by the women she worked with.

'Of course. What is it?'

Her name was shouted from within the building. 'Christ, they don't gi' thee a minute to theesen. Tell Rose that my 'usband has been able to get a conversation goin' wi' the man who reckons he knows who murdered Archie. This man frequents the Blue Pig every night o' the week.'

Daniel frowned. 'I'm not sure this is something Mrs Butterfield ought to pursue.'

Susie Shaw's name was shouted again, more loudly this time. She raised her eyes to the sky. 'Just do us a favour an' tell 'er he said he wants to meet 'er. He wants to tell 'er what happened.'

She turned to run back inside, calling over her shoulder: 'She'll want to know! Just tell 'er to mind 'ow she goes. He'll be proppin' up the bar. His name's Seth – Seth Crookes.'

—

Daniel arrived at the top of the street Rose lived on to witness her walking away ahead of him, quickly disappearing around the corner at the bottom. He paused. He believed it was Rose – he thought he would recognise her gait anywhere – but he couldn't be certain. A fringed shawl concealed her hair and covered her back to her waist, showing a sliver of her jacket, her boots appearing and disappearing beneath the hem of a burnt-orange skirt as she strode along, and was gone. She was carrying a sack, hefting it too easily for it to be full of vegetables or the like. Why was he hesitating?

Daniel set off in pursuit. He was too bashful of the people in the street to call out her name, and hoped she would not have taken another turn by the time he reached the corner, and be lost from view. These few cluttered streets made up a confusing rabbit-warren of shops and cottages and small workshops. It would be too easy to lose her.

But there she was, a hundred yards ahead of him, walking at a brisk pace towards Shales Moor. This would take her to Infirmary Road if she kept on a westerly path, and he could now guess her destination. He broke into a gentle trot, and coughed when he reached her, not wishing to give her a fright.

'Can I take that?'

Rose whipped round, clobbering him with the bag. Luckily, it was not filled with potatoes but was surprisingly soft and light. 'Daniel Housley! That was you pantin' away behind me.'

'I do apologise. I was trying *not* to scare you.'

'I'd hate to see it when you are trying. Sounding like a broken set o' bellows, then offerin' to steal me bag.' Her cheeks were flushed. 'I'm bringin' Oonagh's bits and bobs to her. She's not coming out o' the infirmary any time soon. What are you doin', chasin' after me?'

'I'd come to call on you and saw you, fortuitously. Can I accompany you?'

'Aye, a'course. Has he sacked me again? Old Bright? I'm in an' out o' that place more times than a cuckoo in an' out o' a clock.' She didn't seem perturbed by the prospect. 'Look.' She pointed at a set of evenly spaced columns of coal smoke rising in the sky, torn ragged as they approached the darker grey cloud above. It was the roof of the infirmary, in the distance. 'We're nearly there.'

Daniel fell into step beside her. He was struggling to find the words he wanted to say, but Rose seemed happy to walk in silence for a spell, and that calmed him enough so he could speak without stumbling over his words.

'I have to tell you that I loathe being that man's messenger boy.' The words were out. He had finally admitted how unhappy he was at Bright's and speaking the words aloud strengthened his resolve to leave.

Rose raised her eyebrows. 'Takin' a stand, Daniel?'

'You might say that. I simply didn't want anybody else to tell you, and there is something else that you ought to know, that I am reticent about telling you, although goodness knows it's none of my business.'

'So I am out o' work.' Rose shook her head. 'It's all right, love, I were expectin' it. I'll find another job soon enough. I expect he wants you to check up on Oonagh, an' all. He'll be worried this'll come down on his shoulders, an' so he should be.'

'I consider myself to be your friend, Rose.' He turned up his collar against a gust of cold wind. 'So I hope I can offer some advice without being thought rude.'

She gave him a sidelong glance. 'I'm reight glad we've become friends but I think I know what you're gettin' at, an' I prob'ly won't be takin' this advice. Spit it out, then.'

'Those posters distributed around the town, which Jem agreed to deliver for you.' He paused, wondering whether it was his imagination that Rose had coloured at the mention of Jem's name.

'Aye? What about them?'

'Susie Shaw asked me to forward some information to you. I really don't want to do that.' He looked at her warily. 'I don't think—'

'I know,' she interrupted. 'You don't want me chasin' about. I understand it.' She stopped and stood in his path. 'But I'm afraid you 'ave to tell me what Susie said.'

'Yes.' He hesitated. 'It might come to naught.'

'Well then, you might as well tell me, eh?'

'Let's get over the road.'

Daniel took her elbow and steered her across a busy junction where six roads converged. They waited for a wagon to pass before crossing another street onto Infirmary Road, where there was less traffic and fewer workshops and he would not have to raise his voice to be heard.

'Mrs Shaw has come up with the name of somebody who says he can tell you who was involved in… in your husband's demise. He wants to meet you.'

He heard her sharp intake of breath.

'Did Susie give you the name?'

'The name I've been given is Seth Crookes. He's a regular patron of—'

'The Blue Pig.'

'Yes.'

Rose nodded slowly as they walked on, but didn't speak.

'I hope you're not thinking of going into that establishment alone.'

She snorted. 'I've never set foot in one o' them places in me life. No, I won't go alone. I need to think on it for a while.' She gave him another sidelong look. 'I'm hopin' you might help me.'

'I'll do my best.'

They had reached the estate of the general infirmary, built on the wide expanse of Upperthorpe Meadows. The three-storey building sat on a gentle rise at the end of a tree-lined path between extensive lawns. It was twice as long as it was tall, the two ends bookmarked by rounded bays. Off one of these bays, navvies were balancing on the scaffold of a new extension. Daniel had heard their clatter and calls from some distance off. The sashes of several of the Georgian windows were fully open. The wards would be behind these, the modern idea being that the circulation of air would prevent disease from spreading. It was a fine new building. He wondered whether Oonagh was behind one of the windows that faced the path, sitting on her bed, gazing out at Daniel and Rose as they approached the pillared entrance.

Rose muttered a few words as they entered the building.

'I'm sorry, what did you say?' said Daniel.

'Oh, it's nowt.' She looked embarrassed.

Daniel laughed. 'You can tell me.'

'All right, then.' She shrugged. 'I just saw it, written above the door. *I was sick and ye visited me.* Thought it was worth sayin' aloud, for luck.'

Chapter 20

Rose saw the fleeting expression of surprise cross Daniel's face when she enquired about the whereabouts of Oonagh Ryan.

'I didn't know her surname,' he whispered, as they followed a nurse through a door and up a staircase. 'Oonagh Ryan. Miss Oonagh Ryan.'

Rose understood him. 'Yes,' she said, 'somebody's daughter, p'raps also a sister or a niece or an aunt.'

'She must be longing to return home. England has treated her shabbily.'

'Tha can say that again.'

She hadn't wanted to leave her children today but when she had last seen Oonagh, the girl had been collapsed in Jem's arms, deathly pale, and Rose needed to see her with colour in her cheeks, and to make reparation. She had failed to save Oonagh from public humiliation. She only hoped Annie thought it had been a scene worth engineering. Perhaps Rose was being too harsh; Annie couldn't have foreseen it would end with Oonagh in hospital and Rose locked overnight in a cell. She clenched her fists to still the shudder that ran through her body. She had been left in that cell in her torn dress for so long she thought she'd been forgotten about entirely and would die of starvation. Yet she had wanted to delay an encounter with her jailors, convinced she'd be spirited away to York or Leeds, tried and convicted and put away, and her children left, defenceless, and ultimately consumed by hatred for her, the mother who had abandoned them.

As it was, she could tell Jane hadn't believed Daniel's explanation of her absence. *Back-to-back shifts at the factory.* Rose could never admit to her daughter where she had spent Saturday night, staring into the darkness until her eyes stung, repeating the same litany over and over. *I'm sorry, Archie. I'm failin' thee.* She must have dozed eventually because she had been startled by the rattle of keys. She was being released. She could barely believe it and even on reaching the pavement outside the town hall was expecting to be ambushed, put back in cuffs and dragged away, the victim of a cruel joke.

'A lucky lass,' the constable who led her from her cell told her, 'that's what you are.'

But she was adrift, jobless, in league with the men who would hide Oonagh away, taking their coin, and spending the anonymous donations she received in a perilous quest to find an answer to the question that burned a hole in her soul. Who had taken Archie from her?

'End bed, on the left,' said the nurse, shaking Rose from her thoughts.

'Thank you,' Daniel called after the nurse, who was retracing her steps.

Rose walked the length of the room, keeping her gaze averted from the occupants on the beds she passed. The sound of her boot-heels striking the polished wood flooring served as a counterpoint to the steady groans coming from one of the beds. A gravelly throat was cleared but the entreaty to 'Shurrup, woman!' went unheeded. At the end of the room, coals burned in the fireplace. Daniel's footsteps followed behind, curiously reassuring.

Rose heard him make a *tsk* noise and then there came the clunk of wood sliding on wood. He was closing the window.

'Matron'll be after you,' Rose told him. The smile she directed at the woman in the bed opposite Oonagh's froze on her face. It was impossible to tell the age of the woman, who lay propped up on her pillow, because of the purple bruises that bloomed on her face and neck, the cuts scored into her cheeks, chin and forehead. Some of her hair was missing, burned off or pulled from the roots. She observed Rose through half-lidded eyes. Rose nodded to her and was glad to turn away.

Oonagh's bed was empty.

'She's not 'ere,' Rose said, then lowered her voice. 'Have we been sent to the wrong place, d'you think?'

Daniel scratched his head. 'I'll go and find somebody to ask.'

Rose perched on the end of the bed, the mattress sinking slightly beneath her weight. The bed was neatly made up, the small bureau next to it empty. But that signified nothing. All of Oonagh's possessions were in the bag Daniel had just carried away with him. Rose ought to have taken it from him so that she could set up the girl's framed landscape on top of the bureau – a reminder of home or a dream of somewhere she wished to live, Rose didn't know and wished that she had asked – and put her change of clothes, her woollen stockings and her clogs inside one of the drawers. The bag also contained the library book Rose had borrowed for Oonagh to read. *The Mill on the Floss* was now due to be returned and she thought she could do that while in Upperthorpe, if the library was open.

She examined her hands, which lay in her lap. How complicated her life had become since Annie Whittaker had walked into it. But she could not blame Annie for everything. She'd had no part in Rose's decision to take in a sick girl, to choose to believe she was helping her to convalesce and not to question the unusual circumstances. She'd needed an income.

When a loud curse was uttered, Rose's head jerked up. It had come from outside, from one of the men working on the scaffold. She released the breath she was holding when a shout of laughter followed and the sound of men ribbing one another. A nurse bustled in, drew the curtains around the bed of the woman who had maintained her rhythmical moaning despite the entreaty to be quiet, and informed the patient loudly that the doctor would be in to see her shortly. She didn't pay any attention to Rose, who felt like a fraud, sitting on somebody else's bed, but the nurse saw that the window had been partially closed. She re-opened it to its fullest extent before leaving the ward.

Perhaps Oonagh had been taken to the operating room to have more of the dead bone scraped from her jaw. Or perhaps she had been discharged and here Rose was, mussing up a bed that might be waiting for its next patient. She could not bear to sit alone with her thoughts any longer and got up to poke the coals in the fire, setting orange flames dancing, and releasing tiny motes that flew up the chimney. There were sprigs of dried lavender on either side of the hearth. The scent masked, to an extent, the smell of stale sweat and urine and the metallic tang of old blood. Rose sniffed the bouquets; they reminded her of summer, of the summer she had lost Archie, and all the summers since that seemed so remote now that winter's claw had closed over the land.

The woman with the battered face murmured something Rose didn't catch but she understood her meaning when she lifted a hand and pointed at the window. Rose closed the sash and returned to sit on the end of Oonagh's bed. She wondered what was taking Daniel so long. He had probably got himself lost.

'She's gone.'

These words came from the patient in the bed alongside Oonagh's. It was the woman with the gravelly voice who had told the groaning patient to *shurrup*.

'My friend? Oonagh Ryan? D'you know where?'

The woman wheezed. She hoicked up phlegm and lifted a spittoon to her mouth. Rose looked away, sickened.

'Well, it's one place or t'other. Tha'd think somebody that knew 'er would be able to take a better guess than me.'

Rose frowned. 'What…'

Daniel strode into the room, another man walking at a more measured pace behind him. Rose felt numbness spread through her body, starting in her gut and radiating out, when she saw the stricken expression on Daniel's face and the politely sympathetic look on the face of the other man. She wanted to get up from the bed but couldn't move. Daniel sat beside her and took her hands in his. A nurse came forward and pulled the curtain so that they were shielded from the woman who had spoken, who had told Rose that Oonagh was dead and had been misunderstood. Rose looked into the hooded eyes of the woman in the opposite bed and then back at Daniel. The other man was introducing himself as the medical director of the hospital. She could barely hear his words through the high-pitched whining in her ears.

'The young lady passed away this morning. She had given us your name and address, Mrs Butterfield, but I believe from Mr Housley here that she was under the care of an Edgar Bright so we won't be troubling you with the paperwork.'

'How...'

Rose got no further.

'Mrs Butterfield, there was nothing more we could do. Oonagh had severe wounds' – he paused – 'very severe, and she developed poisoning of the blood and organ failure.'

Daniel squeezed her hands. 'She's been taken to the cemetery out at Sharrow Vale, where she'll be buried in the common grave.' He raised his voice. 'Sir, do you have a handkerchief?' He put his arm around Rose's shoulders. 'Her long suffering is over, Rose, it's over at last.'

A week passed before Rose began examining the *Wanted* columns in the local newspapers. She was looking for factory work within an hour's walk of home and there was no shortage of positions that would suit her, but she decided to wait another few days. She could get by for a little while and her compulsion to spend more time with the children had only heightened since Oonagh's death. She took them out, treating them to their first omnibus ride into the countryside near Hillsborough village, where they alighted to buy hot pikelets from a roadside baker then continued the round trip back to town. Daniel came for tea, bringing with him a meat and potato pie provided by the landlady of the Golden Ball. Rose had baked an orange cake. They talked about Oonagh.

Jem turned up one wet afternoon with paper, scissors and string and taught the children how to make a thaumatrope. Rose watched him cut the paper into a circle, draw a cage on one side and a bird on the other, thread the string through and spin it so that the bird appeared to be inside the cage. Rose had never seen Jane or the twins so engrossed. He left them in the kitchen arguing over who would get the scissors first to make another, and drank tea with Rose that he had purchased from the new teahouse in Market Place. He talked about inconsequential things and made Rose laugh.

She wondered what the neighbours would think about these men turning up on her doorstep, and found she didn't care. She was waiting for a visit from Annie, but when she next opened the door, dusting flour from her hands, it was Albert Boothby who stood before her.

Rose recoiled, stepping back into the house. This gave the man the opportunity of stepping forward over the threshold. He held his hat in his hands and had turned down his mouth into an insincere-looking grimace of apology.

'Mrs Butterfield, I'm so sorry to turn up unannounced. I hope you are not entertaining.'

Rose wanted to snort in derision. Instead, she gestured for him to follow her into the front room. 'What can I do for thee?'

He unbuttoned his coat and sat on her settee. Rose remained standing.

'I can see you're busy. I can smell baking bread. How pleasant that is.'

Rose nodded and folded her arms so he wouldn't see the tremor in her hands. This had to do with Oonagh, and she had no idea what would come next from the mouth of this man.

'I haven't much time either,' he said. 'I have left my gig unattended.' He sprang to his feet and went to the window. 'And as I suspected there are already several urchins climbing all over it.'

He rapped his knuckles on the pane, then turned to Rose, opening his coat and patting at the breast-pocket of his waistcoat. He fished out a wallet and shook coins from it that he held out on the palm of his manicured hand.

'What's this?' said Rose. 'Tha'll know she's gone. Edgar Bright will have told thee.' *Buried in a common grave with no stone or monument.* 'Or have you another girl needing to convalesce far away from her workmates?'

His smile was as thin as a sheet of paper.

'Both myself and Mr Bright wanted to make you a gift of a final payment for your trouble. Ten sovereigns. Here.' He gestured for her to take the money. 'I'm sure a widow with a brood of children who are not yet earning their keep could use some additional funds.'

Rose shook her head. 'A girl has died.' Her eyes filled with tears. She blinked them back. She had not cried in front of anybody. She would not break down before this man. 'I'd like to know who's at fault 'ere.'

'There was an inquest, my dear.'

'Barely a mornin' they spent on that. I were told by a friend that attended it. Worse than useless. She's been used up an' forgotten.'

She was angry now, and the sight of Albert Boothby had given her an idea, a means of channelling that anger. 'I don't want tha coin, if it's supposed to shut me up.'

'Not at all! The very idea.' He put the money back in his wallet, shaking his head in disappointment. 'You're being hysterical, Mrs Butterfield. I shall put it down to grief for an unfortunate young girl and we'll say no more about it.' He replaced his hat and straightened his collar. 'I'll take my leave of you and promise I shall not bother you again.'

He left her standing in the middle of the room. Rose went to the window and pulled the net aside to watch him yank a boy off his buggy by the scruff of his neck. The boy landed in the road and rolled away out of reach of Mr Boothby's flailing leg. Rose shook her head. If that had been Jack or Bobby she'd have been out there with a broom and chased the gentleman down the road. The thought brought a grim smile to her face.

On her way to lock the front door behind him, Rose stopped in the act of reaching for the bolt. Her heart began to hammer. It had been weeks, and she had let it slip to the back of her mind, having other things to consider. But there was no denying it.

On the mat lay a small white envelope, her name printed carefully across it.

Chapter 21

Annie passed between the Doric columns of the gatehouse that straddled the Porter, enjoying a brief shelter
from the intermittent drizzle that accompanied a grey and
bitterly cold day. She could hear the swollen river rushing
by under her feet. Thankfully, Mary Pearson arrived only
a few moments later and the two women walked briskly
through, skirting the Anglican chapel to take one of the
winding paths on the steep north-facing hillside of land-
scaped gardens.

She gripped her cloak and shivered when a gust of
wind tore the overcast sky apart. A watery sun emerged,
glancing off the edge of one of the monuments, a granite
needle that rose above the other gravestones to pierce the
sky. Annie pointed to it and Mary followed her gaze.

'Aye, a new 'un. A fair amount's been spent on that.
Your girl's hidden away beyond the catacombs, an' the
sun won't be kissin' her grave,' Mary said. 'This way.'

The common grave lay in a wide and shallow dip
behind a stand of weeping willows, a black gash –
narrower than Annie had been expecting – in the long
grass. Low bushes rustled against the hem of her skirt.

'Don't get too close,' said Mary. 'It goes a long way
down and tha wouldn't want to tumble in.' She gestured
to an open barrel of what looked to Annie like fine white
flour. Two buckets of water sat on the ground beside it.

'Lime,' said Mary, looking around. There was nobody in sight and all Annie could hear was the squawking of crows. 'There's either just been one tipped in or there's one on its way.'

Annie stopped several yards away from the maw in the ground. Oonagh lay down there, encased in a cheap box, as hurriedly disposed of as if she had died of the plague. The ground would not seal her into her eternal rest until the grave had been filled to its capacity, coffins laid flush against each other, no earth between, like stacks of kindling. Jem had told her all about the common grave, and about the families who begged for their loved one to be lifted out of the pit after they had scraped together enough money for a private burial. And how they'd have to be quick with their request because once a few more boxes and body bags went on top, they'd be denied their wish.

She wanted to tell Mary that she now appreciated more fully the importance of ritual, of laying out, of a mourning period and a funeral service, rites that the living needed, but she couldn't speak past the lump in her throat. So she stood there, hugging herself under her long cloak, staring at the paupers' grave and the few inches of soil that were visible beneath the crumbling lip, wondering what Oonagh's family across the sea had been told, and whether the news had even reached them.

When her face and feet were numbed with cold, Mary spoke. 'Come on, love, let's go and see my Samuel.'

The famous Chartist's grave lay in a glade containing half a dozen other modest stones. Mary touched her fingers to her lips and pressed them to the top of the stone.

'I'll sithee soon,' she said.

'Not too soon, I hope,' said Annie, lifting an enquiring eyebrow.

'Don't worry theesen. Fit as a fiddle, I am.'

The two women stood together, reading the inscription Mary had had engraved on the stone.

SACRED TO THE MEMORY OF
SAMUEL HOLBERRY.

WHO AT THE EARLY AGE OF 27
DIED IN YORK CASTLE, AFTER
SUFFERING AN IMPRISONMENT OF
2 YEARS AND 3 MONTHS, JUNE
21ST, 1842.

Mary sighed. 'They signed his death warrant puttin' him on that treadmill. Illegally, an' all. He'd not been sentenced to hard labour.'

FOR ADVOCATING WHAT TO HIM
APPEARED TO BE THE TRUE
INTEREST OF THE PEOPLE OF
ENGLAND.

'D'you know, there were thousands at his funeral, all them that followed his coffin from the station. What a sight that was.' She read the rest aloud.

VANISH'D IS THE FEVERISH DREAM
OF LIFE:–
THE RICH AND POOR FIND NO
DISTINCTION HERE,
THE GREAT AND LOWLY END
THEIR CARE AND STRIFE,

THE WELL-BELOVED MAY HAVE
AFFECTIONS TEAR.
BUT AT THE LAST, THE OPPRESSOR
AND THE SLAVE
SHALL EQUAL STAND BEFORE THE
BAR OF GOD;
OF HIM, WHO LIFE, AND HOPE,
AND FREEDOM GAVE,
TO ALL THAT THRO' THIS VALE OF
TEARS HAVE TROD.
LET NONE THEN MURMUR
'GAINST THE WISE DECREE,
THAT OPEN'D THE DOOR, AND SET
THE CAPTIVE FREE.
ALSO OF SAMUEL JOHN, HIS SON
WHO DIED IN HIS INFANCY.

She stopped before she reached the final line.

THIS TABLET WAS ERECTED BY HIS
BEREFT WIDOW.

'*The rich and poor find no distinction here*,' Annie quoted.
'But they *do*. Look where Oonagh has been abandoned' –
she swept her arm around – 'and look at that monument
on the hill. The cherub on top is taller than me.'

'Their earthly remains, yes,' said Mary firmly. 'But they
are all equal in the sight of God. Anyhow, the Chartists
paid for Sam to 'ave a private grave. Our baby boy went
in the paupers'.'

'I'm sorry.' Annie stepped back, resting her gloved
hand against the trunk of an ash tree. She could feel the
roughness of the bark through the fabric. The tree's bare

branches rattled like bones in the wind. 'I'm afraid I don't have your strong belief.'

'It doesn't matter what you believe. Oonagh's not in that pit,' said Mary, 'any more than my Sam is under this stone.'

The weather worsened as they made their way back to the gatehouse. The two women stood inside the entrance, watching fat drops of rain chase each other from the gutter to the pavement.

'I can feel snow in the air,' said Mary. 'What will tha do?'

'What do you mean?'

Mary gave her a look and Annie smiled grudgingly. 'I'm not going to allow what happened to Oonagh to be buried along with her. I'll be giving Rose my solemn vow on that.'

Annie welcomed Rob home that evening to a supper of lobster with asparagus and potato pudding, spiced apple jelly and a bowl of roasted chestnuts. They ate in the kitchen, which was enveloped in the warmth of the stove, and afterwards Annie washed the pots while Rob coaxed the coal fire into life in the front parlour and lit the lamps.

She brought him a glass of whisky and squeezed into the armchair he was sitting in, kissing him on his whiskery cheek. He stroked her hair and kissed her back, on the mouth.

'Shall I go up and light the fire in our bedroom?' Rob said. A look of uncertainty crossed his face. 'Only, it's a wickedly cold night.'

'Yes,' said Annie, and kissed him again so that he should be certain of her meaning. 'I'd like that.'

She rested her head on his shoulder and Rob stretched his legs and sipped his whisky. 'What have you done today?'

'This and that. Tell me about your day.'

He told her how well the *Tribune* was doing, pulling in the advertisers, how the print shop business was thriving. He couldn't understand why the previous tenant had let his business die, or why the premises remained closed for so long, even allowing for the tragedy that had occurred there. He said Annie could now place an advertisement for a maid of all work, and a woman to take the laundry, and finances might even stretch to a cook.

'My dear, I gather you've been in contact with Mr Mundella and have invited him to supper.'

'Yes.' Annie sat up. 'I thought you'd like that. Dining with our esteemed member of parliament. Tonight's meal was a rehearsal. What did you think?'

'It was delicious.'

'You see? I can perform my wifely duties *and* have a life outside the home.'

'I'm sorry I was so angry with you.'

Annie put her head back on his shoulder.

'And I'm sorry about Oonagh too.' He reached up to pat her on the head. 'Now, we must put all that behind us.'

'Hmm,' said Annie.

A beam of light flickered across the ceiling where the curtain met the coving. The timbre of men's voices and a horse's neigh carried clearly on the cold night air. Annie felt Rob's body tense then relax when the doorknocker sounded, three sharp raps, a pause, then two more. Jem's signature calling card.

'I hope he won't be staying long,' she said as Rob eased himself out of the chair. 'He chooses the most inopportune moments to appear.'

'We put the *Tribune* to bed today.' He bent to kiss her then went to answer the door, his words trailing behind him. 'Jem's doing the overnight shift and perhaps a change is required, in which case I shall have to go in, although goodness knows the print run is underway and I shall not be popular with the compositors.'

She heard Jem and Rob greet each other and then a woman's voice, firm but apologetic. It was Rose.

Annie stood up and adjusted her dress, her heart fluttering in her chest. She deserved all the opprobrium Rose would heap on her and would endure it without a word of protest.

Jem entered first and kissed her on the cheek. 'What's up, Annie?'

She squeaked out the word 'What—' then Rose walked into the room, and came up to her.

They spoke the words simultaneously — 'I'm sorry' — and then Rose frowned and Annie laughed and enfolded her in a spontaneous hug. The cold air clung to Rose but her response was warm and for a few seconds neither moved. When Jem coughed, Annie relinquished the embrace.

'I thought you'd be angry,' she said, wiping her eyes.

'No,' said Rose carefully. 'I'm not. Not wi' you, anyhow.'

Annie looked from Rob, who stood on the threshold of the front parlour, a confused look on his face, to Jem, who was leaning against the wall, a faint smile on his lips, and back to Rose.

'Who, then?'

'Them that caused it.' Rose folded her lips. She looked like she might burst into tears.

Annie guided her to the armchair she and Rob had just vacated. 'My manners. Would you like a cup of tea?'

'The cab'll be collecting us in an hour,' said Jem. 'I found Rose outside the office...' He glanced at Rob. 'She was distressed and I offered to take her home but she asked for you, Annie.' He looked at Rose, who simply nodded. 'So here we are.'

Annie crouched before Rose and took her hands. 'Why, you're as cold as the—' She'd been about to say 'grave'. 'Why aren't you wearing the fur-lined gloves I gave you? Never mind. What can I do for you, Rose? Just ask. I'll do anything.'

'I want it to be known to all,' said Rose. 'D'you under-stand? I want those men that treated Oonagh so badly to get the comeuppance they deserve. I just don't know 'ow to go about it. You do, Annie.'

'I'm sure my wife can have a quiet word in the ear of our representative in parliament,' said Rob. 'We're hosting a supper for Mr Mundella soon, aren't we, Annie?'

Rose's eyes flashed with anger. 'Good for thee, hobnobbin' wi' the great an' good. Oonagh deserves more than a *quiet word*.'

Rob looked taken aback. 'I beg your pardon?'

'I'm in complete agreement!' Annie rose from her chair and hurried over to the escritoire, pulling open a drawer and bringing out a sheaf of paper. She turned to face the room, hesitating for a second to consider how Rob would react. It was too late now. The deed was done, or almost done.

She put the papers in Rose's lap. 'These are letters I have written, to the London newspapers and the newspapers in York, and to the match factory there, and to Mr Mundella – who, by the way, has been horrified to learn of Oonagh's fate, having met her – and to our police investigators.' She gulped in air. 'Would you like to add your signature, Rose?'

She could see, on the edge of her vision, that Rob had turned on his heel. She looked at Jem, an appeal in her eyes, and he followed Rob out of the room. Rose was leafing through the sheets of paper.

'Who else has signed?'

'Every member of the female association, here in town, and we've got the support of our head office in London. We won't be ignored, Rose. This is what I've been doing, since before Oonagh... since before she passed away.'

She stopped, breathless. Rose got up and took the letters back to the writing desk. She laid them flat under the palm of her hand and looked over her shoulder at Annie, who stood in the middle of the room, twisting her hands together.

'D'you have a pen? An' I'd like to join this association o' yours.' Rose lifted her chin and there was a spark in her eye Annie had never before seen. 'If you'll have me.'

Chapter 22

He'd been on his feet all day but had been asked by the Watch Committee to put in an extra night shift and wanted to show willing. Archie wolfed down his tea while dandling little Jane on his knee and watched Rose follow her massive belly around the kitchen. He scraped the last of the fish and boiled potatoes from his plate and Rose took it away and put it in the sink before lowering herself into the rocking chair by the fireplace, rubbing at her belly with the heel of one hand.

'Is it painin' thee?'

'Aye. Feels like there's a foot jammed in me ribs. Sharn't be long now. I'm the size o' a whale.'

Jane giggled, putting a dimpled hand over her mouth. He tickled her tummy and she tugged at his beard. 'Ow! What does tha think, love? Boy or girl?'

'Girl!'

'Well, I 'ave to say I'm hopin' for a lad. I'm feelin' outnumbered. Got a nice boy's name for us?'

Jane pouted. 'Elizabetha.'

'I were thinking more along the lines o' a Jack.'

Rose rocked gently in the chair. 'Or a Bobby.'

He nodded slowly. Bobby had been her father's name. 'Aye, why not? Reight! I'm off. Lock up the house, would tha? It'll be fully light by the time I get 'ome.'

'I will in a bit,' said Rose. 'I've only just sat down.'

Archie smiled at her fondly. The two of them had been together since he'd knocked into her – nearly sent her flying – at the fish market and by way of apology asked her to eat a plate of shrimp with him. It had been Rose's idea to marry so young; they were only seventeen. *Throw caution to the wind*, she'd said. *When you know, you know.* She'd been right; they were a good match.

'Help your mother,' he said to Jane, setting her down on her feet. 'I'll put thee in charge 'til I get back.'

Rose snorted and he blew her a kiss. 'See you tomorra, love.'

His shift would start when darkness blanketed the town, around half past ten, so he could have taken a nap, and perhaps persuaded Rose to lie alongside him, if he hadn't already told the landlord of the Mason's Arms that he'd show his face tonight. Two of the regulars were feuding with each other over a strip of land between their neighbouring farms. The landlord hoped Archie's presence might deter a promised bout of fisticuffs.

The early summer stench of the mighty Don reached him before he glimpsed the sluggish brown flow at the end of the road between the Union Wheel and Wheatman's saw manufactory. It was a dry and warm evening and there were plenty of people abroad, though nobody he recognised. He accepted a free jar of ale at the Mason's and passed a pleasant evening. The anticipated troublemakers failed to make an appearance, and he left at closing time, turning his back on the river to walk along the valley bottom as far as Upperthorpe, then taking the steep road towards Crookes Moor. It was full dark by the time he got onto St Philip's Road, which would lead him back towards the centre of town.

A light breeze carried the fumes of round-the-clock industry from the bowl of the town into the high street. The shops on West Bar presented blank, shuttered faces, their awnings wound tight. He glanced down a ginnel and saw a shape huddled against a pile of junk awaiting the scrap man. Archie approached cautiously and nudged the sleeping man with his foot. 'Get theesen up an' 'ome.' The man's rattling snores – the sounds a man makes when his belly's full of ale – continued to echo down the passageway. Archie bent and shook the man's shoulder, then stood back, well out of his way. A few nights earlier he'd had a knife pulled on him when he'd asked a group of youths what they were doing outside St Paul's Church at four in the morning. He'd stood his ground and in the end they'd scarpered, to his relief. He hadn't told Rose about that encounter, but it had rattled him.

The man's eyes glittered in the shaft of moonlight that brightened the brick wall where he rested.

'Where d'you live?' said Archie.

The man mumbled something into his chest but managed to stagger to his feet. He leaned against the wall, his head hanging.

'Go an' find your bed,' said Archie.

'Am goin', all right?'

The man pushed himself away from the wall and staggered away towards the other end of the alley. There was a rustling sound behind Archie and he whipped his head around, heart pounding. A sleek fat rat emerged from a hole in the bottom of a sack and scuttled along the gutter. This reminded him Rose had asked him to get more arsenic to mix into rat poison; he'd do it tomorrow after he'd had a few hours' kip.

When, according to the hands of the town hall clock tower, he had less than three hours remaining of what had been an unusually quiet shift, Archie unlocked the watch house near the Corn Exchange to put his feet up for half an hour. He drank two cups of strong tea and ate the cheese sandwich Rose had made for him. She should be fast asleep in their bed, curled around the child in her belly, her long dark hair fanned across the pillow.

Half an hour later he was back in the centre of town, closer to home and his warm bed. He'd let himself in quietly, slide under the covers, trying not to wake Rose, and snuggle up against her back, resting his hand on her belly and hopefully being rewarded with movement from within. He crossed the road to Cutlers Hall, whistling one of the tunes the fiddler had been playing in the Mason's Arms – and saw a figure standing at the bottom of the road. It was a woman.

She stood outside the wine merchant's on the junction of Change Alley. The white oval of her face was turned towards him but he was too far away to make out her expression. She held herself rigidly, as alert as a wild animal caught in the light of a lamp. A prostitute. He wondered why she didn't turn and walk away. Perhaps she was waiting for somebody. At that moment, she craned her neck to look up Change Alley. Yes, she was expecting someone.

He decided not to challenge her. Earn a crust any way you could in this world, that was Archie's philosophy. He turned away, started up Fargate, took a left turn onto Norfolk Row and left again onto Norfolk Street. He soon reached the junction at the other end of Change Alley. He'd been intending to continue on down Norfolk Street to Cranford's baker's. There, he'd be ushered into the kitchen where the ovens were already baking the day's bread. He'd be given a fresh loaf or a batch of breadcakes to take home.

The sudden whinny of a horse, carried on the still air from the stables behind the King's Head Hotel, made him pause.

Was that the tinkle of breaking glass?

A shiver ran across his shoulders and set the hairs on the back of his neck on end. Archie had an undeniable feeling he was being watched. He strained his eyes, peering beyond the black shadows thrown across the pavement, trying to make out whether anybody stood in the doorway of one of the buildings on Norfolk Street, or watched him from a window.

A flicker of movement caught his eye. In Change Alley, a man detached himself from the shadows of a building and ran off, away from Archie. The man was hatless, and pushed back a fringe of thick dark hair as he glanced behind him. It was impossible for Archie to tell whether the man had seen him standing at the top of the road. He was quickly lost from view as the road curved out of sight.

Archie set off after him. Perhaps the woman was in cahoots with a thief, acting as lookout. He ought to have approached her after all.

He gasped when he was jerked back, his cloak caught, and wondered whether there had been a third accomplice at the top of Change Alley. It would explain why he'd felt watched. For the first time, fear crept into his heart. He turned, hoping he would not be facing a steel blade – and saw the end of his cloak was caught up on the window of the print shop. Archie peered closer, and could just make out the shard of glass his cloak had snagged on. The pane had been shattered. He tugged the material free – there was a slight tearing sound: a job for Rose and her sewing tin tomorrow – and made to set off again, then stopped. From inside the shop came a sound that reminded him of a trip to the coast he had taken as a child, the hissing sound of tiny pebbles rolled by the tide. A beautiful sound that awoke his senses to the tang of sea air, the feel of shells as sharp as glass under his bare soles.

Archie strained his eyes. He could see nothing moving in the shadowed interior of the shop. The sound reminded him of something else, something that stirred unease in the pit of his belly, something that he couldn't quite put his finger on.

Then the world turned white. Archie was lifted into a blinding cloud of pain but it was his terrible helplessness in the grip of such a massive, unnameable power that forced a scream from his throat. Then he was falling, into an endless well of blackness, and could do nothing but surrender to it.

When he came to he was sitting on the ground inside a thick white fog. Relief flooded his body. He was alive; there was no pain. Only shock and surprise. He had a tale to tell the boys at work now. He'd been caught up in a bomb blast – he was certain of it, that had been the hissing sound, a fuse burning down, stupid not to have recognised it. But he was now the luckiest man alive. Harsh bells rang in his ears. The white fog stank of sulphur. But he was alive, and filled with a strange euphoria.

He coughed and there was movement in front of him, a jiggle and shift from whatever it was that was sitting on him. He stared down, confused. A fat spear of wood was sticking out of his chest. Archie blinked and looked again. It was still there. He could hear Rose's voice over the ringing in his ears, telling him to get up. *I will in a bit,* he whispered, *I've only just sat down.* Or had Rose spoken those words, to him?

He tried to remember what he'd been doing, but couldn't. He looked away from whatever had skewered him but all he could see was the white fog. Something was wrong but he couldn't put his finger on it. *Well, there's a spear pokin' out your chest, you thick clot.* But there was something else, something that felt more important. The smell of sulphur was fading now, as was the ringing in his ears. Rose would have a fit if he came home with a hole in his shirt. If the wood had made a hole in his clothes then it must have made a hole in him too. Her sewing skills might not stretch that far. He wanted to laugh. A sob hitched in his throat, and it came to him, what had been just out of reach. He should be in pain. There was no pain at all.

A woman appeared, materialising into solidity through the fog, and he watched her take his hand, although he could not feel her touch. Her lips moved but he couldn't hear what she was saying. She had a pretty face but looked careworn, as if she was carrying a large burden. He was her burden, he realised. He was dying and she must be his angel. He breathed out, the last whisper of hope leaving his body. The fog was getting darker, shading into the light grey of coalsmoke, then growing darker still, and quickly – wait! too quick! – was as black as night. He could no longer see his angel. He couldn't see anything at all. A tidal wave of deep sorrow rolled over him and was just as quickly gone. Where was he? And why couldn't he see anything?

Were his eyes open or closed? What a strange dream this was. A dream of dying. There was no need to worry. He just had to wait it out, this dream. He knew he'd wake in a moment, reach out for Rose, breathe in the musky scent of her, stroke the smooth skin of her arm, her lovely round belly... He was home, his pregnant wife lying beside him, and that was all that mattered.

Chapter 23

She kneeled at the foot of the bed, Archie's cloak folded across her knees. The lamp beside her hissed gently, casting a flickering golden glow onto the candlewick bedspread. She'd woken, as she often did, an hour before dawn, in that hush when the ordinary world seemed impossibly distant, almost a dream, a terrible realm where Archie had been taken away from her. Here, where the world was held suspended, she might believe he would return. She'd hear his footsteps on the stairs, the door creaking, and he'd lift her into his arms and take her back to bed and lay his warm strong hands on her body. In this place, there were no men scalded to death in engine houses, no girls disfigured by poisonous phosphorus and no boys growing up fatherless.

Under the covers, she and Archie would discover each other all over again.

The rattle of the street-cleaning cart brought her out of her reverie. *Daft apeth*, she told herself. The problem was she had too much time on her hands, too much time to dwell on what might have been, and what could never be, not in a month of Sundays. She was starting at Morton's scissor and table knife manufacturers in Bridge Street on Monday, wrapping kitchen knives. That ought to sharpen her up again.

The sound of coughing came through the thin wall that separated her bedroom from the children's room. She couldn't tell which child it was. All three had come down with a winter cold and Rose knew she was next; she already had the tell-tale symptoms, a tightening hand around her throat, a heaviness in her skull. She looked down at her hands, at the envelope in them. Twenty sovereigns would put a dent in this little fortune she kept under the bed. Rose shook her head, partly to clear it of the fanciful thoughts she'd been entertaining and partly in disbelief at where she found herself, agitating alongside Annie, getting thrown in jail. What would her husband say about it? *Here I am, keepin' the peace, and there tha goes, stirrin' things up.* Except he wasn't keeping the peace, not any more.

He was gone.

The envelope was a heavy weight in her hand. She had transferred coins from the other envelopes to make it up to the amount of the reward she was offering. What would Archie have to say about *that*? She waited, but couldn't hear his voice. She wouldn't take the money with her, not today. Rose laid the envelope back in the box, tucking it into the corner. Archie's cloak went on top; she smoothed it flat, then pushed the box back under the bed. It scraped over the boards, a screech of complaint.

Lamp held high, she crept downstairs, relishing the opportunity to have a couple of hours to herself. In the kitchen, she made up the fire and set to scrubbing the dirt out of the laundry she had taken in, rinsing out the garments in cold water in the maidening-tub that stung then numbed her hands and arms, then squeezing them through the wooden rollers of the mangle and draping them over the clothes horse she had set up a few feet from the fire. Jane would sort and fold them once they'd dried, ready for collection. Rose sat in front of the fire, warming her hands and sipping from a mug of tea. She would make patties for the children for breakfast, fry them on the stove and dish them up nice and warm with apple slices and a sprinkling of sugar. Jem, who never turned up empty-handed, had brought her a packet of sugar yesterday. 'This is for the next time Annie visits,' he'd said. 'I've never seen anybody take so much sugar in their tea. You don't need any, Rose, you're sweet enough.'

Men would say anything. It was better to keep them all at arm's length. But she found she didn't want to dole out to Jem the same curt treatment she'd given the butcher. She would miss Jem, miss his companionship if their friendship ended. He made her laugh, had charmed all three of her children, and it looked like he'd charmed her too because, look, here she was, daydreaming about him. She'd seen the strange look he'd given Daniel when she had assured him that she was in safe hands for her visit to the Blue Pig. Jem had a meeting to attend, or he would have accompanied them. Rose had thought about telling him that there was no need for him to be jealous of Daniel, but that would mean acknowledging that Jem had feelings for her, and she wouldn't be adding fuel to that fire.

Rose refilled the kettle. There was grocery shopping and sweeping up to do, school for the children, goulash to prepare and pastry to make. She would occupy her mind with the daily routine and try not to worry too much about what the evening might hold in store.

The three-storey inn had two impressive bays either side of a wide black panelled door framed by stone columns and topped with a decorative portico. Lamplight shone from within. Through one of the bays, Rose glimpsed people dining and servers attending the tables. It looked cosy and respectable.

She lingered at the foot of the steps. 'Do we knock, or...'

'That's the White Lion Inn,' said Daniel. He walked a few steps to the end of the terrace. 'Here we are.' He sounded apologetic. 'It's full of rough sorts. Are you sure you want to go inside?'

A hanging signboard jutted from above the door of the squat building that straddled the junction. *The Blue Pig*. The windows were either misted up or filthy. It was impossible to tell in the dark.

'Am not backin' out now.'

Rose pushed down on the handle before her nerve deserted her, stepping into a fug of warm air and pipe smoke. She pulled at her headscarf to hide her face from the enquiring glances of the men standing near the door. There was a noisy group in the middle of the room and a handful of men at the end of the bar, near the fireplace. Her eyes grazed over them. Was he here, the man who reckoned he could identify Archie's killer? Her heart stuttered in fear. Or was the killer here? What about this wizened man in mucky shirtsleeves and waistcoat, standing beside her, raising his tankard to his mouth, and winking to her over the rim? She shuddered.

Daniel took her elbow and guided her towards an empty table, then seemed to change his mind and walked her past the counter and into a wood-panelled room with uneven bleached floorboards and a low, yellowed ceiling.

It was sparsely furnished with long tables, benches and barrels hugging the walls, and was dominated by a large, cold hearth. The room smelled strongly of ale and lamp oil.

There was no one else in it. Rose sat on the end of the bench closest to the fireplace, wondering whether somebody would come to light it.

'I'll go and see if I can find him,' said Daniel, 'if you think you will be all right here for a moment. Would you like anything?'

'To drink?'

Daniel nodded.

'I don't like the taste,' said Rose. She clasped her hands on her lap, glad of the fur-lined gloves Annie had given her. 'I've never been in one o' these places before.' She held up her hand to forestall him. 'I'm not leavin'. Go an' find our man.'

She watched Daniel duck out of the room, then focused on the knotted whorls and stains on the planks under her feet, telling herself the man would be absent tonight, or that he knew nothing and, like Ethel had warned, only wanted to con Rose out of twenty sovereigns. Putting too much store in something only led to disappointment. Hope was the cruellest thing. She told herself this but she couldn't stop the hammering of her heart. Now, so long after the police had washed their hands of the crime that killed Archie, she might learn the truth of it, the reason why her three children had been left fatherless. She was pinning all her hopes on a complete stranger and that was a terrifying prospect. But what if, even worse, it was somebody she knew? Her thoughts circled around; the man was a thug trying to con money out of a grieving widow. That's what she should prepare herself for.

'Rose?'

Daniel stood before her, a shorter man by his side wearing a cloth hat. His beard was straggly, shot through with grey, his eyes red-rimmed and his nose and cheeks as raw as a cut of beef, a drinker's complexion. Rose didn't want to stand up and be in closer proximity to him, and anyway her legs were shaking, so she remained seated.

'This is Seth Crookes,' said Daniel. 'He says he was there, the night Archie died.'

A weight shifted in Rose's chest. She couldn't speak. Daniel sat beside her, leaving the man standing, and took her hand. 'Do you want to go on? We can take our leave now.'

'Ey, ey.' The man shook his head. 'Hold thee horses.'

Rose extracted her hand from Daniel's. 'I'm reight enough. I want to hear what he's got to say.'

She flinched when the man sat down on the other side of her. He leaned forward to address Daniel. 'I'll tell the lass what went on but I'll not say owt in front o' thee.'

Daniel puffed out his cheeks. 'He thinks I'm a police officer.'

Rose finally met the man's eye. 'He's not. Were you there?' She took a deep breath. 'Did you see Archie?'

A look she couldn't interpret crossed his face – a strange cross between shiftiness and sorrow – and he made a pinching motion with a grimy thumb and index finger. 'Am this close to the workhouse, love. I know who did it an' I need that coin off thee. But am not speakin' in front o' him.'

Daniel spluttered. 'That's not—'

Rose put her hand on his arm. 'Go an' get theesen a jar of ale. I'll shout if I need you.' She attempted a smile. 'This little fella won't harm me. He knows I wouldn't be so stupid as to bring the coin along wi' me.'

Daniel went no further than the doorframe, which he leaned against, head tilted to avoid the lintel, elbows crossed awkwardly, staring back at them. Rose felt a rush of affection for him.

'I'll take a whisky, if tha's offerin',' the man called. 'It'll loosen me tongue up.'

Rose threw Daniel a pleading look. He closed his eyes briefly, then stalked away.

—

'It were Joe's doin', really. Me brother. All o' it. I were allus just along for the ride. On this job, there were three on us, one to lay the pipe an' two lookouts. The girl were on the high street an' Joe put me at the top end o' Change Alley where it meets Norfolk Street, tha knows?'

Rose nodded. She couldn't take her eyes from his face. For his part, he stared off into the middle distance and she knew he was back there, in the darkest hour of the night. His hand shook as he raised the whisky glass to his lips. She'd seen ague like that before, in her father not long before he died. Too much drink, and mind and body starting to fail.

Rose examined the man's face as he talked, both fascinated and aghast, but unafraid. He'd seen Archie in the last moments of his life and she wanted to squeeze every drop of knowledge from him. Nothing else mattered.

'Aye, it were all Joe's doin' but I went along wi' it, all the same. It were our final job, Joe an' me, an' then we were done wi' it, wi' all o' it. The town wanted to stop the union trouble, the blow-ups, the shootings, all that, so it were decided that all them that confessed would get let off.'

He cut his eyes at her and she nodded. 'I remember readin' about it, an' the crowds outside the town hall.'

'Aye, bayin' for the blood o' the union leader. Scarpered to America but come back quick enough.' There was a note of surprise in his voice. 'He opened a grocery. Anyhow, they never investigated the blow-up at Change Alley. It were after the inquiry started, but it got swept up in the same pile, that's what I think. Nob'dy wanted to bother wi' it really.'

Anger flared in Rose's gut. 'An inspector came to see me, but 'e weren't interested, I could tell.'

'Sounds about right.'

'What about Archie?'

'Aye, well, I were waitin' on Joe to do the deed and this watchman comes along, walkin' quick like, an' I duck out o' the way. He 'ad a good look about but I don't think he saw me.' He paused, swallowed. 'He must've seen Joe, though, because he set off runnin' down Change Alley. An' then it went off, the bomb.'

Rose clenched her hands into fists. 'Where's this Joe?'

Seth laughed, a bitter sound. 'Long gone, love. Took all me savin's and took his lass wi' 'im.'

'The lookout girl?'

'Nah, not 'er. She 'ad more sense. Ginny, his girl were called. Trouble. Neither of 'em been seen nor 'eard of since. Could be dead for all I know, tho' I come 'ere to wait for 'im every night o' the week.'

'What about this lookout, then, the girl?'

'Oh, she's still about, leadin' a respectable life. She were cut up about it, tha knows. Reckoned she 'eld his hand, before he croak… before he died. That night, she flaked out once she realised what'd 'appened, an' we 'ad to carry her away, me an' Joe, between us. If we'd left her there…' He rubbed his hand over his face and his eyes roamed restlessly across the room before fixing on Rose. 'Nob'dy were meant to get hurt.'

'Somebody did, though.' Surprised by a wave of emotion, Rose put her hand over her mouth and tears sprang to her eyes.

'I'm reight sorry.' Seth Crookes got to his feet and adjusted his cap. 'Tha tells nob'dy, all right? I'll deny it all an' then I'll come after thee. Or tha'll be watchin' over tha shoulder the rest of tha life.'

It was an unconvincing show of bravado but Rose went along with it. 'Who's to say I believe you anyway? I want to speak to this woman, this woman that were wi' Archie when he died.'

Archie might have given the woman a message, for Rose. If he'd had any last words, she wanted to hear them spoken. 'It's my right,' she said. 'Then you'll get the reward, all twenty sovereign.'

'I'd better or tha'll know about it.'

He would give her the information she needed if he wanted the reward. By the time Daniel returned, Rose had a name and an address north of Clay Wood.

Chapter 24

On the walk home, through cobbled streets that were quiet bar the occasional shout or slammed door, Rose related the information Seth Crookes had given her. Daniel fought a growing feeling of incredulity but held his tongue until she had finished.

'Do you mean to say that you are giving a financial reward to one of the culprits responsible for Archie's death?'

'He told me the real villain o' the piece was his brother.' Rose looked thoughtful. 'He were just a weak little man desperate for money. I'd built it up in me mind so much… I were expectin' the devil himself.'

Daniel glanced at her but Rose's face was in shadow. 'You feel sympathy for him?'

'I wun't go so far as that, Daniel!'

They walked on a few paces.

'Although,' said Rose, 'am sorry 'e's got nob'dy, that 'e sits an' waits for his brother to come home. Men don't seem to cope wi' bein' alone as well as women do. We've our children…' She trailed off. 'I din't mean you, Daniel. I don't know what I meant. I'm talkin' rubbish.'

He was glad she could not see his face flush. He might just have to swallow his pride and allow his mother to make him a match after all. Or end up like Seth Crookes, a drunken and lonely sot, spending his days sitting on a stool at the bar of the Golden Ball, making bitter fun of the younger men the way the regulars made fun of him.

'The important thing,' said Rose, 'is that I'm going to meet the woman who were wi' Archie in his last moments.'

'I'll certainly be accompanying you on that visit,' said Daniel, 'and I'll brook no argument.'

'Oh!' Rose's hand flew to her mouth.

Daniel stopped, alarmed. 'What is it?'

'Jem never showed up.'

'Ah. His work must have delayed him.'

'Hmm.'

They walked on in silence until they reached Rose's gate.

'It's been my pleasure to accompany you.' He bowed stiffly. 'Don't go seeking out any more ne'er-do-wells, Rose, not without some male protection.'

He opened the gate for Rose and she snicked it closed behind her. 'I've managed this long wi' out a man,' she said. 'But I'd be glad if you came wi' me, Dan. I'd be grateful.' She wiped her cheek. 'I felt a spot o' rain then. I'm sorry tha's got a long walk home.'

'I should buy a bicycle.'

Rose laughed. 'What?'

'You know, a bone-shaker. Something to get around town on.' He moved his arms as if he was steering a recalcitrant wheelbarrow. 'I've seen one for sale. A spider-wheeled, rubber-tyred bicycle for thirty shillings.' He wanted to hear her laugh again. 'What do you think? Should I buy it?'

'Aye, if you want to make a spectacle o' theesen. Sounds like the daft sort o' thing Jem would do, not you.

Jem would ride about like a circus clown and write it up in his newspaper.'

Her eyes lit up whenever she mentioned Jem's name. 'I think you like him,' he said.

'You sound like Annie.' She rubbed her arms. 'Freezin', in't it? I'll sithee soon, Daniel.'

'Good night.'

He waited until she was inside and then he took a deep breath and strode back up the hill. It was an hour's walk to the Golden Ball if he kept up a brisk pace. He'd complete the journey in less than half the time on a bicycle. He hadn't only been trying to cheer up Rose when he made his suggestion. He was even considering joining the local bicycle club, although its members organised races and did not gad about the streets on the machines, and would be open to ridicule if they attempted it. Dan knew he could never carry off that level of eccentricity.

Still, he pondered, as he skirted the Corn Exchange on Sheaf Street, learning to ride a bicycle was surely as easily done as learning to ride a horse, and would be cheaper to purchase and to maintain. He might invest, were he not certain that the contraption was nothing more than a passing fad.

–

He hadn't called on his mother since the excruciating encounter with Miss Baker but Daniel supposed he ought to pay a visit the next day, if only to tell her that he was resigning from Bright's and going back to his previous employer, on a higher salary and with good prospects. A director of the company, no less. He thought he'd find her in a contrite mood but should have guessed she'd be unrepentant. She had not burned the letters, and had, indeed, added to the pile.

They lay scattered on the breakfast table between them.

'What's the point of making yourself an eligible prospect if you won't entertain my efforts to help?' She attacked her scone with butter and jam as if it had wronged her. 'You don't want to end up alone, do you?'

'I found the right person and made a mess of it.' Mabel wasn't present, or he wouldn't have spoken so intimately. As it was, he feared he was crossing a line. 'I should never have listened to Father...'

'God rest his soul.'

'...or to you.'

'Show some respect, young man. That girl wasn't good enough for you.'

'She was better than me. Is better. I've seen her.'

She released the scone, which crumbled on her plate. 'Do not even contemplate it. That one was carrying another man's—'

'Stop.' He lowered his voice. 'Please stop now.'

He was back on the steps of the horse tram, watching Louisa Leigh cross the tracks, dreading the moment she would turn her head and see him, and at the same time praying their eyes would connect. With just one look, six years earlier, he'd destroyed their budding romance. It had been the moment he had realised she was carrying a child. She had witnessed the horror in his gaze. And the judgement. A fallen woman, spoiled goods, another man's child growing inside her. Daniel had reacted as any respectable man would. It was no excuse. The child, Alice, he'd last seen as a babe in arms, the day Louisa had turned him away, finding him wanting.

'I don't blame you,' he said.

'I should hope not.'

'I blame myself. I was weak and she saw through me.'

'Well.' His mother sat back and sighed. 'You need to relinquish the idea that she was the only love you'll ever find, if it ever was love. I'm just relieved you agreed to speak to Reverend Farrington once you realised she—'

'Mother.'

'Perhaps you should speak to him again. It's long past time you moved on. Long past.' She flapped her hand and rummaged through the letters. 'There's one here that's perfect. She's in here somewhere. Give me a moment.'

His protest died on his lips. Where was the harm in it? He wasn't going to find a bride in the saloon of the Golden Ball.

'Here we are.' She flourished the letter. Unlike most of the others, it was written on plain, high-quality paper in a neat script. No scalloped edging, no hand-drawn bouquets or pressed petals in the crease. No cloying scent. Daniel raised an eyebrow.

'Let me read it,' he said.

She continued to hold the piece of paper out of his reach, her eyes sparkling. 'She's from a respectable family of confectioners, so we'll never want for bonbons and chocolate. Her poor father – who by the way lives in a handsome house at High Bradfield with a gig and stabling for four horses; I sent Mabel to have a look – was blessed with six daughters, and has managed to marry off the other five. She writes that she has a good head for figures, and her father has allowed her to play a role in helping to develop the business.'

She rested the hand holding the letter on the table and peered at him over the rim of her spectacles. 'Unusual, to say the least, but she clearly has a sensible head on her shoulders. Being allowed to step outside her sphere might account for a certain boldness in her approach, for she has suggested you call into the Love Street confectionery and introduce yourself.'

Daniel frowned. 'I don't think I've ever visited that shop.'

'You're intrigued, are you not? And not just because you have a sweet tooth.'

'Can I see the letter now?'

He took it from her and scanned the contents. It was, as his mother said, a plain statement of facts, with no further embellishment.

She leaned forward and tapped his hand. 'Why don't you wander down to Love Street today and see whether you can purchase an ounce of toffee from Miss Clara Fullerton?'

Daniel lifted one foot then the other, examining the soles of his shoes. 'You know, I deliberately chose lodgings close to my place of employment' – soon to be ex-employment; he must speak to Silas as soon as possible – 'but I've done so much walking about the town in the past few weeks, my shoes are wearing out.'

'All the more reason to visit the town, then. Purchase a new pair of shoes. Don't forget my toffee.'

–

It was one of those days that couldn't summon the energy to fully emerge, surrendering instead to the veils of factory smoke that hung in the air and tickled the back of his throat. Through the gloom, the lamplit window of Fullerton's confectionery appeared like a portal to a warmer, sweetened world. Behind the pane, glass-stoppered jars containing sugary delights in all the colours of the rainbow jostled for space amongst ornate biscuit tins and boxes of tea.

Daniel adjusted his collar and was about to enter when he felt a tug on his coat. A boy about half Daniel's height had hold of him. With his other hand, he was holding up baggy trousers that were too big on him and the thinness of his jacket sent a sympathetic shiver up Daniel's spine.

'Got a penny, sir, so I can get some spice?'

'I have.' He fished in his pocket. 'What's your favourite?'

'It's not for me. It's for me ma. She's poorly an' I thought a bit o' spice might cheer her up.'

Daniel beamed at him. 'In that case, have two pennies.'

He remained outside while the boy scooted into the shop. He wanted to prepare his introduction and to see who came forward to serve the boy. He was disappointed to find it was a portly man wearing a white cloth hat and apron, who seemed to be remonstrating with the child but accepted the coins and handed over a paper bag of sweets. The boy yanked open the door and ran off down the road, ignoring Daniel entirely.

He entered the shop and walked purposefully to the counter, on which sat a till, an oil lamp that illuminated a stack of mint-cake bars and a jar of aniseed balls, and a set of scales. Shelving on the rear wall groaned under the weight of jars of sweets of every description, presently partially blocked by the portly man, who was smirking at him.

'Did he fool you, that lad? Tell the tale of his poorly mother?'

Daniel's gut tightened. 'Not at all.' He made a point of peering past the man at the display behind him. 'Is that treacle toffee? I'll take three ounces.'

The smile fell from the man's lips and he assumed a professional tone. 'Right you are, sir.'

He wrapped the toffee and Daniel paid for it.

'Anything else, sir?'

'Thank you, no. Well, there is something.' His tongue was stuck to the roof of his mouth. He coughed. 'Excuse me.'

The man lifted the stopper from a jar and offered the contents to Daniel, who took a lemon-flavoured boiled sweet and popped it in his mouth. He realised his mistake immediately. Now he would have to try to communicate around the damned thing. He couldn't risk trying to bite into it either; it was so hard he would probably crack a tooth. He folded and unfolded his arms. Warmth crept into his cheeks. Eventually, he took out his handkerchief, spat the sweet into it and balled it into his coat pocket.

He would leave, and call again another day. Instead, he found himself blurting out the words he had struggled to form moments earlier.

'Is Miss Fullerton here today? Miss Clara Fullerton?'

'The boss's lass? Aye, she's in the stockroom. I'll fetch her.'

'Oh dear. I mean, I don't want to trouble her if…'

But the man had disappeared through the curtain behind the counter.

Daniel bit his lip. Here he was again, in an awkward situation engineered by his mother. He was frowning mightily when a woman emerged and her welcoming smile faltered for a moment. She was plainly dressed in a high-necked blue shirt and black skirt. Her hair was chestnut-coloured, pinned into a loose bun, and the expression in her almond-shaped green eyes was clear and direct. He realised she was waiting for him to speak.

'Good afternoon, I'm Mr Housley, Daniel Housley. You… you responded to an advertisement.'

'Oh!' She turned away to peer through the curtain, then faced Daniel with merriment in her eyes. 'I have lost a bet with my brother-in-law.'

'I'm sorry?'

'He persuaded me to respond. In fact, he wrote that letter.' She hurried on. 'I read it, of course, before I allowed it to be sent. I thought that would be the end of it.' She tilted her head. 'And yet here you stand.'

Daniel's collar was suddenly too tight, strangling his voice. 'I'm happy to have provided an amusing diversion. I'll take my leave.'

'Oh no, I'm sorry!' She came around from behind the counter and stood before him, hands clasped. 'I really do apologise. I shouldn't have spoken so…'

'Frankly?'

'Well, yes. You caught me by surprise, you see. I'm glad you have called; I genuinely am glad.'

Daniel took off his hat and scratched his head. 'So how do we…'

The shop bell tinkled and a man and a woman, a couple, entered, oohing and aahing over the displays. Daniel picked up a box of biscuits and pretended to examine it. Miss Fullerton assisted the customers; she had a pleasant way about her. He was convinced the couple left having spent more money than they'd intended. She turned to him, smiling.

Daniel swallowed. 'I was going to ask, how do we proceed? If we do proceed.' He was tying himself in knots. 'This is exceptionally unconventional.'

'Are you going to purchase those biscuits?'

'Ah… yes? My mother would enjoy them.'

He watched her long fingers expertly wrap and tie the tin. She put the package on the counter and rested her hand on top. 'A gift, for your mother, Mr Housley. These biscuits are delicious with' – she plonked a packet of tea next to the packet – 'this tea.'

'I see.' Daniel laughed. 'Would you care to take tea with my mother and I, perhaps next Saturday afternoon?'

'What a lovely idea.'

The shop bell tinkled.

Miss Fullerton held up one finger. 'Allow me to serve this gentleman and then I shall go and find a pencil, if you have time. I can take your mother's address down, for the delivery.'

Daniel kept his face turned away from the new customer so they shouldn't see the grin that had spread across his face.

Chapter 25

The shop smelled of spilled ink and industriousness. Annie perched on the edge of one of the desks in the office behind the counter, watching Rob and Jem make a final pass through the book, checking headlines, text and layout.

'It's ready,' said Rob.

'How many court reports are contained in this week's issue?' she said.

'Several,' said Rob. He sounded testy. 'They're what people want to read.'

'Listen to this one, Annie,' said Jem. 'A low sort breaks into a house, raids the larder, taps into a keg of beer, all while the family are in the land of nod, finds and drinks a bottle of wine and falls asleep on their settee. He was still snoring away merrily when they fetched the constable.'

'Why, it's the fairy tale. The story of the three bears,' said Annie.

'Excellent.' Jem scored through the headline he had written, and scribbled a new one. *The Three Bears Burglar.* 'Two months' hard labour. The judge must have been in a foul temper that day.'

Rob rubbed his face, leaving an inky stain on his cheek. 'Are we happy?'

'Happy as we'll ever be,' said Jem, 'barring any last-minute additions. There are a couple of items we can lose if necessary.'

Annie heard the door that led into the back alley open and close and the compositor call a greeting from the back room. He'd check the type box and wait for the pages to be handed over so that he could set them, ahead of the overnight print run. Rob already looked exhausted, and would be up all night, only returning home after the distributor and delivery boys arrived at six o'clock the following morning.

'Can you open up the shop at nine tomorrow?' he asked Jem. 'I could use more than a couple of hours of sleep.'

'I wish I could,' said Jem, 'but I'm off to cover the grand opening of the Wesleyan bazaar. I thought you were employing an assistant for front of shop.'

'I haven't found the time to compose the job advertisement, let alone carry out interviews,' said Rob. 'I shall have to put a cot in the print room. I'm already dead on my feet.'

'Can I help?' said Annie. Standing behind the counter of Whittaker's print shop was a far more agreeable prospect than attending the regular Saturday morning meeting of her sewing circle. 'I have a free morning tomorrow.'

Rob looked up. 'You can indeed help.' He picked up a piece of card and handed it to her. 'Can you proof this? It has to be perfect and you'll know if the dishes are correctly spelled and presented.'

'I meant…' She shook her head. She was becoming weary of pushing against Rob's immovability on what he judged should be her wifely role. 'Of course.'

'What is it?' said Jem.

'Menu card for the annual dinner of the Licensed Victuallers' Society at Cutlers Hall,' said Rob. 'I need to make a good job of it if I want the repeat business.'

'I'm going to that,' said Jem. 'I hear there's upset over the government's plan for more restrictions on opening hours. There'll be ructions.'

'Are there any events in town you are *not* attending?' said Annie.

He peered over her shoulder. 'Let's see what grub we're getting, then.'

They all looked up expectantly when the shop door opened and a top-hatted and frock-coated gentleman entered. Annie was closest to the counter. She would show Rob that she was capable of more than putting a hot dinner before him and darning his socks. 'Give me a job to do,' she had said, during their most recent argument about the letters she had written on the atrocity committed against Oonagh.

'You have a job,' he'd replied, and she had escaped from the room before he could elaborate.

She smiled warmly at the gentleman. 'Can I help, sir?'

He offered a vague smile in return and looked beyond her, at the two men. 'Is Mr Whittaker available?'

Rob came forward. 'I'm Robert Whittaker, proprietor. What can I do for you?'

The man extracted a small card from his breast pocket. 'You were recommended to me. I require a new set of calling cards. Two sets, as my wife has used almost all of hers up too.' He smiled at Annie. 'She distributes them like cherry trees dispense their blossom.'

Rob laughed politely. Annie turned to look askance at Jem, who riffled the pages of the template for the next day's *Tribune* and gestured for her to join him at the back of the office.

'Did you know Mundella has presented your petition to the House of Commons? It came through on wires. Rob's put it in the book for tomorrow's issue.'

She mustered a smile and looked through the book. There was a snippet about the petition on page six, contained within a report on various dull and dry parliamentary proceedings that took up two columns. 'Splendid.'

She heard her father's name spoken in the conversation Rob was having with the gentleman at the counter. Then the man tipped his hat to Rob and to Annie, bade her give his regards to her father, and left.

Jem took the book back from her. 'Here, you'll like this.' He pointed to a correspondence contributed anonymously. Mundella was being challenged to indicate unequivocally – with a simple and firm *yes* or *no* – whether he supported the legalisation of picketing, rather than retreat from the question with platitudes about rights and justice, as parroted by politicians of all persuasion. If Annie had been in a better mood she might have found it amusing.

'Why can't people who wish to broadcast their opinion to all and sundry find the courage to put their name to it?' she said.

Jem shrugged. 'Perhaps it's from Mrs Mundella. Some of these women are harridans labouring under the misapprehension that once married they are allowed to keep minds of their own.'

'Very droll,' said Rob. 'Don't you have somewhere to be, Jem?'

'I do.' He lifted his overcoat from the hook on the door that led into the corridor of the building and shrugged it on. 'Time to charm the constable who has hold of the incidents ledger.'

'I'll accompany you to the town hall,' said Annie. 'I have a headache starting and the fresh air might help.'

Rob laughed. 'Fresh air? In this town? No, I can't have you wandering the streets, my love. Jem, come back by way of the chemist's shop on Angel Street and buy a potion for my wife's headache.'

Annie waited until Jem emerged onto the street from the side door. He sketched a salute as he passed by the window.

'Wandering the streets?'

Rob looked around the office. 'I'm cold. Shall I light the fire?'

He'd taken to adopting this method of avoiding confrontation lately, which involved simply pretending she hadn't spoken. It was infuriating.

'Are you worried that I might incite a riot?'

Rob rubbed his forehead, leaving more ink there, and gave her an entreating look. Annie pursed her lips. 'Look at you.' She retrieved a cloth from under the counter. 'Well, this rag has seen better days but you can't greet customers looking like you've had a fight with a bottle of ink. Come here.'

Rob suffered her ministrations wordlessly.

'I might have bought myself a cup of cocoa from the stand in the high street,' said Annie. 'That would be the extent of my rebellion.' She examined his face. 'All done.'

Rob gave her a chaste kiss on the cheek, no doubt mindful of the compositor in the next room. 'Thank you.

I'm sorry I was cross. I'm exhausted from getting this business going.'

'I do understand. I wish you would allow me to do more to help you.'

'It helps me when you make a happy home for us.'

'Oh, Rob. I wish you would not be so...' She stopped speaking abruptly when the door from the corridor was flung open and Jem entered, an apologetic expression on his face, followed by a man whose portly frame was barely contained in a voluminous black, layered cape. He stepped carefully over the threshold and pinned Annie with a beady eye, like a crow sizing up its prey.

'Your cousin and I collided in the street,' the man said, 'and I thought to seize an opportunity to come and have a chat. Strike while the iron's hot, as they say.' He acknowledged Rob with a bow of the head.

'I thought better here than at your home with the neighbours looking on,' said Jem, grimacing. 'May I introduce Police-Detective Harrison. This is Mr and Mrs Robert Whittaker.'

Rob organised chairs around one of the desks and asked Jem to deal with any customers that might come in. His face had reddened the moment the introductions were made. A detective, in his shop, for all the world to see. Annie couldn't understand why Jem had insisted this was better than receiving a call at home, then realised the detective had probably insisted upon it.

'Have the pages gone through?' Rob said.

'I'll take the book in now,' said Jem, and disappeared into the back room.

'Don't halt your day on my account,' said the detective. 'I can see how busy you are. I'm here to talk with your wife, with your permission of course.'

Rob nodded but remained seated and covered Annie's hand with his. 'Is this about the Irish girl?'

Detective Harrison offered a thin smile in reply and turned to Annie. Over the course of the next hour, he asked her about her relationship with Oonagh Ryan, with Rose Butterfield and with Messrs Albert Boothby and Edgar Bright. She said the two men were strangers she hoped never to encounter. The detective wanted to know what Oonagh had told her of her reason for being in Sheffield and everything that Rose had said in relation to her temporary tenant. She was required to talk through the events in the square where the girl's unfortunate unmasking had taken place. He took notes on a small pad, frequently licking the end of the stub of a pencil and occasionally asking her to slow down or repeat a sentence here and there.

Annie sipped the coffee Jem had fetched from a cart on the corner of the market square. She felt wrung out, and overcome by sadness.

'I should not have asked her to do that,' she said. 'I wanted Mr Mundella, and everyone in the square, to see what had become of a poor working girl, an immigrant far from home.' She gulped, and felt a reassuring pressure on her hand. She'd forgotten Rob was still holding it. 'Working in that match factory killed her.'

The detective sat back and shook his head. 'We're not investigating the practices of the match factory, we're—'

'You should be!'

'Annie,' said Rob, a note of warning in his voice.

'Let me assure you, police-detectives who are based at York are speaking to the factory owner and trying to establish contact with the young lady's family in Ireland, and we are going to be interviewing the gentlemen he is acquainted with here in Sheffield.' Detective Harrison paused. 'This is all as the result of your correspondence landing on my desk, Mrs Whittaker, and a singular request from Mr Mundella to investigate the matter. He was evidently moved by the young lady's plight. Your accusation of kidnapping is being taken seriously, I assure you.'

Jem dropped the stack of paper he was carrying onto the floor, startling them all.

Rob got to his feet and began picking up the sheets. 'What have I said about keeping clear of the fire? Are you planning on burning us to the ground?'

Jem ignored him. He was as pale as the paper scattered on the carpet. 'I hope you're not accusing Rose of colluding in this crime, Detective Harrison.'

Annie gasped. 'Oh no, Rose is absolutely not at fault here. She gave Oonagh her own bed when she realised how poorly she was. She had no idea about her background.'

'Rose had lost her job and needed the money,' said Jem. He measured his words out slowly and calmly, but Annie saw the tell-tale vein that throbbed in his neck.

The detective held up a hand. 'Rose Butterfield is being interviewed by a colleague of mine today. Probably as we speak, in fact.'

Annie stood and laid her hand on Jem's arm, hoping he would interpret this as an instruction to remain silent. 'Is there anything else you'd like to know, sir?'

'I think that concludes our interview, for now.'

Rob dumped the paper on the desk and ran his hands through his hair. 'Annie, you should learn to leave what's well enough alone.'

'But it wasn't well enough, was it?' said Detective Harrison. 'We're grateful to your wife for drawing a serious matter to our attention. The girl should not have been removed to a different town on account of an injury she sustained at work.'

After he had left, Rob reluctantly agreed that Annie and Jem should visit Rose that evening.

'I'll be here all night,' he reminded Jem, 'so I'd be grateful if you would see Annie home afterwards. She'll only get herself into more trouble otherwise.' He kissed her on the cheek. 'What shall I do with you?'

Annie pretended to consider the question. 'You could put a horse's halter around my neck and auction me off at the Saturday market, like men used to do with wayward wives in the old days.'

'So, you admit you are wayward?'

Jem tapped on the counter impatiently. 'Can you put on your bonnet while sparring with your husband, Annie, to save time?'

It was almost dark by the time they left the shop. There was a charred bite in the air that reminded Annie of chestnuts roasting on the grate. She realised she hadn't eaten all day and hoped Rose would have a cake or a batch of scones fresh from the oven. She struggled to keep up with the brisk pace Jem set down Change Alley. He almost collided with the lamp-lighter outside the King's Head Hotel. When Jem took her elbow to cross the busy high street and she caught her heel in the hem of her skirt, Annie refused to go any further. 'That cab missed us by a hair's breadth,' she said crossly. 'Please calm down. I'm sure Rose is well.'

'She might end up locked up again. It's outrageous.'

'Jem, you're inventing outrage where none exists. Let's arrive in one piece, shall we?'

She cocked her head when a series of popping sounds echoed off the buildings. Jem took her hand and pulled her forward.

'Fireworks,' he said.

'Yes, of course,' said Annie. 'I thought people had given up celebrating on November the fifth.'

'Always somebody wanting to burn an effigy and set off a home-made bomb,' said Jem.

'Don't let Rose hear you say that.'

He gave her a look. 'I won't.'

They arrived at the top of the street where Rose lived as she arrived at the bottom. Jem hailed her and ran down, leaving Annie to more carefully negotiate the darkened path. He took Rose's hands in his and spoke urgently to her, before Rose gently disengaged herself and they came up the road together.

Inside, they sat at the kitchen table and watched Rose and her children eat bread and soup and chunks of salty cheese and ham. Annie answered on Jem's behalf when Rose offered food to them. She was hungry but could see there would not be enough to go around. She told Rose about the detective's visit.

Rose replied carefully, glancing at Jane. 'I got a visit, at my work, an' I had to go into a room to be interviewed.'

Rose's daughter put down her spoon. 'Why?'

'Your mother was negotiating an increase in her wages,' said Jem, 'so she can keep you lot fed and watered until you're old enough to look after her.'

Jane frowned. 'I will look after you, Ma.'

'I know tha will, love.'

'I was asked about the two gentlemen,' said Annie, 'and what I knew of you, and… everybody involved. I suppose they wanted corroboration of our accounts.'

'Are you gettin' a pay rise too?' said Jane.

'Yes, I hope so,' said Annie. 'I hope we all get what we deserve from this' – she couldn't help herself – 'which is justice.'

'Can we go an' play?' said one of the twins. Annie could never tell them apart.

'Take them in the front room for us?' said Rose.

Jane sighed. 'All right.'

'Don't go near the fire. Check the guard's on it.'

'*All right.*'

As soon as she could speak freely, Rose told them the constable who had interviewed her – thankfully not one of the men who had been present in Paradise Square on the day of the march – had let slip that the police were also in touch with the girl Oonagh had travelled from Ireland with. 'She's sick, an' all,' she said, 'sufferin' wi' jaw pain an' headaches. She's goin' home, back to Ireland.'

Annie nodded thoughtfully. 'They're missing the point, aren't they, by investigating a kidnapping, though goodness knows I'd like to see Boothby and Bright's faces when the police knock on their door.'

'Sounds like a firm of solicitors, doesn't it?' said Jem. 'Boothby and Bright.' His equilibrium had been restored as soon as he'd been assured by Rose that she hadn't been mistreated. Annie wondered how Rose failed to see how devoted he was, then checked herself. Rose knew very well.

'Tell us about your meeting at the Blue Pig,' she said.

'There's nowt to tell, not really,' said Rose. 'He were a sot, a weak man. He were part of the crew, settin' the bomb, though he didn't do the deed himsen. The man he called the real culprit emigrated soon after. But there is a woman too, an' she were the last to see Archie alive. I'm goin' to visit her.'

'When?' said Jem.

'I don't know when. Soon.' She got up and began to tidy away the plates. 'I'm tired out.'

Annie took the cue. 'We'll be off, then. We wanted to see how you were, and it looks as though you took it all in your stride, Rose, as you always do. Shall we walk up to the cab stand, Jem?'

'Yes, will you wait outside for me? For just a moment? I have a question I'd like to ask Rose.'

Rose frowned. If Jem was going to ask her to begin courting, Annie feared he would be disappointed. She buttoned up her cloak. 'All right. Don't be long or I shall be iced over.'

She was surprised, and touched, when Rose came forward and lightly embraced her. 'I'll sithee soon, love.'

On the pavement, Annie stamped her feet to keep warm. She ought to have worn her earmuffs. No sensible creature would be outdoors now; even foxes would remain in their burrows, and birds in their nests. The only sounds she could hear were man-made, the factory whistle and hum carrying on the cold night air from the bottom of the valley.

Jem bounded out of the house, closing the door behind him, and, waiting a moment, tensed, for the sound of the lock turning. He took Annie's arm.

'Well?'

'She said yes, eventually.'

Annie couldn't see his expression in the dark. 'Yes to what?'

'She's agreed to accompany me to the bazaar tomorrow.'

'Ah, I see. Chipping away, still, are we?'

Jem tugged her arm playfully. 'I'll win her over, you just wait and see. Come on. Let's hope the cabbies aren't sozzled by now, or it's shanks' pony all the way to Walkley. Oh.' He stopped.

'What is it now?'

'Can I borrow the lovely cloak you're wearing?'

'This?'

'Yes please. Only I neglected to tell Rose that the bazaar is a bit of a grand affair, and I don't want her to feel out of place.'

'Am I allowed to wear it home first?'

'Oh yes,' he said airily. 'I might as well borrow a bonnet from you too, if you've one handy.'

Chapter 26

'I do love this, if tha can get excited o'er a daft bonnet,' said Rose. She put her hands up to adjust it. The brim was soft, but unyielding, the midnight-blue nap decorated with pale blue ribbon.

'The colour suits your complexion,' said Jem.

'You shouldn't have taken Annie's cape, though.' She pulled on the gloves Annie had given her: a little girl trying on her big sister's clothes, about to be found out and punished for her audacity. She looked down at her feet. 'An' these scuffed boots'll gi' me away.'

'Nobody will be looking at the ground,' said Jem. 'And Annie will find something else to wear to her sewing circle, I'm sure, or she'll stay at home, which will suit Rob.'

'Gi' me five minutes.'

Rose went back into the house. She'd set spellings for the little ones to learn, with the promise of a treat as a reward on her return, provided they behaved themselves. Jane was doing the mending and keeping an eye on the boys. They were in the front room, the twins cross-legged on the rug, arguing over who would hold the board and who would write with the chalk. 'Take it in turns,' said Jane. She was sitting in the armchair by the fire, the sewing tin on the table at her side. 'I'll not tell thee again, I'll stick the pair o' thee with this needle.'

Rose picked up a scrap of paper from the mantlepiece. 'Pop this in the tin, would you, love? It'll end up in the fire at this rate.'

'What is it?'

'Just a name an' address I don't want to lose.' She could see Jane would not be satisfied with this. 'Somebody who might 'ave a bit o' extra mendin' work for us.'

She stopped on her way out of the room. 'Will you be all right?'

Jane sighed. 'I'm eleven.'

'That's not what I asked thee.'

Her daughter gave her an appraising look. 'You're very pretty all dressed up, Ma.'

'It's nowt much. A borrowed bonnet.' Flustered, Rose looked back at Jane from the door. 'I'll only be an hour or so, all right?'

When they arrived on Church Street, she restarted the earlier argument she'd been having with Jem after he'd admitted they were visiting the grand banqueting room of Cutlers Hall. Hemmed in by buildings either side, this was one of the town's finest venues, where the master cutler hosted an annual feast that was as important commercially as it was socially. As a humble knife wrapper, Rose wouldn't ever be invited to such an event. She'd never before stepped foot inside the hall, although she'd passed by the elegant façade often enough.

She stood on the pavement, gazing up at the polished pillars of the entrance. 'When you said *fair* I was expecting stalls on the common or summat. Donkey rides an' apple dunkin'.'

'I said bazaar, didn't I, at Cutlers Hall?'

His eyes were round and innocent and Rose couldn't help but laugh. 'Don't gi' me that. Last night, you said it were a fair an' you din't give me the location, though I asked. You said there'd be trinkets I'd like and I might find summat for Christmas for the children, so they'd have to stay at home or it'd ruin the surprise.'

'Goodness, I'll treat it as a compliment that you're able to repeat my every word.'

'Aye, it's a shame tha leaves so many out.'

'I do have to say your fair with the donkey rides sounds a lot more fun than mine.' Jem offered his arm. 'But please come inside. You never know, you might enjoy it.'

Rose turned her back on a spatter of rain blown up the high street by a cold gust of wind.

'Well, we're here now,' she conceded. 'I'll go in to get out of the wet.'

Rain that had begun to speckle the pavement moments earlier began to fall in sheets. The foyer was soon crammed with people, some peering out and exclaiming over the sudden shower, others ascending the staircase. Rose overheard a man tell his companion that he was looking forward to seeing how the Wesleyans had managed to conjure an Eastern theme in so provincially English a setting.

Jem whispered in her ear. 'It's a shame they couldn't give the weather an Eastern aspect too.'

She smiled uncertainly and touched the side of her neck with her fingertips where she could have sworn his lips had brushed her skin. The space they stood in seemed suddenly too small to contain the swelling chatter of the crowd. Her ears whined with the effort of processing the noise, while the fusty smell of wet clothes plugged her nostrils. Rose stepped away from Jem, almost panicked in her need to create a space between them, and found herself on the bottom tread of the sweeping staircase.

'Excuse me.'

There was a man close behind her, smelling of stale tobacco and damp wool, who had obviously assumed she was ascending to the banqueting hall along with everyone else on the staircase. Rose murmured an apology and, not wanting to turn and fight the tide, trotted up to the top of the stairs. She cast a quick glance behind her but could not see Jem. She was carried along by the crowd, through a set of wide-open doors, into the bazaar. Rose could barely believe Jem had tried to pass this off as a fair. She craned her neck to look up at the vaulted ceiling high above, from which hung an enormous chandelier. Rain lashed at the half-moon panes of the clerestories that ran the length of both sides of the room. Below these windows hung elaborately framed oil portraits of men she didn't recognise. Under their stern gazes, the wood-panelled walls were lined with turreted stalls draped in white cambric and decorated with brightly coloured glass lamps, embroidered rugs, white feathers and dimpled cushions the colours of emeralds and rubies.

A string band played at the far end of the room and the floor was filled with people browsing the stalls. Jem had been right. Nobody would notice her scuffed boots in this melee. Rose turned to look behind her and was relieved to see him reach the top of the stairs. Her heart fluttered when he caught sight of her and a wide smile lit up his face.

'Thought I'd lost you,' he said. 'What do you think?'

'That there'll be nowt 'ere I can afford to buy.' She gave him a sideways glance, stifling laughter.

Jem put on a mock-injured look. 'Did you not read the poster? Costly *and* cheap articles, ornamental and *useful* items. I'm sure we can find something you'll like amid all the frippery.' He spread his hands. 'It's all to a good cause.'

'What's the cause?'

'The restoration of the chapel over on Norfolk Street. The Wesleyans need six thousand pounds all told, and hope to raise over a thousand with this event. A committee of bachelors organised it but of course all the actual work has been done by the ladies.'

'I wonder how they find the time.'

'You mean, between inviting one another to lunch and instructing their cook on what to prepare for dinner?'

They stopped in front of a tasselled screen, one of several placed around the room. This one depicted a magnificent castle and grounds and was bordered with beaded needlework on ebony velvet. Rose played a tassel through her fingers.

'Twenty-five guineas,' said the man standing beside the screen. 'Free delivery.'

Rose snorted. 'It'd 'ave to be. I'll think about it.' She moved on; Jem followed.

'I thought you were part of that set?' she said. 'Fancy suppers an' carriage rides to Birley Spa?'

'Not really,' said Jem. 'I'm Annie's poor relation, from a side of the family mired in disgrace, but the job I do gives me a free ticket to most things, and acquaints me with those personages who run the town.'

Rose picked up a slim tortoiseshell case, one of several fanned out on a velvet mat. There were silver ones too, and some made of ivory. 'What are these?'

'Calling-card cases.'

'I sharn't be needing one o' them.'

She returned it carefully to the display and moved on to a stall devoted to silver tableware, wondering if any of the cutlery came from Morton's, her new employer. She bent to examine a fish knife and fork set presented in a glass case, the bulge of the knife blade figured like the underbelly of a fish, the point its head and eye. The tines of the fork were the most delicate she had ever seen. This was cutlery for royalty. Rose looked around for Jem. He was trying on toppers and bowlers nearby.

'What d'you think, Rose?'

He looked handsomely rakish under a sleek black top hat. 'How much is it?'

'Too much. And I have one at home.'

'Call theesen a poor relation?'

'A poor relation, on the up,' said Jem.

'Hmm.' Rose moved on. 'Oh, these're lovely.' She ran her fingers over the lacquered lid of one of several musical boxes lined up in a row on the next stall. The man standing alongside them smiled at her and picked up the box.

'Listen,' he said, and wound the metal key on the underside, placing it back down before Rose and lifting the lid to reveal a shallow space lined in some satiny material. A cascade of notes like birdsong floated out. 'A gift for your delightful lady?'

'How mu—'

Jem interrupted her. 'It is delightful. Would you like it, Rose?'

'No.' Although she spoke the word quietly and firmly, her heart was pounding with something close to fear. 'Sorry, I mean, it's lovely but it's too extravagant. I can't let thee buy it for me.'

She turned, and collided with a man holding a large cushion in his arms.

'Oh, am sorry!'

'Don't worry, miss,' he said, 'I have this padding to protect me.'

His laughter rang in her ears as she marched towards the entrance. Jem caught up to her on the stairs leading back to the foyer, his face full of concern. She spoke before he could. 'I need to get home.'

The foyer had emptied of people but was filled by the sound of the unrelenting rain.

Rose peered out. 'Annie's fancy bonnet'll be ruined.'

Jem plucked an umbrella from the stand beside the door. 'I'll liberate this.'

'You can't nick somebody's umbrella!'

He put it back, shamefaced. 'I want to do right by you, Rose.'

'What does that mean?'

Jem came to stand alongside her and gazed out at the street, at the church across the road that was blurred by the torrent of rain, at the passing carriages throwing up sprays of dirty water.

'What a downpour,' he said. 'This will surely pass soon. There'll be no moisture left in the heavens.'

'Let's wait for a bit, then,' said Rose. 'Five minutes.' She was enjoying the cooling effect the air was having on her cheeks. She had over-reacted to Jem's offer to gift her the musical box but didn't want to admit to that, for reasons she couldn't even articulate to herself. She'd asked him, foolishly, what he meant when he'd said he wanted to do right by her and was relieved he hadn't answered the question.

'What I meant just now,' said Jem, and her gut tightened, 'was that I'd like to court you, Rose, to properly court you. I think you know I'm falling in love with you.'

She closed her eyes briefly, tried to quell a rising sense of panic, then looked at him. But Jem wasn't looking at her; he was staring out, into the rain. He blinked and she followed the sweep of his lashes. Time stood still. Even the raindrops seemed suspended in the air.

She broke the spell. 'I can't.'

'I won't die on you, Rose.'

She curled her lip and stepped away from him. 'What a thing to say.'

'Or I might.' He finally turned to look at her. 'There's no guarantees, not in this life.'

She shook her head. 'I've done the hard bit. I've learned to live wi'out 'im. D'you think I need rescuin'?'

'No.' He smiled gently. 'But I think you harbour feelings for me, too. Now you'll say my head's too big to get through this door, won't you?'

Rose frowned. She realised she was twisting the wedding band on her finger, around and around. 'I'm married.'

''Til death do you part.' He was still smiling but his eyes were hooded.

'That's a terrible thing to say.'

She stepped outside. The downpour would shelter her, would prevent any further conversation as they hurried home. But she could sense he had not followed her onto the street. She looked over her shoulder. Jem stood in the doorway of the Cutlers Hall, unmoving. She couldn't make out his expression.

Rose hesitated, then turned away and set off for home.

Chapter 27

Susie Shaw detached herself from the group of workers huddled in the factory yard and approached Daniel with a triumphant look on her face. *What now?* he wondered, his resolve to hand over his resignation letter strengthening by the second.

'Has tha heard?'

'I've only just arrived,' he said. 'Heard what?'

'Edgar Bright's had the police at 'is door, an' he's bein' questioned about some young lass that died.' Her eyes were hungry for gossip. 'What's goin' on? Tha must know summat.'

'I know I want to get out of this rain. Excuse me.'

He hoped his face didn't betray the glow of satisfaction spreading in his chest. If the police had apprehended Edgar Bright then the letter signed by Rose was being taken seriously. Daniel hoped she wouldn't suffer for it.

But Susie Shaw wasn't finished with him. She followed him up the stairs and into his office.

'Did Rosie find the man she were lookin' for, at the Blue Pig?'

'Yes. Yes, she did.' Daniel nodded vigorously in an effort to compensate for the fact he intended to give her no further information.

'Well, that's all right, then.'

He was aware of her observing him as he walked behind his desk, fiddled with the paperwork on it and checked the level of ink in the pot. 'Excuse me,' he said, drawing out his chair and sitting down.

'Only,' she said, finally, 'I know that reward were quite a big 'un. Twenty sovereign, it said on the poster. How's she got that to spare, on such a fool's errand?'

Daniel blew into his hands, aware of the window pane rattling at his back. He wondered whether he could find an excuse to visit the factory floor, to get some warmth into his bones.

'Unless she's got hersen a rich man on tap. It's allus the quiet ones.'

He rubbed his hands together briskly and took up his pen. 'What can I help you with, Mrs Shaw?'

'I were thinkin' some o' that reward should be goin' in me husband's direction, an' mine for passin' it on.' She pulled her shawl tightly around her shoulders. 'Winter's 'ere and coal in't gettin' any cheaper. I thought tha might mention it to our Rosie, now she's gone from 'ere, an' tha pair bein' as thick as thieves.'

Daniel thought about giving her the two guineas and loose change he had in his wallet but knew that wouldn't be the end of it. Rose had made her escape and he'd be gone from this place soon enough. He adjusted his spectacles and opened a desk drawer at random, hoping she'd take the hint.

'If you'll excuse me.'

'All right, well, I'll no doubt sithee later, Mr Housley.'

Daniel waited until the sound of her footsteps on the stairs had faded then sat back and sighed. His breath misted into the cold air and he recalled the fierce heat of the fire-breathing convertor at the Hinchcliffe steel works that had prickled his skin from the far side of the factory floor. Silas was on the up, while the wire mills might not survive a scandal involving the owner, especially on top of the tragedy in the boiler-house. Tongues wagged in this town and reputations could be destroyed in a day.

It took a few minutes to compose a letter of resignation and slip it under the door of Edgar Bright's office. He'd tried the door first, gently rotating the knob. It was locked. Daniel wondered whether his employer was sitting inside, behind his desk, head in hands, or standing at the window watching the dense smoke rise from the wire mills' chimney. He inclined his head towards the door but there was no sound from within.

He worked on for most of the morning, undisturbed, then got up and left his office, tucking his chin into the raised collar of his coat and walking quickly through the yard to the main entrance. He had an appointment to keep and might not be back until mid-afternoon but felt no qualms about it, now that he'd resigned his position. A flicker of excitement ignited in his belly. The last time he'd seen the Hinchcliffes, Silas had clapped him on the back. *It'll soon be me an' thee again, Dan. Me an' thee takin' on the world.*

He stood on the opposite side of the street from Morton's cutlery works and raised his hand when Rose emerged, his spirits lifted by the sight of her, although she had a frown on her face as she waited to cross. Her first words to him were lost in the wheels of a passing cart.

'…an' I've been given dispensation to take a full hour, but no more.' She was already striding along, and Daniel hurried to keep up.

'Try not to be too anxious,' he said.

'Am not anxious.' She acknowledged this blatant untruth with a smile. 'All right then, a bit, maybe. So 'ave you done the deed?'

'Yes. If he comes in today he'll find my letter.' He debated whether he should tell Rose about Bright receiving a visit from the police. It would only cause her more worry. 'How far have we to go?'

'Oh, not far at all. She's on Pond Lane.' Rose glanced at him, then turned her attention back to the road ahead. 'I've been wonderin', what if she's not there? I should've written a note to leave, but then I'd be tippin' her off an' she might refuse to talk to me, if she's forewarned.'

Daniel spoke as gently as he could, considering the pace they were keeping. 'She might refuse you anyway.'

'Aye. Aye, she might.'

He inhaled the rich odour of freshly cut wood as they passed a timber merchant's and turned the corner onto a sloping road of terraced houses. A large lead mill squatted at the foot of the street. Rose slowed, and pointed. 'It's this one.'

She stopped outside the second house from the top. It looked well-kept to Daniel, with a pristine step, brick walls that the town had not yet fully blackened and clean nets in the single bay window. He looked up. Smoke rose from the twin pots of the chimney above the eaves of the attic. Movement caught his eye, a twitch of the curtain that hid the room behind the bay. He stepped aside to allow a group of men to pass, coal miners by the look of them, the creases of their faces ingrained with dirt. They disappeared around the corner.

Rose was staring at the house.

'Shall I knock?' said Daniel.

She shook her head.

'We can leave,' said Daniel, 'if you've changed your mind. I would understand if you had.'

'No, I—'

The door opened. The woman who stood on the threshold wore a house dress the colour of russet apples and a knitted shawl in cobalt blue. It matched her eyes. Her hair was pinned up, blonde tendrils framing her face, and her open look of enquiry shaded into surprise and then consternation. She looked from Daniel to Rose and back again. Her cheeks dimpled when she smiled.

'I wondered who were lurkin' outside but I weren't expecting to open the door to thee, Dan.'

He had to trust what his eyes were telling him. There was no mistake. Still, he tested the word he had whispered from the steps of a horse tram, months earlier when the heat had risen from pavements that were now wet and cold.

'Louisa.'

He was aware of Rose's curious look and straightened his shoulders. 'Miss Leigh. We apologise for calling unannounced. This is my friend, Mrs Butterfield.'

He looked helplessly at Rose. She had not given him the name of the woman who had been the last to see her husband alive. He tried to order his jumbled mind. Louisa was probably the lodger of the accomplice in crime, or perhaps a companion, like Mabel to his widowed mother. He knew she had started her working life as a maid. But she was dressed too well to be a servant – that expensive shade of blue wool – and by all accounts now managed the cab business. A visitor, then, and he and Rose had intercepted her bidding her farewells inside the house so her host would not have to linger on the cold doorstep, and now she would leave. Then what would he do? Follow her? He couldn't leave Rose to enter the house alone, to face an accomplice in a terrible crime that could not – must not – be Louisa.

He gave a fleeting thought to the confectioner's daughter. He couldn't recall her name or what she looked like. Nonsense to believe he would court her, or anybody else, or that anybody would ever show an interest in him. He belonged to the woman standing before him. It was as devastatingly clear and simple as that.

Daniel cleared his throat. 'Mrs Butterfield has come to see… to see…'

Rose folded her arms, hugging herself tight, and when Louisa spoke, his frail hopes dissolved.

'Me,' said Louisa. 'She's come to see me, an' I think I know why.'

—

They followed Louisa into a narrow hall that ran alongside a carpeted staircase. The door to the front room stood open, revealing a crackling fire, shelves crammed with knick-knacks and a table in the bay window with an open newspaper spread on it.

'I were readin',' said Louisa Leigh, 'in the light, what little o' it there is today. Let's go in the kitchen.' She led them into the room at the end of the hall, where a fire blazed in the hearth, and closed the door behind them. 'I'll put the kettle on, shall I? 'Ave a seat.'

Daniel pulled a chair back for Rose, who hadn't yet spoken a word, and sat beside her. 'We're lucky to find you at home,' he said.

'Nah,' said Louisa. Her quick smile pierced his heart like a dagger. 'Day off. I work weekends so Mondays are mine, to do what I like.' She looked at Rose. 'Though women's work is never done, is it, love?'

Rose nodded. 'Thanks for lettin' me in,' she said. She coughed nervously. 'How do you know Daniel?'

'We were in love,' said Louisa. 'I thought we'd get wed but I were foolin' mesen.' She laughed. 'Don't look so shocked, the both o' thee. Tha's not come to pass pleasantries, has tha?'

She poured tea and sat down opposite them. 'Can I ask thee how tha found out, Mrs Butterfield?'

'Seth Crookes told me.'

'Seth? But he dun't know owt about it.' She took off her shawl and draped it over the back of her chair before turning to face Rose. Her mouth was set in a grim line. 'I think we're at cross-purposes 'ere. Why has tha come to see me, Mrs Butterfield?'

Chapter 28

The midday hour had arrived and flown and here they were still breakfasting in the dining room of the King's Head Hotel. Annie removed the linen napkin from her lap and dabbed her lips, before dropping the napkin on the table. She drained her cup, sat up straight and adjusted the sleeves of her jacket. She declined an offer of more coffee and pushed her plate away. With these small gestures, she hoped to encourage Rob or the other man they were dining with to declare the meal over. They had been given the coveted table in the bay window but there had been little to see through the rain-streaked panes, other than the occasional carriage or wagon pulled by miserably sodden horses. Pedestrians hurried by, faces hidden under umbrellas or hats or shawls. Oonagh had kept her face hidden until Annie had exposed her wounds for all to see. Had she made the right decision? Rose didn't believe so. What would Mary Pearson have to say about it? She would have an opinion, that was certain, and she would speak the truth, or her truth, which was all anybody could do.

Annie sighed and scraped her chair back a few inches on the polished wood, catching the edge of the rug that covered most of the floor.

The problem she had was that Rob was too enamoured of being seen in the company of Mr Mundella and would happily ignore his wife, if he picked up on her cues at all.

Meanwhile, the member of parliament was magnanimously accepting handshakes from other diners, assuring the various gentlemen who appeared at the table that he could tolerate the interruption – *Always a pleasure. Have you tried the curried eggs?* – and clearly enjoying himself enormously. During a lull in the general adulation, Mr Mundella scraped the remnants of his final course – kedgeree and cold chicken – from his plate and forked them into his mouth.

'Did you enjoy your breakfast?' said Annie, after a few moments.

'I did indeed. Thank you for the invitation, Mr Whittaker.'

Rob smiled. 'It was my pleasure.' He would foot the eleven-shilling bill for their feast and as far as Annie could tell had certainly obtained value for money, putting away porridge, kidney and bacon, kedgeree, cold chicken and what appeared to be a gallon of tea. Annie had eaten her fried whiting, but most of the bacon rashers and omelette she had ordered remained on her plate. During the course of the morning, Mr Mundella had given her enough food for thought to over-rule any physical appetite she might have had. There was a means by which Oonagh's story could be published to a wide audience – a national audience – and Annie needed to see Rose as soon as practicable to discuss the idea with her.

'You've hardly eaten anything,' Rob said quietly as they rose from their seats.

'Nevertheless, I feel quite full,' said Annie. 'You see? I can hardly fasten the button of this jacket.'

Rob's eyes lit up.

'No, no. It's not that.'

Although of course she couldn't be sure. The family Rob longed for might have taken root. Each time the tell-tale cramps began, Annie experienced a strange combination of relief and regret. She was thirty, had been married for five years and was now anticipating Rob or more likely her father to utter the dreaded word. *Barren*. Annie wanted a child but the freedoms she continued to enjoy in the uneasy truce she had made with Rob would be irrevocably curtailed. He indulged her involvement in the female association, provided the housekeeping was done, and grudgingly acknowledged that she had brought him into the sphere of one of the town's leading dignitaries. But pregnancy and motherhood would imprison her behind the bars of their unequal union. What a terrible thought; she loved her husband. Mary Pearson had children and managed to pursue her causes, although Charlie did seem to be more accommodating than Rob.

Annie glanced at him guiltily as they walked through to the hotel foyer and said their farewells to Mr Mundella.

'I shall look forward to seeing you both very soon,' he said, 'but now I must hasten back to London.'

The men shook hands.

'I hope your little publication prospers,' said Mr Mundella, 'and will continue to treat me kindly. Good morning, Mrs Whittaker. It's always a pleasure to see you. Give my regards to your father.'

'Good afternoon, Mr Mundella. I'll give your suggestion some thought.'

On the slick pavement, Rob marched ahead, his back stiff. Annie was tempted to keep walking when he opened the side door to the print shop, to avoid what she surely knew was coming, but instead obediently followed him inside. The volcano would only erupt later; she might as well get it over and done with. He began to spout in the corridor, flinging open the door to the office, throwing words back at her.

'I'm not going to allow it, Annie. You will tell him that you have given it thought and you will turn his generous offer down or be damned with you. You imagine yourself a martyr to your causes but what have you achieved, really, except the public humiliation of a poor child? And why did you have to correct him on the time of day? That was childish and beneath you. Well, Jem, you do look relaxed.'

Jem swung his feet down from the top of the desk and tapped his fingertips on the edge of it, a fast drumbeat to match the pounding of Annie's heart.

'It's our quiet day, news-wise,' he said, 'and who wants to venture out to buy stationery in weather like this?'

'Have we had no customers at all?'

'A few.' Jem smiled uncertainly at Annie but she could not muster a response. 'How was your lengthy breakfast with Mr Mundella? I'm surprised he has the time.'

'He needs to show his face to the town occasionally,' said Rob. 'Annie was not the reason he came up, although she would like to think it.'

Jem grimaced sympathetically at Annie and picked up a pencil.

'I've been waiting patiently for our editorial meeting, Rob, and I have several calls to make this afternoon, in all parts of the town. Shall we get on with it?'

Annie refused the seat Rob gestured she should take. He shook his head impatiently and pulled out a chair, dropping into it with a huff. Annie went to the counter and gazed out of the window, her eyes idly following the passers-by, aware of Jem swivelling about in his chair. Did

he never sit still? Rob was telling him about their breakfast, and the diners who had come up to greet Mundella.

Jem interrupted him. 'Why don't I pen an anonymous
letter to the editor? Let's see. I note that Mr Robert
Whittaker, proprietor of this venerated title, had the ear
of our liberal member of parliament, who was said to be
exceptionally liberal in his praise of' – he paused, and
Annie held her breath – 'the King's Head culinary.'

'Why not?' said Rob.

Jem laughed. 'I was joking.'

'Well, I'm serious. Let's make the most of this.
Mundella will be gone in a year, turfed out at the next
election. He's too soft.'

Annie turned to look at him in disbelief. 'I thought you
agreed with his manifesto and all he is trying to achieve,
for children in particular.'

Rob banged his fist on the desk. 'You're all for the
poor, Annie, but neglect—'

'Steady on,' said Jem.

Annie turned away. 'Oh look,' she said, 'the rain has
almost ceased.' She retied the ribbon of her bonnet with
trembling fingers. 'I think I'll take the opportunity to go
for a walk. With your permission, of course, husband.'

He opened his mouth to speak but Jem interjected. 'A
fine idea, cousin. We'd best get to work, Rob.'

The high street buildings were blurred by a fine mist
of rain or by the tears in her eyes, she couldn't be sure.
Annie skirted the edge of the market square and had
reached West Bar before she admitted to herself that she
was walking in the direction of Mary Pearson's house at
Port Mahon. She slowed her pace when she reached the
bottom of the road Rose lived on. She would call in on
her afterwards. Let Rob wonder and worry about where

she was. It was a small, mean victory and it saddened her to think that pettiness was all she had in her arsenal.

–

'Don't be daft, girl,' said Mary Pearson. She had ushered Annie inside and sat her by the fire in the front room, explaining that Mr Pearson had gone to the Seven Stars in Trippet Lane to help the new landlord with a delivery. 'That's Charlie's excuse, love. Really, he misses the place an' wants to have a good nose round an' listen to the regulars tell him it's not the same wi'out him. Anyhow, tha can speak freely. Tell me what's up.'

A ginger cat sprang into Annie's lap. She scratched at the soft place between its ears. 'I thought she belonged to the tavern.'

'Aye, so did we. She turned up a few days since. A good mouser, tho' she dragged a half-dead rat into me kitchen yesterday. I 'ad to finish it off wi' a spade.'

'How awful!'

'Aye, but I 'ope she deigns to stay. Cats'll do what suits them, won't they?'

'I wish I could do what suits me.'

'Husband's nose out o' joint again, is it?'

'Do you think I humiliated Oonagh, on the steps in Paradise Square?'

Mary tilted her head. 'She gave 'er permission, din't she?'

Annie nodded.

'Well, sometimes it takes summat like that to seize attention. It worked. Am reight sorry the girl has died but don't think tha had a hand in that, Annie.' She sighed. 'Death came wi' her from that factory.'

'What about Rose? I put her in jail.' Annie had unwittingly tightened her grip on the cat. It yowled and wriggled from her grasp, jumping to the ground and stalking off, tail held high.

'An' she's out, an' back wi' her kids. I wun't worry about Rose. She's got 'er head screwed on, an' tha knows that. So what's really up wi' thee?'

Annie stared miserably into the flames. 'I've been given the opportunity of being published in a prestigious journal. It will bring the plight of girls like Oonagh to wider attention. Rob forbids it.'

Mary got up and held a sheet of newspaper over the fire to fan the flames. 'Love, honour an' obey, eh?'

'His patience has worn thin of late.'

Mary screwed up the paper and threw it onto the flames. 'Then ask theesen, can tha sit back and do nothin'? There's nowt wrong wi' that, if it eases the way.'

Annie tried to swallow the lump in her throat. 'I was so excited when Rob decided he wanted to publish a newspaper. I suppose I thought I'd play a bigger role, that I'd be working alongside Jem in some way. It was my dowry that paid for it, after all.' She paused. 'I know that sounds churlish.'

'It's anger speakin'. Nowt to be ashamed of.' Mary cocked her head. 'Take a step back, love. The picture blurs when tha tries to look too far ahead.'

'What do you mean?'

'I mean, what does tha want to do today?'

A weight that was not unpleasant settled in Annie's gut, a sense of inevitability.

'I'm going back to the shop,' she said, 'and then I'm going to call on Rose at teatime, once she's finished work.'

Mary got up. 'Wait a minute.' She left the room and returned wearing a heavy shawl. 'I'll come wi' thee.'

'I'll be glad of the company, and a stroll amongst the falling leaves has to be better than bludgeoning vermin to death.'

Mary's cackle brought a smile to Annie's face. 'A truer word were never spoke.'

Chapter 29

'I'll tell it straight.' Louisa folded her hands in her lap. 'It's up to thee what tha does wi' the information.'

She faced them squarely but Rose saw the uncertainty in her eyes. 'I were in dire straits at the time.' She paused. 'I got pressured into bein' a lookout for Joe Crookes. I needed the coin. The woman that he were courtin' were meant to be there, not me. I'm not tryin' to excuse mesen.'

Daniel mumbled something and cleared his throat and spoke more clearly. 'Was this Ginny?' He sat with hands clasped and head bowed as if he was praying.

Louisa smiled gently at the top of his head. 'Aye. Our Ginny.' She looked back at Rose, and seemed calmer now. 'She were a friend. Well, I thought she were. She ran off wi' Joe, who you'll have 'eard all about from his brother. Not been seen since, neither of 'em.' She paused. 'But I were there, yes, in his last moments.' She held Rose's gaze. 'It were the low point of me life.'

'An' mine,' Rose whispered.

She experienced a moment of dizziness that passed as quickly as it had arrived. Her throat was dry and she desperately wanted to sip the tea Louisa had provided but was afraid that she would blow apart like a dandelion clock if she so much as twitched her little finger. She held herself still, and a numb hollowness grew from the pit of her stomach to fill every part of her. The clock ticked.

'You were a lookout an' you saw him, before… it happened,' she said.

'Aye, I first saw him walkin' down the high street,' said Louisa. 'I thought he'd come right up to me but he din't. I remember 'e were whistlin' a tune. He went up Fargate' – she paused – 'an' he must 'ave circled round.'

'He were allus whistlin',' said Rose, 'an' singin'. He used to say he allus 'ad music playin' in his head. He sang to me, an' he sang to our girl, but he never got to sing to our lads.'

She swallowed. Neither Daniel nor the woman spoke. It was as if Louisa knew she was gathering herself up for what she needed to ask, and a spark of anger briefly illuminated the black emptiness – she didn't want this woman's sympathy, while Daniel seemed lost in past history that Rose knew nothing about.

Eventually, she spat out the words. 'Did he say owt? Did he suffer much?' She only realised as she spoke that her next question was the one that had haunted her dreams. 'Did he know he were dyin'?'

Louisa reached out a hand, then seemed to think better of it and replaced it in her lap. 'He din't say anythin', Mrs Butterfield. He looked at me. He were quiet. I don't think he were in pain.'

Rose took a quick, shallow breath. 'Just tell me, did he know?'

She could see how difficult it was for the woman sitting before her to recall those moments during which Archie's life ebbed away. She was glad of it. She felt Daniel's touch on her arm. He was offering a handkerchief and Rose realised only then that tears were rolling down her cheeks. She shook her head.

Louisa rubbed a hand over her face and kept her mouth covered when she answered, as if she could muffle the meaning away from the words. 'Aye, I think he knew, at least he did when I… when I got to him. It were in his eyes. Then he closed them, like he were fallin' asleep.' She dropped her hand onto the table as if it was a lead weight, palm up, and sighed. 'I were holdin' his hand an'… he went. I'm sorry. An' to thee an' all, Dan. I hid a lot from thee, din't I?'

'It doesn't matter,' he said quickly. 'I was more at fault, in the final reckoning.'

Spite rose in Rose's throat, an acid bile. 'Will you get a final reckoning, d'you think, Louisa Leigh?'

The look Louisa gave her was open, guileless. 'I've no idea. I'm not a religious woman, an' I don't expect owt from thee, forgiveness or owt like that. I wouldn't burden thee so.'

Rose's mouth twisted. 'Not even a penny o' reward money?'

'You came lookin' for me, not the other way round.' Louisa tilted her head and directed at Rose the same gentle smile she'd given Daniel. 'And not for the reason I thought.'

'What other reason is there?'

'Let me just say this: why would I want to be takin' coin back off thee?'

Rose's heart lurched but it was Daniel who choked out the words.

'It was you.' He stared at Louisa. 'You're the…' He laughed, a strange, strangled sound. 'And it's led us here, your money. It's led us back to you.'

He said something else, something about a terrible irony, but the roar in Rose's mind drowned out his words.

Her vision clouded. All she could see was Louisa's face, her halo of hair, her nod of assent. Rose covered her mouth with both hands, as if she would be sick, her mind replaying a recent memory – a blonde tendril of hair escaping from a headscarf, a woman turning her face away, striding away from Rose up the steep incline of the street on a hot and hazy Saturday afternoon, Rose returning home to find another donation, and hurriedly concealing it from her daughter.

Putting it in the box with the rest, hiding the blood money under Archie's cape.

'Every time I found one o' them envelopes,' she said, 'it scared the life out o' me.'

Louisa looked distraught. 'I'm sorry, love. I 'ad to do summat to atone an' I thought it might help thee...'

Daniel finished her sentence. 'In a practical way.'

Louisa nodded.

'I din't know what to do with 'em.' Rose sniffed and Daniel offered his handkerchief again. This time, she took it, wiped her face and blew her nose. 'Ah. I can't...'

'You're overwhelmed,' said Daniel. He touched her arm but she shrugged him off. He put his hand against the side of the teapot. 'Do you think we could have another pot, please? This one's gone cold.'

'I'll put the kettle on,' said Louisa, pushing her chair back. 'If you 'ave a rummage in that cupboard, Dan, there should be some biscuits if Alice hasn't eaten 'em all.'

Rose swiped at her cheeks, watching the two of them move about the kitchen, acting as if this were a normal scene, a cosy chat over a cup of tea with old friends. Daniel opened a cupboard and brought out a biscuit tin. Everything was backwards. A burst of laughter startled them all. Rose realised it had come from her own throat.

She couldn't catch her breath. 'You paid,' she gasped, 'for the posters an' the reward.' She squeezed her eyes closed, tears falling onto her cheeks. This was the funniest thing she had ever heard. 'Sorry, sorry.' She snorted. 'Why am I sayin' sorry?'

'I'm sorry,' said Louisa quietly, and Rose stopped laughing. She let out a long breath.

When she spoke again, her voice was ragged and low. 'I wouldn't 'ave been able to afford it, to learn who killed Archie' – she saw Louisa flinch as if she'd been struck – 'if it weren't for you. I hope you don't expect me to be grateful.' Finally, her anger came raging to the fore like flames from a blast furnace. She wanted to scratch this woman's eyes out. The hurt she'd inflict would be a drop in the ocean to the injury that had been done to Rose, but it would be something.

This woman offered tea and biscuits when what Rose really wanted was her head on a plate.

Where the numb hollowness had been, she was now filled with a rage so enormous she could not contain it. She stood up, knocking her chair over, but instead of obeying her instinct and swinging at Louisa, who stood with the iron kettle in her hands, her mouth open, Rose backed away, towards the door that led into the hall, her fists clenched. She would fetch the police. She would bring them here and then she would take them to the Blue Pig, dragging Louisa Leigh by the hair if necessary, and find Seth Crookes and watch the pair of them shackled and dragged off to jail.

Forged in white-hot fury, her words emerged calmly and slowly. 'You should hang for this.'

In the shocked silence that followed, the kitchen door swung slowly open, creaking on its hinges. A child's blonde head appeared around the doorframe, a dimpled smile on her face. She was unmistakably Louisa's child, with the same candid blue eyes.

Louisa's voice shook with fear. 'This one can hear a biscuit tin bein' opened from a mile off.'

'Is this Alice?' said Daniel.

'It is. Tha can take one, Alice, and then leave us grown-ups to finish our business. I'll gi' thee some dinner in a bit.' She looked at Rose, an appeal in her eyes.

Daniel held out the tin and the girl took two biscuits from it. She smiled up at him and thanked him in a reedy voice that reminded Rose of Jane at a similar age to the twins. This woman had a daughter too, and was raising her fatherless.

'I said one.' Louisa laughed shakily. 'Oh, go on then, 'ave them both. I'll gi' thee some dinner in a bit. Now leave us be, all right?'

'All right, Ma.'

After she had gone, closing the door behind her, Daniel cleared his throat. 'I last saw her as a babe in arms.'

Rose's knees buckled and she sank back into her chair. 'Is that your daughter, Daniel?'

'No, but I would have liked it.' He sat back at the table, crossed and uncrossed his legs and looked at Rose with such a raw and hopeless expression in his eyes that her heart went out to him. 'No good would come, Rose, of seeking revenge. You won't feel better for it.'

'Tha would say that, still bein' in love wi' her.'

But she was calmer, for the interruption; there was no denying it.

'I'm sorry, Daniel,' she said. 'None o' this is your fault.'

Louisa put down the kettle and opened the back door, letting in a blast of cold air. She returned to the table, took up their cups and threw the contents outside. Then she poured a fresh pot of tea and returned to sit down again, opposite Rose.

'I don't want tha money,' Rose said. 'It's tainted. I'm givin' back what's left. Daniel can fetch it to thee.' She looked at him. 'Is that all right?'

He smiled weakly. 'If Louisa can tolerate another visit from me.'

'I don't want it back,' said Louisa. 'Gi' it all way. Gi' it to a beggar, if tha likes. Make his day.' She turned to Daniel. 'Is there owt we have left to say to each other?'

'Yes.'

Louisa nodded. 'All right, then. What will you do?'

Rose realised the question had been addressed to her. 'I'll not do owt,' she said, 'on account of your girl. How old is she?'

Louisa sipped her tea. Her eyes were wary. 'Six, nearly seven.'

'Same age as my boys.'

Daniel leaned forward, as if something had suddenly occurred to him. 'Do Silas and Harriet know?'

Louisa shook her head. 'The only ones that know are me an' Seth, and now thee, an' Rose. I don't count the other pair that ran off. We'll not see them again.'

'All right. We'll keep it that way,' said Rose.

'Thank you,' said Louisa.

Rose couldn't look at her, afraid that the anger she had succeeded in tamping down would well up again.

'What happened, between you and Daniel?' She felt she could ask anything, that she was entitled to, and that Louisa must answer.

'I were pregnant wi' Alice when I met Dan. I were alone.'

'Oh aye?'

'Not like thee,' Louisa said. 'Not widowed. I mean, it were a mistake, gettin' in the family way. I weren't married an' I don't know' – she seemed to check herself – 'where the father is, an' I don't want to neither.' Louisa looked at Daniel. 'I should 'ave told Dan, a'course I should, but we were gettin' along so well, an' I suppose I kept puttin' it off.'

'Until I saw for myself,' Daniel said quietly, 'and reacted in an ungentlemanly way.'

'It's all water under't bridge,' said Louisa. She looked at Rose guardedly. 'I am sorry, love. I'll allus live wi' this. I know it's no consolation to thee.'

Rose stood up and Daniel and Louisa followed suit. 'I've to get back to work,' she said. 'I sharn't be seein' thee again.'

'I'll walk you back,' said Daniel.

'No.' Rose put her hand on the knob of the kitchen door. 'Stay a bit, Daniel. I think you pair 'ave some catchin' up to do.'

––

For once, the monotony of the job worked in Rose's favour and – being the new girl – she could get away with not joining in any of the conversations around her. The others would assume she was shy and not josh her too much. She took her place on the production line and her hands worked confidently and capably, belying her racing mind. She'd never experienced that level of pure rage before, not during the times she had birthed and nursed the boys without a husband by her side, not even when her daughter had asked, consternation on her sweet round face, when her father would be coming home. But if Rose could go back in time, back before the encounter with Louisa Leigh, right back to when Annie made her suggestion to offer a reward, and decline it, would she?

The answer was no. She had some knowledge now that eventually would be a source of comfort. Archie had felt a human touch in his last moments.

When the whistle went, she waited on the pavement outside Morton's, allowing the other workers to stream past. It had stopped raining. Rose looked up at the sky that was visible between the tall buildings on either side of the street. It was a narrow patch, already star-sprinkled, but it took her breath. 'Look!' The word burst from her and she was mortified, but a few of those around her lifted their faces, only to look back at her, puzzled. A shooting star, to see out the day. 'It's nowt; it's gone.' Rose lifted her shawl to cover her hair and set off for home.

She could walk via Change Alley. It would add only ten minutes to her journey. Rose hesitated, then turned in the opposite direction. There were better ways to remember Archie. She could see him in her children's faces. She could feel his touch when Jack or Bobby climbed into her lap, when Jane grudgingly succumbed to her mother's arm around her shoulder. She would not think about the last time she had seen him, lifeless flesh laid out on a table, but instead the time before that, when he had dandled Jane on his lap and his daughter had pulled at his handsome black beard. The compulsion to visit the place he had breathed his last was gone.

Rose was thinking about what she had in the larder for the children's tea as she turned the corner onto her street. Below, a figure detached itself from the lamp post he had been leaning against and waved to her. Rose waved back, uncertainly. She couldn't make out who it was in the dusk but was unafraid. She had faced her demons today and was the stronger for it. When she realised who it was, waiting for her, heat rose from the pit of her stomach to warm her cheeks.

Rose stepped into the pool of light cast by the street lamp. 'Ey up, Jem.'

'Rosie! Where've you been?'

''Ere and there.'

'I'm sorry, for what I said…' He trailed off.

'It's all right, Jem.'

His smile dazzled her. He put his hands on her waist and she thought he was going to kiss her – right out in the open – but instead he lifted her, and swung her in the air, depositing her on the other side of the low garden wall. He hopped over it to land awkwardly beside her.

'That could have gone better,' he said. 'I don't know what you're laughing at, young lady. It's freezing out here.'

He tucked a strand of hair that had come loose back behind her ear and whispered into it. 'Are you going to let me in?'

Chapter 30

Rose sat by the fire in her small front room, the heat warming her face, and listened to Mary Pearson, who had taken the other armchair, regale her audience with tales from her life as the landlady of the Seven Stars inn. Daniel squatted on a three-legged stool but was shooed off it by Jem, who begged him to swap for one of the chairs he'd carried in from the kitchen.

'I'm sorry to say it, Daniel, but you look like a grasshopper trying to balance on a grain of salt.'

As soon as Daniel relinquished the stool, Jem took it and placed himself at Rose's feet. She only just stopped herself in time from reaching out to caress the back of his head.

Daniel and Jem had taken the children's bedsheets and pillows and created a den in their room, which Jane pretended to disdain but was soon deciding who would sit where in the shelter to eat their cheese sandwiches and drink their mugs of spicy carrot soup. For a few moments, Rose had leaned against the doorframe, head tilted, and watched her play mother.

Jem had brought whisky – Rose declined a measure but went in search of glasses for the others – and raised a glass in Oonagh's memory, coughing to disguise the quaver in his voice. Rose recalled that he had sat on the cold steps of the Freemasons' Hall in Paradise Square with the girl in his arms after her collapse, and had never spoken of it. She gazed into the flames, thinking about what Annie had told them. She had turned up with Mary Pearson in tow, babbling about an opportunity to be published in a famous London journal of literature and science. The Sheffield member of parliament was on friendly terms with the editor and had arranged it all. Next, Daniel had arrived, full of apologies, explaining that he was anxious about how Rose might be feeling after her encounter with Louisa Leigh.

'I feel all right, Daniel,' she'd said, and found that it was the truth.

She looked at the faces around her, animated by fire-light and lamplight. She had never had so many people in her house before. There was one empty chair by the fireplace, recently vacated.

Rose smiled along with the others although she wasn't really listening to Mary's story about the wife of a regular, a baker, who turned up armed with his own rolling pin to give him a bashing. She put her hand on Jem's shoulder – he covered it with his own, his warm fingers sending a thrill through her body – then stood up and went into the kitchen. She found Annie sitting at the end of the table, at her side the oil lamp she'd taken from the shelf by the back door. She was unpacking the box of writing implements she'd brought from the print shop – a blotter, ink, dip pen and wax – and laying them out. She looked up and grimaced.

'Charles Dickens once reported on this, you know, many years ago. He described it as one of the evils of match-making, writing about the poisonings in a style I could never master.'

Rose folded her arms. 'Then don't try. Just tell what Oonagh told thee, and what you saw wi' your own eyes.'

Annie nodded slowly. She laid a blank piece of paper on the blotter. 'My husband has forbidden it.'

'Aye, so you keep tellin' us. Then why did you bring along all this paraphernalia? Seems to me tha wants to get published in this fancy journal.'

'It's not a given,' said Annie. 'Mundella knows the editor but if it's not good enough, they won't use it. I don't know what *good enough* means.'

'Me neither. Is there enough oil in that?'

'Yes. What if it makes no difference, is just ignored, and I've gone against Rob for nothing?'

'I don't 'ave the answer to that.'

'I'm not as brave as you, Rose.'

'What?' She laughed. 'I'm not brave, love.'

'Oh yes, you are.'

The two women smiled at each other.

'Best leave tha to it, then.'

Rose paused at the kitchen door. She could hear laughter from the front room, and a series of thumps from upstairs. She'd better go and check on them, make sure they hadn't murdered each other. She looked back at the glowing oasis of calm where Annie sat, and watched her dip her pen in the ink, and begin to write.

Author's Note

A sea change in working lives in the nineteenth century – from rural to urban, from specialised trades (like the skilled craftsmen known as the 'little mesters' in Sheffield) to factory production lines – resulted in grim, and often dangerous, conditions for many. Today, it seems unfathomable that workers, including children, were required to clean heavy machinery while it was still in motion. Change was slow in coming. Charles Dickens published an article about phosphorus necrosis, or 'phossy jaw', in 1852 and named it 'one of the evils of match-making', but the poisonous substance continued to be used to make matches up to the turn of the twentieth century. All the characters in *The Watchman's Widow* are fictitious, with the notable exception of Anthony John Mundella, the son of an Italian immigrant, who served as MP for Sheffield from 1864 until his death in 1897 and was responsible for major reforms to protect workers, particularly women and children.

Acknowledgements

Sincere thanks to everybody who got me over the finish line with this third novel in the series, especially my agent Kate Nash and editor Emily Bedford, and my beloved writer buddies. The most satisfying part of this journey so far has been the wonderful reader feedback. I'm grateful to everyone who is enjoying reading or listening to the Sheffield Sagas.